BEETHOVEN'S STRING QUARTET OPUS 74 'THE HARP'

A novel by JANET WHITE

This book is a work of fiction. Any references to historical events, real people or real places are used fictitiously. Other names, characters, places and events are products of the author's imagination, and any resemblance to actual events, or places, or persons, living or dead, is entirely coincidental.

ISBN-13: 978-1983429040
ISBN-10: 198342904X

With thanks to the Manhattan String Quartet, whose conference in Kraków held in January 2017, was the inspiration for this story.

Chapter 1 – Creation

Vienna, Spring 1809

Thud. Ludwig van Beethoven felt the cellar floor shake beneath his chair, and the candle flame guttered, casting eerie shadows on the roughcast wall. Little Karl, his three-year-old nephew, wailed, his cries piercing the pillow that Ludwig pressed around his own head, penetrating even the constant ringing that plagued him in his ears. Ludwig extended a hand to the lad and drew him close into a one-armed embrace, while a sob escaped him. What if this terrible din were to further diminish his failing hearing? He pulled Karl on to his knee and laid his head down on the boy's dark curls. The cellar smelled of cabbage and coal dust. The dim light from the window at street level, that was splattered with mud from outside and cloaked in cobwebs on the inside, barely penetrated the gloom below. To Ludwig it seemed like a prison, the confinement of the rough stone walls closing in on him, an untidy heap of chests containing the possessions that he'd moved there for safety, a broken bedstead of Caspar's and Johanna's, a scant few bottles of wine of dubious quality, musty root vegetables and crocks of sauerkraut and cherry preserves. To comfort them both, Ludwig began to wonder out loud how beautiful the countryside outside Vienna, where his friend and patron the Archduke had fled, far from Napoleon's troops, must look now that it was late spring.

'The hawthorn trees that skirt the pastures are dredged in pink and white blossom, and the cattle tread on a carpet of yellow cowslips. The willow shakes the pollen from her catkins on to the merry water of the brook; the trout leap for mayflies. Let's close our eyes and imagine we are there, with the breezes bearing the scent of springtime to us!'

The little boy calmed and Beethoven gained some comfort feeling the warm, squirmy little body relax in his lap. He missed Archduke Rudolph intensely – his optimism and his encouragement never failed to lift Beethoven's spirits. Never had

Beethoven felt more in need of his friend's cheering presence. This had been a difficult year – he had been miserably ill and his hearing had gotten worse. After the triumph of his fifth and sixth symphonies he had been profoundly disappointed with the lukewarm reception of his set of three string quartets dedicated to Count Razumovsky. Schuppanzigh had complained that they were too difficult and the critics hadn't understood them. Beethoven wondered whether his best years were behind him now. To cap it all, Therese had refused him, and now his heart was sick, on top of his stomach ailment and the noises in his head and outside. Would Beethoven ever find a wife and sire a son? He held little Karl tighter. His brother Caspar may have made a foolish choice – that slut as Ludwig privately thought whenever he saw his sister-in-law Johanna – but little Karl was a bright spark, a source of hope for the future.

Beethoven glanced around the cellar and sighed. His younger brother had little to show for his life's work to date – the meager possessions, the broken-backed chair, the mismatched glasses on the shelf. Yet what did he, Ludwig have? Even less. He rented a poor apartment and all he owned of value were his compositions and his piano, and the piano pleased him less as his hearing faded. He thought of Therese, of her plump white wrists and hands on the piano keys, the bead of sweat hanging from the damp wisp of hair that fell in front of her ear, the faint chaste scent of lily-of-the-valley that tickled his nose when she moved closer to him on the piano bench. He winced as he remembered her rejection of his passionate advances. Ludwig had even less to show for his life than Caspar.

Ludwig dropped the pillow and reached for his quill. Thinking of nature never failed to inspire him, and he needed to make progress on his compositions to have something to show for this, his thirty-eighth year. This latest quartet would please both Schuppanzigh and the critics – built on classical form with opportunities for the violinist to show off his virtuosity. Maybe it would be Beethoven's swan song. Adieu to the archduke and adieu to Therese. The slow movement theme had been brewing in his head for some days now and he wanted to capture it on paper. He jabbed the nib impatiently in the inkpot and just as he set it to the page, another bomb crashed close by and the fright made him grind the pen into the paper, breaking the nib and leaving a large ugly ink blot on the page. He leapt from his chair, cursing. It was impossible to work under such circumstances. He threw himself down on the mattress that Caspar had dragged down the stairs for him to sleep on during the bombardment, little Karl in his arms, and pulled the blanket and pillows over them both. He pressed the pillow more tightly around his head, holding it over his ears as the thudding continued outside, screwing his eyes shut to block out the horror. He felt little fingers tugging at his knee and opened his eyes. It was Karl.

'Onkel Ludwig, Onkel Ludwig! There's someone at the door.'

Ludwig dropped the pillow for a second time. The pounding at the door continued. He stumbled up the stairs to see who it was. He fumbled with the door and pulled it open. Although his eyes hadn't yet adjusted to the brilliant daylight that flooded through the gap between the door frame and the figure that stood there he recognized immediately the portly silhouette of his friend Schuppanzigh.

'Friend Beethoven, what took you so long? I've been knocking a full five minutes!'

'Ah, Schuppanzigh, you made such a racket I thought the sound was more bombs dropping. Come in, come in! We are sheltering in the cellar.'

Schuppanzigh set down his violin case, drew two bottles of wine from his coat pockets, which he placed on the hall table before hanging his coat on the stand. He ruffled little Karl's hair, picked up the violin with one hand and the bottles with the other and followed Beethoven down the cellar steps.

Beethoven pulled the second chair with the broken back up to the table for his friend, and trimmed the wick of the candle so that it burned brighter. Schuppanzigh gingerly lowered his bulk on to the seat. The legs held under his weight. He peered at Beethoven's face in the candlelight.

'You don't look well, my friend. Have you been able to sleep during the bombardment?'

'Not really. I have been trying to distract myself by composing.'

'How's your new quartet coming along? I hope it's easier to play than the last one. Our audience is impatient to hear more of your compositions, Herr Beethoven.'

'Patience, patience, my friend! These things take time. I'm no longer a young man. Now that you have taken the string quartet out of the living room and into the concert hall, my work must be even more perfect.'

'Ach, Beethoven, the Schuppanzigh Quartet feels the pressure as much as you do. When we used to play privately for the princes at the palace they would forgive the odd wrong note or mistake. We could laugh it off together. Now that we play for the common people we must prepare, we must rehearse. So many more ears listening may spot a mistake.'

'Surely the people are not as refined or educated in music as Prince Lobkowitz and the like? I would imagine an error is more obvious when you play in a small chamber beneath their noble noses, than when you sit on a distant stage with the rumbling and muttering of a large audience to mask your sound.'

'Ah, it's not so much the common people as the critics. Herr Beethoven, Lobkowitz is loyal, he loves you and is always proud of your music. But the critics, they are the ones that can make or break Beethoven and the Schuppanzigh Quartet!'

The friends settled into silence. Schuppanzigh had touched a raw nerve. The critics had panned Beethoven's most recent quartets, dedicated to

Count Razumovsky, around which Schuppanzigh had formed and debuted his quartet, the first professional string quartet to challenge the common perception that chamber music was for the enjoyment of amateur players at home rather than the stage or the concert hall.

A strangled sob interrupted the silence and to Schuppanzigh's dismay he saw his friend's shoulders shaking and his mouth drooping slack at the corners.

'Now now, Beethoven, this won't do. Don't mind the critics. You know how highly our quartet regards your music. Come, I brought some of your favorite claret to cheer us both. He stood and walked over to the shelf by the wall, found a couple of mismatched glasses and hastily wiped the dust from them with his shirt sleeve. He set the glasses on the table and reached for the bottle of wine, rummaging in his pocket for an opener. With some effort, sweat beading on his forehead from his exertions, he plucked the cork from the bottle, poured two glasses and held his own aloft.

'Now here's a toast to you, your music and to the future première performance of your next quartet!'

Beethoven sat still, his sobs subsiding. The reflection of the candle flame glowed ruby red from the dusty facets of Schuppanzigh's raised glass. To Beethoven it seemed that his good friend's kind heart radiated from the vessel. With a gulp and a sniff, Ludwig snatched up his glass and struck it fervently against his friend's. A few drops of claret slopped on to the table, recalling the time Ludwig had shed a few drops of blood to become brothers with his youthful compatriot.

'Bruders!' he cried, defiantly tossing back the toast.

'That's better' beamed Schuppanzigh, reaching across the table to slap his friend heartily on the shoulder. 'There are few ills that wine can't cure. And for all else, there's the string quartet. A string quartet is a safe haven – it's a place of utopian democracy where all voices, through different, are equal and everyone has a unique and important role to play. A string quartet can express all the emotions of life – a party for a wedding, or a birth, or a lament for a funeral. The bond between the players is so strong that they can communicate without words, even just by sensing one another's breathing and movement with their eyes closed.

They integrate their four voices into one, and know each other so well that they can seamlessly finish one another's sentences. Now Beethoven, show me your new quartet. My fingers are itching to play it!'

Beethoven grimaced.

'It's only half done. But I would like your advice on some technical matters in the violin part. Despite your teaching, I still fumble with the violin; my fingers are fat and stupid and I cannot play in tune. Will you try it for me so I can see the effect?'

Schuppanzigh carefully set down his glass and reached under the table for his violin case. A button popped on his waistcoat as he leaned forward. He grumbled as he felt it break. Beethoven was oblivious; he could not hear the soft plunk as the wayward button landed on the cellar floor. Schuppanzigh groped for the missing button in the shadows, and when his fingers closed on it, he stuffed it with some difficulty into his straining trouser pocket.

Beethoven shuffled through the pile of manuscript sheets and pulled out the movement he had been working on. Schuppanzigh peered at the page in the candlelight, raised his eyebrows and lifted his violin to his chin. He tightened his bow and tested the tuning of his strings, making a moue and adjusting the pegs until the instrument resonated correctly. He looked once more at the page and then stood and began to play. The music spun a wreath around him in the glow of the candlelight.

Beethoven watched the violinist's bow gliding across the strings, anxiously regarding his visage for a clue to his friend's reaction to the music. The whistling in his ears drowned out the high notes and he had written the lament high on the E string. He held his breath. Schuppanzigh's mouth curved upwards and his eyes closed. He swayed on his feet and his forehead grew smooth beneath the greasy curls. He stopped playing, lowered his violin from his chin to hang by his side and looked enigmatically at Beethoven, who cried out 'Well, don't keep me in suspense! What do you think?

Deliberately raising his voice, Schuppanzigh spoke. 'It's perfect, Beethoven. This is your best melody yet. It's full of loss and yearning but also of beauty. Well done, my friend.'

Beethoven nodded gruffly. 'Yes, I thought so too. And the violin part, how does it play?'

'As naturally as a swallow flies south at the end of summer.'

'Ach, my friend, I see you understand me.'

Schuppanzigh laid his violin carefully back in its case and the two friends sat and drank in silent companionship. The music expressed their feelings exactly so no more words were necessary.

When they had drained the bottle, Schuppanzigh got up to leave.

'Farewell, my friend. And finish your quartet soon so that we can play it to the people.' With some difficulty, he lumbered up the cellar steps, panting from his exertion. 'I'll let myself out.' He squeezed through the cellar door, shutting it behind him. Beethoven could not hear his steps receding down the wooden hallway above, and he strained to hear the muffled bang of the front door as Schuppanzigh left. With new-found fervor, he seized his quill, trimmed the tip with his knife, added the dregs of wine to moisten the ink in his inkwell and paused a moment to gather his musical ideas before taking a fresh sheet of paper and beginning to write furiously on the page, scribbling down the notes as fast as he could.

Vienna, May 20, 1809
My dear Schuppanzigh,

Words cannot express how much your visit during my darkest hours in the cellar during the bombardment, has encouraged me. My dear friend, I thank you for your kindness to me and for inspiring me to continue composing my quartet. I am delighted to inform you that it is finished! Indeed, I have just returned from delivering the manuscript to my publisher. As I walked back to my apartment – I quit my brother's basement as soon as the shelling stopped – my steps were light and gay. I took a detour to the Schönbrunner Gardens where all of nature seemed to share in my good spirits; the linden leaves quivered merrily as they scattered the pollen from the sweet-smelling blossoms, and the early rose buds pouted flirtatiously at me, teasing my nose with their faint perfume as they peeked from their green calyx casques. Even the sparrows sported, fluttering from the trees down to the lawns and back up again into the branches. It is so good to be able to walk outdoors in safety again beneath the warmth of the sun, rather than to have to cower in cellars.

My friend, you must come and dine with me soon, when my publisher sends the proofs, and we will play my quartet together, taking care all is properly annotated. Thank you again from the bottom of my heart for the gift of your friendship when I was most in need of it.

Your loyal friend,
Beethoven

Chapter 2 – Preservation

Berlin, December 1940

Dr. Wilhelm Pöwe reached into his pocket for the key. It felt warm and solid in his gloved hand. He paused for a moment to look up at the façade of the Haus Unter den Linden, home of the Prussian State Library. The massive edifice with its classical portico stood there unchanged, reassuring. Wilhelm had hardly slept a wink, afraid to fall asleep lest he should miss hearing the drone of the bombers or the whistle of the bombs as they plummeted through the night air, or the terrible thud as they landed. It was hard to tell just by listening which part of the city had been struck. Every morning after an air raid he walked to work with the same trepidation. Would the great library still be there? Had any bombs fallen nearby? He picked his way along Berlin's broad streets. The bare trees on Unter den Linden shivered, a few lone shriveled leaves still trembling on their branches. One or two brave souls sat on the benches, their shoulders hunched beneath their winter coats as they puffed on their cigarettes, clouds of smoke and steam rising from their lips. Dr. Pöwe sighed. Usually, at this time of year, the Christmas markets would be in full swing, the fragrance of the potted fir trees spiriting the city streets into a magical forest hung with gingerbread hearts and gaily painted wooden toys. Now instead of families with round-eyed, rosy cheeked children, the streets were filled with militia and Hitler Youth parades. Gone were the cozy evenings when one could stroll in the throng, sipping a steaming glass of glühwein; now the streets lay cold and empty in the night-time curfew. The red banners of the Third Reich now replaced the cheery Christmas garlands, while so many small shops, the butchers and bakers and delicatessens were closed, their windows blind and boarded, daubed with the ugly letters 'Juden'.

He unlocked the front door and slipped into the library, locking the entrance behind him. After the fearful night-time noises, he let the blissful silence of the library envelop him. Unconsciously he breathed a little deeper and let his shoulders fall.

Even during public hours, the library was a sanctuary of peace and quiet. All you could hear even when the desks were all occupied was the occasional turning of a page, or the scratching of a pencil on paper, soft as a mouse. The opening hours were greatly reduced now; they were short-staffed with all the young librarians having been drafted. Dr. Pöwe shuddered. He remembered the last war, so disastrous for the Prussian state. He was glad to be too old to enlist this time. Still, he had much work to do. The most valuable books and documents must be taken down to the safety of the basement where they could be catalogued and carefully packed.

Dr. Pöwe walked briskly towards his office, removing his gloves and tucking them into the pockets of his heavy winter coat as he walked. His secretary Helga was already there, bending over the coffee pot, an auburn lock straying from her tightly pinned bun.

'Coffee, Dr. Pöwe?' Their morning ritual hadn't changed in the twelve years since Wilhelm had become Library Director and Helga had been hired shortly afterwards. Wilhelm looked fondly at Helga. She was the closest he had to a daughter. He'd never married and his mother had given up hinting after a while, teasing her Willi that he was married to the library.

'I'm afraid it's only chicory coffee today – they have run out of the better kind.'

Dr. Pöwe beamed at Helga and patted her shoulder in an avuncular kind of way. 'As long as it's hot, that's enough. We all have to make sacrifices in wartime.'

Helga's face fell and Wilhelm kicked himself, remembering that Helga's brother and her sweetheart were both away, fighting in France. How tactless he had been. He took the coffee and cradled the cup in his hands, enjoying the warmth. 'It's still quite cold in here this morning. Do you know if they have stoked the furnaces? We have a lot of work to do in the basement today; we'll need to keep warm down there.'

The phone jangled, startling Wilhelm. He slopped his coffee on his fingers. Helga trotted over to pick up the handset, her short, clipped steps constrained by her tight skirt. 'Hallo? Prussian State Library, Office of the Director. Who is speaking please? Heil Hitler.' She looked at Wilhelm and held out the handset. 'It's Carl Weichert, Dr. Pöwe, Director of the Antiquities Division.'

Wilhelm took the receiver. 'Good morning, Dr. Weichert. Heil Hitler.' He pictured the tall, faded academic. He had to strain to hear Weichert's voice, as self-effacing as the man himself. Rumor had it that the transition from academician and museum curator to working for Hitler's Ministry had been a difficult one for Weichert. The voice on the line sounded breathless as if Weichert had been running. The Pergamon Museum had suffered some damage overnight and the protective casing erected around the massive and priceless Pergamon Altar had been blown away. In an agitated whisper, Weichert repeated 'It was just as if the big bad wolf had blown away the house of the three little pigs in the fairytale. With a huff and a puff, the whole house fell down.' Thankfully the altar had survived unscathed and Weichert needed to know if the manuscripts held at the Library were safe. He'd already had Goebbels berating him on the phone this morning.

Dr. Pöwe shuddered involuntarily at the mention of Goebbels, at the thought of those chilly dark eyes that seemed to bore into your brain and read your innermost thoughts, and the immense power that he wielded to dismiss you from your hard-won position for the slightest perceived infraction or disobedience. 'Thank you for calling me, Dr. Weichert. I can assure you, all the manuscripts are safe in the basement.'

'Goebbels orders that you pack them ready for transportation. Be sure to separate the most valuable pieces and to document everything.'

'Certainly, Dr. Weichert. It will be done immediately. Heil Hitler.'

Wilhelm set down the phone with a trembling hand and sat heavily in his chair. The Führer had promised them a short war, a *blitzkrieg*, and then it would all be over. But Russian armies loomed unstoppable close to the eastern front and the British bombing raids sent Berliners cowering to their cellars at night. Any hopes of returning to a normal life soon had been dashed. He reached in his desk drawer and fumbled for the little metal tube of Pervitin, hastily dashing down a tablet with a swig of coffee. His anxiety subsided, and his body filled with energy for the task ahead. He clapped his hands. 'Well, Helga, let's get started. We have much to do today.'

The ever-efficient Helga handed Dr. Pöwe a typed list of documents to be packed away for safety. He ran his finger down the list. 'Ah, the musical manuscripts!' He handed her back the list, which she attached to a clipboard. Helga scurried along behind her boss as he strode down the echoing corridor and descended the marble staircase that led to the basement.

To Dr. Pöwe's senses, sharpened by the Pervitin, the dry air in the cellar seemed to suck all sound and breath – the perfect place to store fragile paper and parchment. Bare lightbulbs strung in single file along the rough brick ceiling illuminated the rows and rows of bookshelves that stood to attention as he walked along the ranks to inspect their contents. Open packing cases lay at intervals down the center aisle. He explained to Helga the instructions he'd received.

'Let's start at A'.

The pair moved slowly and methodically down the aisle, Wilhelm selecting the volumes and directing Helga in which case to place them. By mid-morning they were well into the B's. The Pervitin had worn off a little and Wilhelm couldn't resist opening and perusing some of the manuscripts as they worked, while Helga perched on the edge of the nearest packing case rubbing her woolen-stockinged calves.

'Ah, Helga, to think this is the double violin concerto in Johann Sebastian Bach's own hand. Every note is so clear, so neatly marked.' Wilhelm sang the first few notes of the opening theme.

'Do you play the violin, Dr. Pöwe?'

'Sadly, no. I used to sing in the chapel choir as a boy. That's where I found my love for music. Bach is so perfect, so timeless. I have a recording of this at home, Helga. I'll have to listen to it this evening.'

The collection contained no less than twenty-five autograph scores by Bach – cantatas, the concerto for two pianos as well as the concerto for two violins. They moved on to the Beethoven manuscripts, under whose weight an entire book stack groaned. Wilhelm placed his hand over his heart, waxing sentimental.

'Ah Helga, here is Beethoven. Who else has better captured our German psyche, the very essence of nature and humanity than Beethoven?' He ran his fingers lightly along the spines on the shelf, reading the letters tooled in gold on the leather binding. 'Here's the Ninth Symphony!'

He thumbed through the several volumes, identically bound, pulled the last one from the shelf and carefully opened it. 'Here you see where the celli and bassi begin the recitative.' He continued to turn the pages. 'And here is where the bass solo enters "*Oh Freunde*" – Oh Friends!'

Wilhelm felt like kneeling as he held the revered manuscript in his hands and traced the brown ink from Beethoven's quill with the tip of his finger. It was like communing with the great genius himself. Surely this was worth fighting for, this epitome of German culture, the pinnacle of artistic expression. His heart swelled in patriotic pride. He closed the volume and handed it reverently to Helga. She wrapped it gently, winding it in a linen cloth.

'This is of tremendous value' explained Wilhelm. 'We should pack it separately from the other volumes in case, heaven forbid, some of the collection should be lost. Go, put this one in a new packing case over there.' Helga complied, and then started to pack the other volumes of the symphony in the case at foot of the stack.

'What shall we put with these?' mused Wilhelm. His eye fell on a volume on a higher shelf. He blew off the light film of dust and craned his neck to read the inscription. 'Ah, the string quartet Opus 74. Do you know this one, Helga?' Helga shook her head. Wilhelm opened the volume. The first page bore only the title of the work and then boldly scrawled beneath it 'L V Beethoven' underscored with a heavy line. The pages swarmed with impatient energy as if Beethoven had dashed down the notes in the moment they came to him. Although the writing was uneven, each note, including the intermittent bluish gray lead pencil corrections, was clear, each instruction precise. Perhaps it was the last traces of Pervitin circulating in his veins, but Wilhelm felt as if the vitality in the pages he gazed on pulsed through his fingertips and quickened his very heart beat. Reluctantly he closed the volume and extended it in both his hands to Helga, who swaddled it in linen and placed it on top of the Ninth Symphony. Together they catalogued twenty more autographs by Beethoven including the entire seventh symphony, the eighth symphony whose third movement Dr. Pöwe separated from the others, which he had Helga pack in the special case, parts of each of the late string quartets, including Opus 127, 130, 131, 132 and 133, the Grosse Fugue as well several of Beethoven's sketchbooks from the same period.

The worked through the day, diligently cataloguing and packing their way through Cherubini and Mendelssohn. There were one hundred and nine scores by Mozart, which by themselves filled ten packing cases; eleven of his symphonies, including the famous Prague and Jupiter symphonies, parts of three operas including the Marriage of Figaro, the Magic Flute and Cosi Fan Tutti. By five thirty they had reached the P's and Dr. Pöwe's heart was bursting with the intoxication of being surrounded by so much great music all at once. 'I think that's enough for today, Helga. It's hard to keep track of time down here. We can finish packing the rest tomorrow.'

Helga followed him back up the stairs. Dr. Pöwe closed and locked the massive doors, grimly patting the bolts as if to assure that the cellar and its priceless contents were secure for the night. He helped Helga on with her coat and then buttoned his own coat and escorted her to the exit.

By now night had fallen, and their exhalations puffed visibly in the crisp chill air. Wilhelm bade Helga a good night and turned to make his way

back to his apartment. The night sky was cloudless
and he marveled at the stars, so clear in the black-
out. Beethoven's glorious music played in his head
as he walked. As soon as he reached his room,
before even removing his coat, he went straight to
his gramophone, thumbed through the stack of
records and with a sigh of contentment, selected the
string quartet Opus 74. He lowered the needle into
its groove and as the music unfurled, took off his
coat, lit the gas fire and settled into his chair with a
glass of schnapps to listen. Alone in the dark, the
fire warmed his toes and the schnapps warmed his
heart, but most of all, Beethoven's music warmed
his soul.

Chapter 3 – Flight

Lower Silesia, December 1943

'Attention' barked the guard 'Two men are missing. Where are they?' Jakob Goldberg cautiously raised his hand. 'Yes, you. Where are they?'

'They have the typhus fever. Sir' he added as the guard raised his eyebrows menacingly.

'Scheiss' cursed the guard. Construction on the tunnels was already behind schedule due to the unexpected early snow that had held up delivery of the wooden beams used to support the roof. The typhus epidemic ravaged his workforce as easily as a wolf tearing into a herd of sheep. 'You'll just have to work harder to make up the difference' he spat back at Jakob.

Jakob's shoulders drooped. He'd had little sleep, lying on his straw mattress listening to the delirious moaning of the sick men next to him. He'd lost his brother Ephraim to the epidemic three weeks earlier. Jakob shivered as he remembered the purple rash that spread like a net across Ephraim's chest, his body burning up despite the thick snow lying outside, his cries and raving. The guards had made them bury the bodies in a common pit, then shaved their heads, burned their clothes and ordered them to scrub their bodies with carbolic soap to kill the lice that spread the disease. Those who had fallen ill most recently must already have been infected by then. Underneath the traces of carbolic, the wooden barracks still smelt like a barnyard, sweat and fever on top of moldy straw.

The prisoners climbed into the truck that transported them daily from the camp to work at Schloss Fürstenstein. The heat from the tailpipe running under the floor soon crept through their worn boots, warming their feet a little, together with nauseating diesel fumes. Every day Jakob thought, as they bounced and lurched over the rutted gravel driveway, about the irony that they entered by the ornate wrought iron gates as if they were guests arriving for a ball hosted by the Prince of Holberg and his mad English wife Princess Daisy, instead of forced labor. The only entrance to the castle was via the front gate and along the driveway that wound its way through the formal park. Only as they neared the castle with its gothic towers and spires did the truck lurch off the driveway to bump over the churned and frozen mud that had once been the croquet lawn to deliver them unceremoniously to the construction site behind the Schloss, where they were employed to dig out several layers of tunnels. They had already finished the upper level but the work was back-breaking, especially once winter came and men started falling sick.

Jakob was assigned to throwing into carts the rubble that had been blasted away. The carts were then hauled by men to the mouth of the tunnel and from there the rock was transported away in rail cars, to be used, Jakob assumed, for construction elsewhere. By the end of their shift he could barely stand, so tired were his legs and back from the constant bending and stooping to pick up rocks. He was grateful for the thick gloves that protected his hands. On learning that he played the violin, his captors had insisted that he lead a string quartet assembled from other prisoners within the camp, to provide music at their parties and functions. As such, Jakob received special privileges; he was assigned to relatively light duties that spared his hands, and on the occasions that the quartet performed, they could count on a hot shower and a decent meal afterwards.

The guard seemed particularly on edge today. Jakob asked Frieder, one of the estate workers who had been kept on to oversee the construction work, if he knew why the guards seemed tense.

'I heard them talking about a special delivery coming in this evening. They're expecting a train with some special load. That's what we're building these tunnels for – to store valuables, I've heard.'

'That makes sense' mused Jakob. 'Our quartet has been ordered to play at a party here at the Schloss on Saturday night. They never tell us who will be there or the reason for the celebration. Unusually this time, we've been given strict instructions what to play - particular quartets by Beethoven.'

The men set to work, methodically piling stones in the carts and hauling them out along the tracks. The work had a certain rhythm to it. At least deep inside the tunnels they were sheltered from the cold outside and the chill wind that howled around the entrance. At four, a sharp cry echoed down the tunnel. The men stumbled towards the entrance. Their shift still had a good two hours to go; what was happening?

As Frieder had predicted, six rail cars waited at the train track entrance. The guard instructed the workers to unload the cars and push the contents in carts into the upper tunnel. Jakob stepped forward. The cars contained wooden packing crates, each stamped on the sides with the letters 'PSB' in gothic script. He wondered whose monogram it was. The crates had slots into which long handles could be slid so that two men could easily lift them and carry them down into the waiting carts. They then pushed the carts along the rails down to the far end of the tunnel, where the guards directed them where each crate should be placed while consulting a list. Only once the last crate had been unloaded were the men taken back to the truck, waiting to transport them back to camp.

Jakob slumped on the hard wooden bench as the truck jolted and rattled along the roads. His hands ached and he flexed his cold, stiff fingers. He looked forward to being able to wrap them around the warm baked potato invariably served for dinner, to ease the stiffness. After dinner, the quartet would rehearse. The Beethoven piece they had been ordered to play had a difficult virtuosic passage that he needed to master, that required supple fingers and a sharp brain. Later that evening he fetched his battered violin case, took out his instrument and began to tune it. The crumped velvet interior still carried the faint smell of rosin and of home. It never failed to remind him of better days, especially sitting in the darkness, where he could almost imagine being back in the drawing room, practicing for his violin lesson. He tried to remember the magenta velvet curtains, the gold-flocked wallpaper, the scent of Papa's tobacco in his pipe, Mama sitting quietly by the fire with her hands folded in her lap, her head on one side and a sweet smile on her lips as she listened to his music. He'd received no word of them since they'd parted at the train station. He remembered sitting on the train, clutching his violin on his lap, looking down through the grimy window at their upturned faces as they stood on the platform below. Hearing the faltering tone of his strings, his colleagues in the quartet crept quietly from the darkness, carrying their instruments. Jakob looked up and acknowledged them with a silent nod. The other three players pulled up their broken chairs and began to tune. The cellist, Tobias, fetched the lamp and propped the pages of music in front of the players.

'Shall we begin with the second movement?' Jakob asked. As the three lower strings gently spread a carpet of sound beneath him, Jakob began to play the sweet melody that sighed with loss and regret. He heard his colleagues' breathing slow down and watched their bodies relax. He saw tears begin to flow down the violist Leon's cheeks. Poor Leon, his brother was one of the two workers most recently stricken with typhus. The grinding work might numb your soul but playing music unlocked your feelings again, brought back memories and activated the senses once more. You could lose yourself in the music and temporarily forget this miserable place and the hardship.

Now that his hands were warm and his fingers flexible, Jakob could tackle the first movement with its pyrotechnic passages. The quartet played the rest of the piece. When they had finished, Jakob nodded in approval and his mouth spontaneously twisted up in a rare smile. 'Very good, gentlemen. I think we are ready for Saturday.'

On the day of the concert, the quartet members only worked a half shift. The truck brought them back to the camp to collect their instruments and then took them to the Schloss itself, to the servants' entrance. The guard led them to the bathroom, where four dress suits hung on hooks on the wall. The men stripped and stepped into the steaming showers. Performing provided a rare opportunity for a hot shower and a good meal, rewards that they keenly anticipated, not least as a way to purge themselves from the taint of having to entertain Nazis. Even their instruments enjoyed the steamy warmth of the bathroom. The wood greedily drank in the moisture, becoming smooth and plump. Jakob could almost hear the fibers expanding and relaxing after the weeks in the rough cold of the barracks. The bathrooms in the servants' quarters were rudimentary but clean with gleaming white tiled walls and porcelain sinks. Jakob had seen the bathrooms upstairs in the Schloss, which they were allowed to use once they had changed into concert dress. The Prince and Princess had furnished their palace lavishly, sparing no expense. The bathroom floors and washbasins were carved from the same creamy marble veined with ochre, set off with dull gold fittings. Jakob luxuriated in the torrent of hot water, flexing his hands and scrubbing his nails clean. The soap suds smoothed away the ground-in grit and dirt and the faint stink of carbolic. He wrapped his body in the soft towel and wiped the fog from the mirror so he could see to shave and comb oil through his hair. The dress jacket hung loose and heavy on his shoulders.

The guard returned to escort them upstairs. The ballroom had been decorated with an exquisite eye for detail, from the intricate design of its parquet floor, and the gilded mirrors that lined its walls, to the ceiling crisscrossed by heavy beams with ornate carved wooden flowers and faces painted in gaudy colors in every alcove. Jakob wondered how much was original and how much was a reconstruction of a grand past re-imagined by Princess Daisy and her squire. He could imagine knights and ladies of old dancing the courtly steps of a minuet in such a room. Ranks of chairs with elaborate gilded frames and rose velvet upholstery were lined up with military precision to face the stage. Jakob shivered. It seemed unnatural to sit and perform with the cold eyes of so many of their persecutors like the eyes of boiled fish trained upon him. 'I feel like a performing monkey' he muttered to Tobias, who patted him on the shoulder and whispered back 'Forget them. Just play for us. G'd will hear you.'

'Hurry up' the guard nudged him. 'No time for daydreaming.' He led the quartet into an ante-room through a door that opened directly on to the stage. The quartet sat nervously in the ante-room waiting to be called. Tobias eyed the side table heaped with platters of ham, cheese and purple grapes, his mouth watering. 'Do you think...?' Leon shrugged. "Why not? What can they do to us if we eat it? They need us to perform.' Jakob swallowed. Surely G'd would forgive him for eating the ham. His stomach growled. Meat was hard to come by. He gingerly took a plate and piled it high. His colleagues followed suit. As they gobbled down the food, they heard voices in the ballroom outside as guests began to drift in. The noise swelled to a hubbub and then they heard a bell and the scraping of gilded chair legs on the parquet as the audience took their seats. They hastily wiped their greasy fingers clean on damask napkins. Applause followed and Leon opened the door a chink so that they could listen to the speeches.

'*Meinen Herren und Damen*' began the speaker, a stout man, his white swallowtail coat straining at the buttons, his lapels sagging under the rows and rows of ribbons pinned to them. 'We are here this evening to celebrate the safe arrival of the archives of the Prussian State Library. These archives will be stored here below Schloss Fürstenstein, a home fit for none less than the Führer himself.' The audience laughed and cheered, stamping their feet in appreciation on the parquet floor. 'That's what the monogram PSB on those crates must stand for' said Jakob. 'Prussische Staats Bibliotek. Now it makes sense. Those boxes we carried, they must contain the archives.' The speaker tapped his cane on the floor to regain the attention of the audience.

'Among the national treasures and priceless manuscripts that now lie directly beneath our feet are several autograph manuscripts by none other than Ludwig van Beethoven. What other composer better epitomizes our proud German heritage than Beethoven? What can better express our national identity than the music of Beethoven? He is the greatest composer of all time; his music speaks of the superiority of the German race, the beauty of our countryside, the intellect of our poets, writers and scientists. And now, right here, we have preserved his manuscripts for posterity.'

With much scraping of chairs, the audience rose to its feet with shouts and more applause. The speaker tapped his cane once more. 'And now, for your patriotic enjoyment, you will hear this very composition performed – Beethoven's string quartet Opus 74. But first, our National Anthem. He struck his cane three times on the stage, giving the signal for the quartet to enter. Taking a deep breath, Jakob rose to his feet, clutching his violin by the neck with his bow in his other hand. He led the quartet on stage, walking stiffly with his head held high, neither looking at the speaker nor the audience. The quartet made their way to the four rose-and-gold chairs on the stage and set their music on the gilded wooden stands. The speaker cleared his throat. 'Please stand for *Deutschland Uber Alles*.' The chairs scraped once more and the quartet played the anthem. Tobias whispered to the others 'Don't think about the words. Just think of Papa Haydn. We are just playing a movement of his Kaiserquartett, that's all.' They tuned their ears to block out the sound of two hundred Nazi elites lustily belting out the hateful supremacist words, hearing only each other's pure string sounds. The audience sat again and the house lights dimmed.

Jakob closed his eyes, sweating under the glare of the stage lights that roused terrifying memories of being interrogated when he was first rounded up and imprisoned. He gave a cue and the quartet began to play. The dark, dissonant chords of the slow opening stole across the hushed ballroom.

Poco Adagio

The opening harmonies are insecure, doubting, halting abruptly. The first violin breaks into lamentation punctuated by rising cadences broken by a violent diminished sixth chord. The lower strings play their rising cadence again, interrupted by a second chord. The first violin creeps slowly and chromatically upwards until it the quartet resolves into an emphatic E flat major chord.

The quartet focused on each other, aware only of the music. The audience faded into the darkness and they barely noticed the tapping feet and nodding heads as they transitioned to the lively *Allegro*. As they reached the triumphant cadence at the end of the first movement, the lusty cries of '*Bravo*' and '*Heil Beethoven*' startled them.

After the concert was over, the guard patted Jakob on the back. 'Well played, Jews' he grinned, his breath laced with beer and garlic sausage. Jakob tried not to shrink back, wordlessly inclining his head to acknowledge the compliment. The guard led them downstairs back to the bathroom, where they changed back into their work clothes and carried their instruments tenderly to the truck waiting to drive them back to the camp. Lost in feelings generated by the music, none of the four spoke. The glow in their fingers and bellies from the warmth of the Schloss, the taste of fine food and the feel of clean dress clothes on their bodies dissipated bump by bump as the truck rattled its way back to the campground.

Tobias was the first to break the silence. 'So now we know what was in those cases. To think today we literally carried the music of Beethoven. How about that? Being so close to the very notes that he wrote on the page. I wish I could see the manuscripts with my own eyes. Do you think…?'

Leon spoke up bitterly. 'You're crazy, man. My brother lies dying in those huts and you want to risk your life prying into crates filled with Nazi treasure?'

'Now, now' said Jakob 'let Tobias dream. Beethoven would never have condoned what the Nazis have done. He believed in brotherhood and freedom for all men, not just Aryans.'

The four men fell into silence again. Jakob lay on his mattress for a long time before falling asleep, Beethoven's music still resonating in his ears.

Wilhelm Pöwe tossed and turned, unable to sleep despite the sumptuousness of the bedchamber to which he has been assigned at the Schloss. Privately, he'd been shocked by the decadence and luxury of the Schloss. And what he'd witnessed must represent the merest dregs of what it must have been in the heyday of Hans Heinrich XV of Holberg and Princess Daisy's reckless rule. His bed, a four poster, dripped with emerald green silk hangings embroidered with gaudy birds of paradise. The dressing table was topped with a slab of polished onyx and its drawer pulls were cast in silver. As Library Director, Dr. Pöwe had traveled with the cases to assure their safe delivery to Liebichau and the tunnels beneath the Schloss. The conditions in the tunnels appalled him. The walls were rough-hewn earth and moisture dripped down from the ceiling in several places. This was no place to store priceless documents – the damp and mold would destroy them in a matter of months. A better and safer hiding place must be found. He resolved to seek an audience with the General first thing in the morning.

At eight thirty the agitated librarian appeared before the General to voice his concerns. Dr. Pöwe paced up and down, his eyes hollow, running one hand distractedly through his hair while gesticulating with the other.

'General, I am personally responsible for the preservation of these manuscripts, and I'm telling you, this place is not suitable. The Führer would be furious to hear of this. I beg you, let me take them somewhere less damp. We don't need to announce their removal from the Schloss. Surely that will improve the security; after last night's concert, the more people who think they are still here beneath the Schloss, the safer they will be.'

The General scratched his moustache as he pondered Dr. Pöwe's proposal. While it would be a serious blow to lose the artifacts from the storage facility whose construction he had personally supervised, the librarian raised some good points. He didn't want to be held accountable if the books were damaged. He could always justify the need for secrecy as the reason for moving the collection elsewhere. He reached a decision and nodded. Yes, the library collection could be taken elsewhere.

Dr. Pöwe bowed and clicked his heels as he saluted 'Heil Hitler'. He asked if he could use the telephone. A couple of calls to Berlin later, he had procured a train to transport the cases to their new storage place.

Jakob couldn't believe his ears when, a week later, his shift was instructed to remove the very crates they had unloaded just days earlier, and to load them back on to a new train just arrived from Liebichau. What were the Nazis playing at? The boxes stamped with the 'PSB' moniker were not destined to rest at Schloss Fürstenstein, but where they were headed, no-one could say.

Chapter 4 – Concealment

At midnight, Father Benedict waited anxiously with four brothers who had been sworn to secrecy. They had been told to prepare for the arrival of a special delivery. They were to take it into the Grüssau Monastery and await further instructions. They must conceal the delivery under cover of darkness and guard it with their lives.

He had summoned four of his strongest and steadiest brothers: Brother Francis, massive and silent, who managed the livestock, wrangling the cow and pigs into their stalls in the barns; Brother Hubertus, who rang the bells in the monastery church of the Blessed Virgin Mary; Brother Peter, who tended the monastery gardens; and Brother Andreas, his second in command, whose shrewd judgement Benedict trusted above all others. They shifted uneasily, the hoods of their black cloaks raised over their heads to stave off the cold, hands tucked in the folds of their robes, their breath rising in steaming clouds into the starry night, stamping their feet to keep warm. Father Benedict noted the sharp sliver of the new moon and wondered whether the Germans had deliberately chosen this darkest of nights for their secret delivery. In the distance, he heard the thrumming of an engine and then he saw the twin beams of headlights at the bottom of the hill. It must be them. As the lights approached he saw it was not one vehicle but a convoy of three, no, four trucks approaching. Crossing himself, he tensed his muscles and prepared for the arrival.

The trucks drew up to the monastery gate and an officer leapt out.

'Father Benedict?'

'Yes.'

'Is the hiding place ready?'

'Yes, in the Abbey Church of the Blessed Virgin.'

'Show us the way.'

Father Benedict bowed and led the way through the Abbey gates, across the graveled courtyard to the massive doors of the church used by the monks. The officer walked beside him and motioned the trucks to follow. The ground was frozen solid and the monks' steps made no sound. All that could be heard was the low throbbing of the engines. The convoy drove through the gate and pulled up outside the church. Father Benedict drew a large key from his pocket and opened the door.

'Come in, let me show you the place.'

He crossed himself again as he stepped over the threshold of the Abbey church, picked up a lantern from the table just inside and lit it from the candle that burned at the feet of the statue of the Madonna. The strange procession led by the Father, followed by the uniformed soldiers, with black-garbed monks bringing up the rear, advanced up the aisle to the heavy carved rood screen. The stained-glass windows glittered in the lamplight and the officer could just about make out the stations of the cross marked by paintings hung along the walls at intervals between the windows. Beyond the screen lay the choir stalls and then a few steps led up to the altar.

Father Benedict turned to the left and led the way to a small door at the base of the screen. He sorted through the keys on his ring and selected one to unlock the door. The small room behind it held a row of hooks with surplices hanging on them above low shelves neatly stacked with hymn books.

'For the choir' explained Father Benedict.

In the far-right corner of the choir room he unlocked a second door which led to a steep flight of stairs.

'These go up to the loft above the choir. They are only used rarely, when the organ tuner comes. There is plenty of space up here to store…' Father Benedict let his voice trail off as he raised a quizzical eyebrow. What exactly were the monks being asked to hide and 'guard with their lives'?

The officer swept a critical eye around the loft, assessing the space.

'This is good but I fear it may not be large enough to store everything. Do you have other attics in the monastery?'

Father Benedict swallowed. What on earth could it be? He looked at Brother Andreas, who spoke up.

'There is a similar loft above the choir in our other church, St. Joseph's. This one is used only by we monks; the services at St. Joseph's are for the townspeople.'

The officer frowned. 'It will have to do. You must ensure that the townspeople don't suspect anything. Come now, help us move the cases. The trucks will return to the station to bring the next load.'

Brother Andreas glanced at Benedict as he led the way back to the porch. Benedict tightened his lips – he didn't have any more information than his brothers. The soldiers rolled up the canvas sides of the trucks and the brothers saw that they were stacked to the roof with wooden packing cases. Brother Andreas sidled closer so that he could decipher the lettering stamped on the side. 'PSB'. Prussische Staats Bibliotek. His eyes widened beneath the shadow of his hood.

The soldiers slotted the carrying handles into the crates and two by two, the monks took them up through the choir room and into the loft. As soon as one truck was emptied, its driver took it back to the station, where the train was being unloaded, returning with a fresh stack of crates. Francis and Hubertus were sweating now, their hoods thrown back, as they carried box after box into the loft, stacking them tidily one on top of the other until the loft was full. They stood and rubbed their aching arms, and wiped their tired faces on their sleeves as they rested from their labors. Benedict estimated they must have taken up over three hundred crates by that time. He guided the convoy of trucks over to the other side of the courtyard where St. Joseph's church stood, and opened the door. St. Joseph's, the original monastery church, had been built one hundred and fifty years earlier and its walls were lined with monuments and memorials to three centuries of parishioners. The rood screen here was carved from oak, lighter and more delicate than the one in the newer, baroque church whose loft they had just filled. The stream of monks and men carrying cases, like ants foraging and returning to the nest, was redirected into the loft of St. Joseph's.

The last cases were deposited as dawn was beginning to break. The brothers stumbled wearily downstairs and dropped into the pews at the back of the church near the entrance. Benedict raised his head and looked directly at the officer.

'We have labored all night for you. Won't you tell us what it is that we are guarding?'

'That's top secret.'

Benedict persisted 'For purely practical reasons, we need to know, in case of a fire, or a leak in the roof, so that we can keep whatever is in those boxes from harm.'

The officer relented. With a harsh laugh, he said 'I suppose I may as well tell you to stop inquisitive holy fingers from prying open the lids as soon as we turn our backs. I imagine you may have guessed from the stamps on the cases that they are books from the Prussian State Library. But these are no ordinary books; they are priceless manuscripts.' His chest puffed with pride. 'We have been entrusted with protecting original autographed musical scores by German's greatest composers – Bach, Mozart and Beethoven, no less. That's what these cases contain. We'll be placing a guard at the church and we'll need to billet our men here. I trust that will be arranged immediately.'

Father Benedict bowed slightly, inscrutable. 'Of course.'

'And you will not breathe a word of this to others in the monastery or to the townspeople.'

It was Benedict's turn to laugh. 'Surely you know, officer, we Benedictines are a silent order. We do not engage in idle chatter. You could not have picked a better place to hide a secret.' He held up the lantern and looked earnestly at his brothers.

'You heard the officer. Not a word of this to anyone.' The four monks nodded solemnly. 'How shall we explain the presence of guards to the monks and the townspeople? We hold services in the Abbey Church daily and in St. Joseph's four times a week.'

'You will tell them that the Third Reich has taken over the monastery to become a garrison to protect the local population from Russian attack.'

Benedict pressed his hands together as if in prayer. 'Very good. Brother Peter, will you show these men to our guest quarters? And Brother Francis, will you show them where to park the trucks out of sight, inside the large barn?' Benedict waited with Hubertus and Andreas as the soldiers left. 'Hubertus, you spend more time in the churches ringing the bells than any of the rest of us. I charge you with keeping an eye on these chests and the guard. Make sure they stay safe – and that the guard does no damage.' Hubertus nodded solemnly. Benedict continued 'Andreas, come pray with me.'

The two elders approached the altar and knelt on its steps. Benedict glanced at the ceiling. The weight of the treasures hidden up in the loft pressed on his mind as he prayed. 'Holy Father, we entrust to Thy heavenly care these works of art that glorify Thee. May we protect them faithfully and may they be not a burden but a blessing to our community.' He finished his prayer and turned to Andreas with a mischievous grin. 'Just think, Andreas. Bach, Mozart and Beethoven will be listening to our choir now. I like to think of their sacred songs floating up and permeating these cases and the very pages of music themselves like incense.' Andreas said nothing but smiled beneath his hood. Words were not necessary.

Chapter 5 – Discovery

Poland, March 1946

Brother Peter stood and brushed the mud from the knees of his cassock. He squinted up at the morning sun and beamed as the rays warmed his face. He surveyed the rows of lettuce and radish seedlings and smacked his lips at the thought of fresh salad after a winter diet of sauerkraut and boiled turnips. Brother Francis called to him from the barn.

'Peter, can you help? The cow is calving and I could use a hand.'

Peter chortled with delight. A calf meant fresh milk, butter and cheese. God was gracious after the years of wartime deprivation.

'You go around and hold the cow's head' said Francis. 'I'll help the calf come out.' He wore a rubber apron and long rubber gloves up to his elbows. Francis positioned himself behind the cow and grunted with exertion as he felt for the calf. The cow mooed urgently and pushed out her calf, which slithered to the floor at their feet. Francis grabbed a handful of straw and wiped away the mucus that covered the little creature. 'It's a healthy one!' he said with pride.

'Good, good. I hope we'll have enough milk to give to the parishioners. It can only help strengthen our relationship with the townspeople.' Peter's voice tailed off. After the occupying Nazis had been driven out the monks had enjoyed only a brief respite. Posters announced a new decree to expel all those of German descent from Poland, and their Benedictine order originated in Germany.

'Do you really think they will force us to leave?' asked Francis, looking up from the calf, which was now being licked clean by its mother. 'This is our home. Surely we belong to the community.'

'But the notices posted in the town square say that no-one of German descent may remain, without exception. We were all born in Germany even though we have made Grüssau our home.'

'What else can we do to make the townspeople trust us?' Peter looked significantly at the tower of St. Joseph's church. 'You don't mean…?'

'Why not? The Nazis have fled. It's our secret. What better way to prove our loyalty to Poland than to give the manuscripts to the Polish people?'

'Have you spoken to Father Benedict?'

'Not yet, but I've been thinking about it a lot recently.'

'Let's speak with him before Evening Prayers. Grüssau is our home. No-one wants to leave.'

Father Benedict rubbed his chin thoughtfully when Peter drew him aside and whispered his suggestion confidentially in Benedict's ear. Taking Peter by the arm, Benedict led him to his study and closed the door. 'Sit down, Brother Peter.' Peter sat facing him across the desk. Father Benedict had aged during the war. His hair was now snow white and his thin lips were pinched in his sunken, gray face. His hands trembled a little as he rested them on the crucifix on his desk. 'I must confess, the burden of care the Nazis placed on us has weighed heavily on me. We swore an oath to protect these manuscripts but I fear I no longer have the strength to do so. Our roof is in poor repair – what if rain or rot should weaken the rafters? All those heavy cases up there…Moreover there are rumors that the Russians are on the move, looting as they go. If the Russian army were to come here, we would have no means to defend ourselves or the manuscripts. I think our best course is to surrender them to the Polish Government. They will surely find a safer hiding place, and have the means to keep these treasures from falling into the wrong hands. Go, fetch Andreas, Hubertus and Francis. We should all make the decision together.'

The four monks stood in Benedict's study as he wearily laid out the proposal. He looked at each of them in turn. 'Do you agree?'

Hubertus gasped 'Father, at last! Every day as I ring the bells I fear that we cannot keep the manuscripts safe. I feel the weight of responsibility in my legs as I climb the bell towers and in the very ropes I pull as I ring the hours. It would be such a relief to give them to Poland.'

Benedict twinkled at Hubertus. 'Well. I suppose we should take a look to see precisely with what the Nazis entrusted us.'

Hubertus blushed. 'Forgive me Father, I already have. The very day that the guards fled, I was consumed with curiosity and I pried open the lids. In fact, I have made an inventory of all five hundred and five packing cases. It's folded inside my Bible - here.' He hung his head as he sheepishly reached inside his robe and handed the folded papers to Father Benedict.

Benedict took the folded paper and ran his eyes down the list. His mouth fell open. 'Heavenly Father! I had no idea' he murmured. Sinking heavily into his chair, he handed the paper with a shaking hand to Andreas, whose eyebrows shot up in surprise as he read the list. 'Well, well. To think we've had Beethoven's ninth symphony and the late string quartets resting quietly above our heads these last three years. Works inspired by God, indeed. We'd best keep this as quiet as possible so that we can find a way to get them to safety in secret. Let us pray this evening for wisdom and guidance how we can make this happen.'

The following morning found Brother Peter working busily at the beehives, opening them up in preparation to receive the pollen and nectar building up in the spring buds. The bees buzzed contentedly and he was so engrossed in his task that he didn't hear the car pull up at the monastery gates. The slam of the door broke his concentration and he looked up to see two men in suits and hats waving at him to get his attention. He carefully replaced the lid on the hive, and walked over to see what they wanted, pulling off his protective hat and gloves. The older of the two men swept off his hat and stuck out his hand in friendly greeting.

'Good morning, Father! I'm Dr. Stanisław Sierotwiński and this is Dr. Kalecki. We're from the Monuments Service. May we come in? We are cataloguing historic buildings and items of cultural heritage taken by the Nazis, for the Polish government.'

Peter was dumbstruck. God certainly worked in mysterious ways. He'd never had a prayer answered so quickly. Dr. Sierotwiński smiled patiently. He was used to getting a puzzled reception and to having to explain his team and their mission, and mistook the monk's silence for misunderstanding. He repeated 'May we come in? And could you please take me to the Abbot?'

Peter threw his head back and laughed, thanking God for the clear answer to their prayers. 'You are most welcome. Please, come this way.' Dr. Sierotwiński was now puzzled. He'd never been greeted with hilarious laughter before. These friars seemed very jovial. Peter showed the two Monuments men into Father Benedict's study. They shook hands and introduced themselves. Dr. Sierotwiński was Head of the Art and Music collections at the Jagiellonian Library in Kraków and Dr. Kalecki was a curator at the National Museum in Warsaw. The government had established a task force headed by the pair to travel the country and catalogue what was left of Poland's heritage, as well as to seek out places where artworks looted by the Nazis had been concealed. Father Benedict clasped Dr. Sierotwiński's hand and his voice shook with emotion.

'God has sent you here. You have come to the right place. We have housed and protected over five hundred boxes of musical manuscript from Berlin here in the Abbey for the last three years. Praise God that you have come to find them.'

Dr. Sierotwiński almost fell off his chair. He'd been working his way from one small Silesian town to another ever since the winter snows melted. They had uncovered a stash of paintings here, an altarpiece there, but this was staggering news. 'Five hundred cases?' he faltered.

'Yes. Come and see!' Father Benedict rose stiffly from his chair, drew his key ring from his belt and shuffled, stooped, out across the courtyard, to unlock the door of the church of the Blessed Virgin Mary as he had done three years earlier for the Nazi soldiers. Dr. Sierotwiński's eyes widened as they reached the loft. So, there had been substance to the rumors of the Nazis sweeping up wholesale priceless works of art from across Europe, although no-one had suspected that this monastery, requisitioned as a garrison, had also been used to store treasure.

The Monuments men got to work quickly. There was no time to lose with movement increasing on the Russian front and another invasion looming. A few evenings later, watched only by the ghostly narcissi that poked up through the frozen crust of snow along the roadside, the last remnant of winter, the cases of manuscripts left Grüssau for Kraków. The convoy rolled into Kraków around three in the morning, hours before the farm trucks began to trickle in to the market. Any citizens woken by the sound of vehicles knew better than to peek out through their lace curtains. Twelve years of war and occupation are good training for minding one's own business and keeping secrets. Dr. Sierotwiński's staff waited inside the Jagiellonian library, drinking chicory coffee to keep warm and stay awake, ready to spring into action and hustle the packing cases into the bowels of the library where they could be secured.

The librarians tensed as they heard the rumble of tires on cobblestones in the alley outside, then the soft clunk as a car door opened and closed, and footsteps approached the side door of the library. They heard a key grind in the lock, and as the door opened, and they recognized Dr. Sierotwiński, they let out a collective sigh of relief. He beckoned them to follow him out into the alley, where dark figures bundled in long coats were descending from trucks. The librarians formed a human chain, passing boxes from one to another into the unlit library as quickly and quietly as they could. Within an hour all the cases were safely inside and the trucks had dispersed. It was still dark outside, but inside the library he could hear the muffled footsteps of his staff as they rearranged the cases in the storage rooms below.

Dr. Sierotwiński sat down on top of one of the cases, pulled his pipe from one pocket and a tin of tobacco from the other. He filled the pipe, lit it and took a breath, sitting in the darkness, savoring the smoke. He still couldn't believe the magnitude of his discovery, and that they had managed to successfully bring the music to safety. Filled with sudden gratitude, he leapt to his feet and tugged at the lid of the box he'd been sitting on. He took his flashlight and shone it on the contents, each volume individually wrapped in linen. He unwrapped the first bundle and opened the cover. In the torchlight, he made out Beethoven's signature in faded brown ink on the yellowed page. String Quartet Opus 74. He shook his head in amazement and then, carrying the score, made his way to the record section of the music library where he ran his hand along the bakelite discs until he found the one he was looking for. He took the record and the score to his office, closed the door, turned on the lamp and set the record on his gramophone. As Beethoven's music played he traced the notes with his finger in the score, and his resolve grew to keep these treasures hidden. No-one outside of Poland, no Russian or German, must ever know of their existence. Although he'd been up all night, supervising the loading of the trucks, riding at the front of the convoy and overseeing the unpacking, his mind buzzed as he formulated his plans for how the collection would be stored and managed. He was elated to have brought these priceless documents to his own institution. Researchers and musicologists (Polish only, of course) would be allowed access but with strict confidentiality. How this would elevate Polish musical scholarship! Although he had to return to the field, to continue seeking the repatriation of Poland's cultural heritage, he knew that little could surpass this find.

Chapter 6 – Rumors

For twenty years the manuscripts stayed buried at the Jagiellonian library. Knowledge of their existence was kept to a very few people who needed to know, only the top Polish musicologists who were sworn to secrecy. Inevitably though, tongues wag and academics brag, and rumors began to circulate in the wider musical community. In 1968 an article appeared in the Deutscher Zeitung postulating that the Poles had discovered and kept possession of the manuscripts listed as still missing from the Berlin Library after the war. Professor Zofia Lissa had apparently been boasting of the collection in Kraków and word had reached Horst Kunze, the new director of the Berlin Library. The East German musicology community began to lobby their government to demand the return of the manuscripts to Berlin.

Professor Jan Stęszewski chairman of the Polish Composers' Association, leaned back in his chair contemplating his hands pressed together in front of him on the desk. Jan had been only ten years old when the Nazis invaded Poland. Too young to enlist, he had helped with the resistance. He'd known for many years about the secret 'Berlinka' music collection of course, and had accessed it to study for his doctorate. Poles who had suffered through the war remained bitter about their treatment and deprivations at the hands of the German occupiers. The Polish economy still struggled, unemployment was high, and people resented the powerhouse economy that neighboring East Germany had rebuilt. Many argued that war reparations awarded and repaid by Germany to Poland represented but a fraction of the cost of restoring the large-scale destruction and theft that the Nazis had inflicted on Poland over so many years. However, times were changing. The summer of love had come and gone, together with the Prague Spring. Young people were impatient. They wanted to mend bridges, to share wealth, freedom of speech, and equality for all. He wasn't going to be able to keep a lid on the open secret hidden in the Jagiellonian library much longer.

He looked around the table at the Committee of the Composers' Association, gathered for the meeting he had called to discuss the issue, and to decide how to respond to the rumors and the calls for the collection to be returned to Germany. One of their more radical members had proposed an audacious yet inspired plan. They would go public on the existence of the collection and would present a few token manuscripts to the German government at a ceremony in Berlin. The whole affair would be used however to demand adequate reparations for war damages from Germany to Poland. This approach would cast Poland in a positive light – while being hailed as the saviors of a treasure that transcended political boundaries they would at the same time send a strong message to Germany. Who could fault the generosity of the Poles in handing back some of the choicest pieces to Germany, while keeping the rest as collateral for future negotiations? The plan was brilliant. Jan couldn't wait to see the look on the Germans' faces when the Poles came clean and taunted them with what was just the tip of the iceberg. The only challenge was deciding which manuscripts to return.

The Committee reviewed the typed lists on the table and noisy and vigorous debate ensued. Which of the works of Bach, Mozart and Beethoven would be considered most significant? After only two hours they reached consensus. The Bach works to be returned were the Concerto for two pianos and the Sonata for flute and piano. Mozart's finest compositions were unanimously agreed to be the Magic Flute, the Mass in C Minor and the Jupiter Symphony. These would be returned. To complete the set, Beethoven's Ninth Symphony would be returned, to be reunited with its final choral movement which was repatriated to Berlin soon after the war ended, and his Piano Concerto No. 3, dedicated to Louis Ferdinand, Prince of Prussia. The middle and late Beethoven string quartets would remain in Kraków.

Jan closed the meeting and the committee members dispersed. Now that the decision had been made, he realized his time to enjoy access to these autographed masterworks was limited. He grabbed his coat and headed for the Jagiellonian library, to the room where the scores were kept and to which he had ready access. He reached for the scores that were to be returned and brushed his fingers lovingly across the pages, before setting them aside with instructions for them to be packed for presentation to the German Chancellor.

Chapter 7 – Recruitment
London, 2017

Gunther Erdogan sat in the coffee shop at the Barbican Center in London, his precious Vuillaume violin in its case at his feet. His armpits were clammy, his nervous sweat now chilled by the draft from the door. He wiped the grease from his forehead with his handkerchief, which carried the sticky, aromatic traces of the rosin that he'd dusted from his instrument before the audition. He just wanted to sit for now and gather himself, to recover his composure. The hiss of the urn, the clatter of silverware, the scraping of chair legs on the linoleum floor, these were the sounds of normalcy and everyday life that he craved after the intimidating hush of the concert hall, the feeling of walking out on stage and peering into the cavernous darkness of the auditorium. The disembodied voice from the darkness instructing him to begin sounded like his conscience speaking in his ear, and he choked down the panic rising in his throat so that he could focus on producing a clean, rich sound that floated up to the balcony that loomed high above the orchestra seats.

Gunther had just auditioned for, he mentally calculated, the fifteenth time for the London Symphony Orchestra. It had been challenging to find the time to practice this year's selection of orchestral excerpts, but he'd forced on himself the discipline of carrying the parts with him in his case, to take fifteen minutes to practice here and there between one student departing and the next arriving, or before a rehearsal, or even late at night before he allowed himself to collapse into bed. Gunther's fervent hope that this time things would be different wracked his nerves. It was impossible to tell from behind the screen how the judges were reacting. Their voices were so matter-of-fact and emotionless, they never gave a hint of what they were thinking. He'd agonized over his personal post-mortems after each previous audition. Had that G sharp been a fraction too sharp? Were his bow strokes even in that rapid passage? Had his vibrato been the correct speed or had he overdone it? Then came the two weeks of waiting in purgatory for the letter telling him if he'd been accepted into the orchestra, followed by the plunge into despair when the telltale thin envelope with its standard rejection letter eventually arrived on the doormat in the morning mail.

Gunther had been second violinist of the London Quartet since graduating from the Royal Academy of Music over fifteen years before. While he was thankful to have the work for at least this one long-term permanent position, the string quartet alone didn't pay enough to cover his bills, and he aspired to a position that provided more hours, better pay and a pension. And he still longed for that lucky break, the opportunity to shine and move into the limelight, just for once. He'd studied so hard at the Royal Academy, and he knew he could play as well as the best. He'd invested in his Vuillaume violin three years ago, determined to get a better instrument since he worried that the factory-made German violin that had carried him through college wasn't up to the demands of a professional violinist. Anyway, now that the audition was over, he'd better get back to practising for the London

Quartet's next concert. He'd had to neglect his study of the pieces they were programming and they would be rehearsing that afternoon with their new cellist. Gunther wanted to make a good impression on the quartet's newest member from the outset. His hands still trembled from the adrenaline of the audition that seeped back from his fingertips as he unzipped his violin case and pulled out the Dover scores for the two string quartets, Shostakovich No. 8 Opus 110 and Beethoven's Opus 74 'The Harp', to study.

Gunther lived in a small flat in Kilburn, North London, above a music store. He taught private violin lessons from his flat – it wasn't ideal but he couldn't afford to rent a studio, and at least the flat was right by the bus stop which made it easy for his students to come by after school. Also, he didn't have to worry about disturbing any neighbors, which meant he could take students early in the morning as well as late into the evening. Gunther couldn't afford to turn work away, not with the loan he'd taken from the bank to buy the Vuillaume. The struggle to find jobs was endless, to raise enough cash each month to pay the rent, let alone the installments on his loan. He even stretched out the playing life of his violin strings, trying to make them last as long as possible for practicing and teaching, and reserving a good set that he put on the violin for concerts and auditions only.

He ate as cheaply as possible, just as he had done during his student days, getting by on ramen noodles and peanut butter sandwiches. Jacek, the viola player in the string quartet, enjoyed food and took charge of finding restaurants for the group when they toured together. Gunther always chose the cheapest dish, worried about being able to pay his share of the bill. The only luxury he allowed himself was good Turkish coffee, which he brewed on the stove each evening when he finally got back to his apartment. The delicate taste, the sweet pinch of the sugar and the texture of the powdered grounds on his tongue transported him back home, to his grandmother's kitchen, before he had left Germany to go to college in London. Anneanne had given him the set of tiny coffee cups when he left home. 'Never forget your roots, Gunther' she'd said as she crushed him in a hug. He so badly needed a break, like a job at the Symphony.

Gunther always seized any opportunities that came up for studio sessions at the BBC in Maida

Vale. The BBC was a great place to make connections and find out from the grapevine what was happening in the local classical music scene. As well as playing second violin in the London quartet, he played first violin in a gigging quartet. His friend David who was even more strapped for cash than Gunther played second violin and they used a roster of freelance players on viola and cello, whoever he could get, mainly students from the Royal Academy who were also in dire straits financially. David was still waiting for his lucky break and eked out a meager living from freelancing and teaching. He had a passion for string quartets by obscure – or as David called them 'unjustly neglected' – composers and an encyclopedic knowledge of the chamber music literature. Gunther had aptly named his moonlighting group the Nightingale Quartet, a suitably romantic name that appealed to brides. He'd had cards printed and left them at bridal stores and registry offices. Even if he couldn't play a gig himself he got a finder's fee for putting the group together, which helped a little. But at thirty-eight years old, Gunther was still just scraping by, increasingly disillusioned whether all the hard graft would ever pay off and make his slaving round the clock worthwhile.

'Herr Erdogan?' A quiet voice in his ear addressed him in his mother tongue. Gunther had been so absorbed in reading his score, the music playing in his head, that he'd not noticed anyone approaching. Gunther spun around to see a man in a long raincoat standing behind him. It wasn't someone he recognized – the man was not much taller than Gunther, who was sensitive about his lack of inches; he was clean shaven, with short cropped brown hair and a bland face with no distinguishing features. Not only his accent but something indefinable about the cut of his clothes marked him out as a foreigner, a German. Gunther detected the faint scent of naphthalene mothballs as well as tobacco – a pipe smoker, perhaps – emanating from the raincoat. He guessed the man must have been in the audience for the auditions – they sometimes allowed selected individuals to attend. Or perhaps he was a music lover and had been to one of the London Quartet concerts. Usually when the quartet traveled together, Gordon James, the charismatic first violin with the floppy blond fringe got all the attention. Gordon was the one that the women, usually the grey-haired matrons, but also the pretty younger ones, and the critics and enthusiasts clustered around like bees buzzing around a honey pot. Gunther skulked around feeling invisible and unattractive. He'd inherited his Turkish forebears' dark skin and his large hooked nose sat prominently on his pinched face. Even his family name Erdogan, which means tall and handsome, felt like a cruel joke life had played on him. He'd been teased and bullied at the Gymnasium he attended in Essen, finding solace in playing his violin. He felt flattered, and surprised that the man had recognized him. He held out a hand in greeting.

'Ja, I'm Gunther Erdogan. Nice to meet you. Were you at the audition?'

'Holger Heimlich. I've been looking for you.' Heimlich's palm was cold and dry. He didn't smile.

'What do you want?' asked Gunther, suddenly cautious. His neck prickled, Heimlich didn't seem like a fan. In fact, he didn't seem particularly friendly.

'It's complicated. We need to talk. May I buy you a coffee?'

A wave of irrational fear flooded Gunther. Who was Heimlich? What did he want? He fervently hoped that the man wasn't a debt collector – he was significantly behind on his loan payments for the violin. He closed his scores and picked up his violin case, instinctively cradling it on his lap to keep it safe. But why send a German debt collector when his loan was with Lloyds Bank? His stomach lurched as the awful possibility that Heimlich was from the Federal Office for Immigration. Gunther's parents had paid dearly for his forged passport; the family had overstayed their Turkish visas when they had brought him to Essen as a baby, in the hope of giving him a better future as a European citizen, and he'd only learned of his status through the whispered discussions at the kitchen table when he'd won the scholarship to the Royal Academy in London. His parents had agonized over how to get his documentation, the passport that would allow him to travel freely within Europe. He twisted around to watch Heimlich as he ordered two coffees at the counter and then walked back over to sit at the table with the violinist. The coffee shop had emptied and now only the two men sat there, as the waitress brought the cups to the table. Gunther tried to calm himself but internally his mind was racing. He kept silent, waiting for Heimlich to speak. His companion waited until the waitress was out of earshot, and then he sighed and shook his head.

'Mr. Erdogan, you are in big trouble. The BZSt is after you for unpaid taxes. Did you really think you could leave your problems in Germany?' Another wave of fear rose within Gunther's throat. Didn't he have enough problems already without this new, completely unforeseen one?

'There must be a mistake. I left Germany when I went to College. I live in the UK now, I pay taxes here.'

'Ja, Herr. Erdogan, but you've given many concerts in Germany. How were you paid? In cash, I presume? Large amounts of cash on multiple occasions, ja? But you've not paid a penny in German taxes. We've been investigating you.'

Gunther began to panic. His cheeks grew hot and his fingers, suddenly sweaty, slipped on the handle of the case. He'd never heard of having to pay taxes in countries where he'd performed but maybe it was one of those things like a television license, or an M.O.T test for your car that everyone else seemed to know about but no-one ever told you, until you got into trouble for not having one.

'How come I've not heard about this before or received any tax statements? What do I owe?'

Heimlich leaned forward, his elbows on the table, and pressed his fingertips together. He seemed to be taking sadistic pleasure in watching Gunther squirm. 'You tell me. You haven't declared your income in Germany so we have had to make our own estimates. Let me see, over the last ten years you've given, let's say, some thirty concerts. Let's say you make five hundred euros a concert. Based on that, you owe the BZSt about two thousand four hundred euros. But that doesn't include the penalties for ten years of non-payment.'

Gunther gritted his teeth and the veins bulged in his temples with the effort not to cry out. He glanced across at the waitress, but she didn't seem to have noticed anything was off. He swallowed and took a deep breath to calm himself. Then he faced Heimlich and said quietly.

'Well, we both have a problem then. I don't have that kind of money. That's way more than I make in a typical month. So, what happens now?'

'We thought as much. So, we have a proposition for you. There is something that we want that we think you may be able to help us acquire. If you would be willing to cooperate, the BZSt might be able to overlook your debts. Wipe the slate clean as it were.'

Gunther wondered what was being asked of him. And who were 'We'? He tried to summon as much bravado as he could.

'Well, that depends. What sort of cooperation are you looking for? Is it something or someone I know?'

For the first time since he'd introduced himself, Heimlich grinned. Or to be more accurate, he bared his teeth and smirked in a most unpleasant way.

'Funny you should ask. In a way, yes, it's something you know very well. In fact, it's right at your fingertips.' He reached his hand across the table towards Gunther, pointing towards the table with a neatly manicured finger.

Gunther jerked back from the table, almost dropping his violin. Surely not the Vuillaume? What would the German government want with his precious violin? But then Heimlich dropped his finger on the Dover score. Gunther's puzzlement grew. You could buy a Dover score for thirty pounds, much less if you bought one second-hand, online. He blurted out 'Beethoven's quartets?'

Heimlich withdrew his finger and pressed it to his lips.

'Quiet now, Herr Erdogan. We don't want to draw attention to ourselves.' He leaned forward and whispered. 'Listen very carefully. The London Quartet is planning a concert in Kraków later this year, yes?' Gunther nodded. 'There's a certain musical manuscript that needs to be liberated from the Jagiellonian Library there. We want you to help us acquire this document and bring it back to Germany, where it rightfully belongs.'

Gunther stared at him, dumbfounded. They were asking him to steal a manuscript to order? Who was Heimlich really working for? He began to protest.

'I really don't think I'm the right man for the job. You've got the wrong person. There has to be another way.'

Heimlich shook his head and grinned again. 'Oh no, Herr Erdogan, I think we have the right man. I can see you are in desperate straits, you have debts you can't pay. Perhaps we can add some additional incentives for your cooperation. This manuscript is none other than Beethoven's Harp Quartet, the piece you will be performing in Kraków. It would only be natural for you as a professional musician to ask to see the autograph score which was stolen by the Poles after the war and has been held hostage at the Jagiellonian Library ever since. The rest we leave up to you.'

Gunther suddenly felt cold, the kind of chill you feel when the sun goes in after you have taken a swim in the lake too early in the spring. He didn't know what Heimlich was insinuating by 'additional incentives' but he suspected these might be negative inducements – threats of physical violence for example – and he wasn't prepared to take that risk. Heimlich had him cornered and he couldn't think of any other way out other than to accept.

'OK, OK. I'll try' he muttered, desperate to get out of there and away from Heimlich's cold stare. 'So, what happens next?'

'I thought you'd come around' said Heimlich, holding out his hand once more to shake Gunther's and seal the deal. 'Don't worry, I'll find you. I'll be in touch with further instructions when you embark on your European tour.' And at that he rose to his feet, thrust a hand in his pocket, and pulled out a crisp, clean ten-pound note, which he placed on the table between their coffee cups, both untouched, the coffee now tepid with an unattractive layer of scum on the top. 'I'll be seeing you soon' he said and left.

Gunther's heart was pounding and he could feel his cheeks burning. He picked up the coffee cup and chugged its contents. He needed the caffeine and it was a waste of good coffee not to drink up. He steadied himself and went to pay the waitress at the counter, leaving a small tip and keeping the change for himself. The waitress looked sympathetically at him.

'You all right, love?'

'I'm just tired, it's been a long day. Thanks' mumbled Gunther. He picked up his violin and scurried out, looking fearfully from side to side and behind him in case he was being followed. But Heimlich was nowhere to be seen.

Chapter 8 – Rehearsal

Allegro

The quartet begins with bright chords and then the second violin meanders merrily like a bubbling brook as the first violin floats over the top with a jaunty whistling song. The viola takes over the tune in a throaty tenor. The violins join in bouncing chords while the cello and viola trade off their plucked arpeggios and then the two pairs switch roles, echoing the harp an octave higher.

The viola starts the cascading scales of the second theme, joined in unison by the cello and passed first to the second violin and then taken over by the first who ascends into the stratosphere while the viola and cello join back in turn descending to the depths. The cello and viola chase each other with scales running up and down, and the second violin joins in, taking the lead for a brief moment while the first violin soars above his tune in octaves. The upper and lower pairs move in octaves towards a classic cadence that smacks of Viennese pomp and circumstance.

In the development, the key shifts to a nervous G minor. Now the viola and then the cello whisper in the darkness the melody that the second violin played in the sunlight. The group tiptoes back towards the light as the cello breaks into song back in the major key, bathing in the sunlight. The inner voices scrub away the cobwebs as the cello and first violin play the glorious melody in canon. The pairs of voices break up, answering each other, the inner voices now scrubbing fragments, the outer voices echoing each other as they fade away to stillness.

Out of the calm, the pizzicato arpeggios start to ripple up from the bottom, accelerating and fanning out into a spectrum as they return to the opening E flat major chord. The violins play the tune and the merry undercurrent. Now it's the cello's turn to play the tune, starting on a high B flat and descending all the way down to a low E flat on the C string before resolving on B flat, while the first violin sails heavenward to a suddenly whispered top B flat. The theme repeats and the Viennese court bows out down to a whisper. But it's not over. The cello creeps out like a little mouse, with the other three strings tiptoeing behind and all of a sudden, we are in another key. What is going to happen next? The tune comes back in the upper strings and the excitement builds as the cello holds double stopped chords that morph from minor to major. The first violin breaks into urgent arpeggios as the three lower voices play their pizziccati, and then the cello is bringing home the harmony while the second violin and viola play the familiar tune as a dialogue and the first violin throbs in ecstasy overhead. One last Viennese curtsey and the plucked chords climb the stairs to put the movement to bed.

Gunther opened his violin case, the familiar muted cacophony of sounds at the Royal Academy taking him back to the optimistic days of his student hood. As alumni of the Academy, the London Quartet were able to book practice rooms there for their rehearsals. The background noise was a good way to test your focus – unless you were a hundred percent concentrated on your own music, it was easy to get distracted, to start trying to dissect the sounds with your ear and work out what piece each of the neighboring groups was working on. If you were paranoid, you might start making comparisons and wondering if your own playing was up to scratch with the muffled snatches you heard through the practice room walls.

Gordon, the first violinist, was already in the rehearsal room when Gunther arrived, practicing scales up and down three octaves, then in thirds, sixths and lastly, tenths. Gordon the perfectionist as always. Gunther vacillated between hating Gordon, jealous of his precision and his success, and grudging admiration of the way he projected his tone and made the passagework sound so effortless. He remembered his first day in class, Gordon strutting forward with such confidence, commanding the accompanist with his plummy patrician accent, immediately making Gunther feel inadequate. How could he, short, dark and skinny with a strong German accent, compete with the tall golden English schoolboy? Gordon reeked of privilege, from his fine old Italian violin, the patina of a private education to the polish of his expensive handmade leather shoes. Gunther's parents had scrimped and saved, living in a tiny apartment so that their son could go to the best Gymnasium in

Essen to prepare him for college, but he'd been bullied and teased, not only because of his Turkish heritage and small stature, but also because his trousers were faded, the seat and knees shiny from wear, and his shirts were tinged with grey and had frayed cuffs despite his mother's best attempts to scrub them clean and mend them. But wanting to beat Gordon had spurred him on to try even harder throughout the four years of his degree, and to his great surprise, Gordon had invited him to form the London Quartet together when they graduated. They'd managed to maintain an uneasy truce for the last fifteen years, like warring spouses in a marriage of convenience, reluctantly acknowledging that they needed each other for the success of the quartet as a vital element of their respective professional careers.

Jacek Kowalski, the quartet's viola player, observed the tension between Gordon and Gunther with detached amusement. His prime objective in coming to London for his studies at the Royal Academy had been less about the music and much more about escaping from the restrictive society of his native Poland. His natural brilliance had meant he never had to work hard to rise to the top, and he'd deliberately chosen to play the viola not only because he enjoyed its darker, richer sound (just as he'd always preferred boys over those boring, prissy Catholic girls) but also because the parts were easier and there was less competition, ergo less practising which meant more time to enjoy life. On first meeting Jacek, many people mistook him for an introvert, as he didn't say much. His modus operandi was that of an astute observer. He watched and listened, and summed people up, and only then would he launch an acerbic dart into the discussion with as much truth and wit as any Shakespearean Feste. Gordon had invited him to join the London Quartet since he was clearly head and shoulders above any of the other violists in his class, without even trying, and Jacek had accepted since it was an easy option requiring little effort on his behalf. While Gordon and Gunther competed to select repertoire, and find gigs for the group, Jacek made their physical and mental wellbeing his responsibility. He'd lost count of the number of times he'd had to intervene with a barbed comment in a spat between the two violinists or serve as a peacemaker to bring them back together after one of their regular fallings-out. Jacek paid particular attention to creature comforts and spent hours finding the best hotel, weighing the pros and cons of soft sheets in one with convenience to the concert venue in another. He also took responsibility for seeking out interesting restaurants for dinners when they were on tour, always eager to sample the best of the local cuisine.

The fourth founder of the quartet, cellist John Roberts, had exerted a stabilizing influence on the group. He sat with his cello, calm and steady as a rock while the temperamental storms of his fellow players had played out. John was responsible for logistics – for good reason, as his was the largest instrument which required meticulous planning of flights, trains and cars to ensure that the cello was suitably and safely accommodated. John had married soon after graduation and he and his wife Susie now had three children. Family had been John's reason for leaving the group in September. His youngest child had just started school and John and Susie were finding it difficult to manage the various school runs, music lessons and doctors' appointments that three energetic children needed, when combined with the punishing touring schedule of the London Quartet. John had built a thriving teaching studio and was able to support his family by teaching from home as well as freelancing with several local community orchestras. It was impressive that the original group had managed to stick together for so long; a quartet rarely kept all its original members for fifteen years. This spoke volumes of Jacek's and John's abilities to temper the rivalry that simmered between Gordon and Gunther.

The quartet had auditioned several cellists to replace John, and had unanimously agreed on a new graduate from Juilliard, Jennifer Rose, who'd come highly recommended by a Royal Academy alum now teaching cello there. Jacek had some private reservations about bringing a woman into the group, and how that would irrevocably change the dynamics of the quartet. He sensed trouble brewing, especially given the competitiveness between Gordon and Gunther over everything, not just music, or who was working hardest, but over attracting women as well. But there was no question that Jennifer had stood out above all the other candidates; as a new graduate the pay they could offer her was comparable with the going rate, and they could tell immediately on meeting her that she would bring a breath of fresh air and new ideas to their music.

Jennifer had moved to London a month ago and had been getting used to the way the quartet worked, and to integrating her unique sound with theirs. Gunther looked at his watch and shook his head. Where was she? It was five minutes past the hour, and they needed all the rehearsal time they could get, especially Jennifer, as she was less experienced than the others. The practice rooms were in great demand and they only had a two-hour session booked before the next group would arrive and kick them out. He heard footsteps hurrying down the corridor and stuck his head out of the door. Yes, it was Jennifer. Her face was flushed and her long golden locks tumbled messily over one shoulder, as she half jogged towards him, her cello case slung awkwardly over her other shoulder. Gunther held open the door, wordlessly as Jennifer burst in, breathlessly apologizing for her lateness. She dumped the cello unceremoniously on the floor, straightened up and threw her coat on a chair, tossing back her hair.

'I am sooo sorry, guys! I thought I had plenty of time, but the strap on my cello case got caught in the turnstile when I got on the tube at Kings Cross, and I just missed one train and had to wait fifteen minutes for the next, and then the train was running so slow that I thought I'd get off at Regent's Park and walk, but I didn't realize there's no escalator so I got my workout in already today!'

The torrent of travel information bemused Gunther. He wasn't used to having such a talkative colleague.

Gordon stood up affably to greet her.

'Well, better late than never. Remember for next time, Baker Street has elevators. Take your time Jennifer, we'll tune when you're ready. We'll be starting with the Beethoven.'

Jennifer took out her cello and propped the empty case against the wall. Its white lacquered surface was plastered with stickers and slogans. She sat down between Gunther and Jacek, adjusted her endpin, pulled the music stand towards herself, and wrapped her long legs in faded denims around the cello.

Gunther couldn't help staring at her. Jennifer was strikingly different from most of the pale Englishwomen one saw huddled on the tube in a London winter. A classic California blonde, her tanned hands and face stood out against the fluffy white angora sweater that no sensible English girl would dream of wearing in the grimy city. Jennifer hadn't yet acclimatized to the damp, chilly November weather and Gunther had yet to see her without the sheepskin Uggs on her feet. She tucked her hair behind her left ear so that it wouldn't get under her fingers on the cello, and with her right hand, pulled a tube of lip balm from her jeans pocket and applied it to her lips. Gunther caught a trace of the strawberry scent of the balm, warmed by her lips. She reminded him of early summertime.

'Who's got a good A?' she asked to no-one in particular, and Gordon obliged by drawing his bow cleanly across his string to give a pure pitch for tuning. Gunther checked his tuning for the sixth time. Jennifer took up her bow from the stand, tightened its hair and checked her own strings. Jacek waited until Jennifer had finished and then asked her to play her C so he could tune his viola's lowest string to hers. Jacek, always the joker, growled in his thick Polish accent 'that's a pert bottom' and Jennifer laughed. She knew by now that Jacek was gay and that he liked to have dalliances with buff younger men. She liked Jacek best of all the quartet members. He didn't say much, but when he did speak he was very insightful, and he could be very, very funny. Jennifer couldn't believe some of the things he came out with, poking fun at people. He was an excellent mimic too. Jacek said outrageous things but he got away with it with the twinkle in his eye, and his humility. Jacek truly loved the music for its own sake, he wasn't into being competitive, as she was learning Gordon and Gunther could be. Most of all, knowing that Jacek was gay, she could relax and feel safe with him. She wanted all the guys to like her but she could already sense a bit of sexual tension brewing between Gordon and Gunther.

This was Jennifer's first job after graduating and she wanted to be successful. She'd read 'Mozart in the Jungle' and was well aware of the perils and pitfalls of being a young woman professional working in an all-male environment. Blair Tindall's true story was a cautionary tale for any young woman wanting to make it in the music world. Jennifer had concluded that the moral of the story was never to compromise on your principles, and don't even think about sleeping your way into a job. She was determined to keep her working relationships and her private life strictly separate.

She'd recently broken off a two-year relationship with Kent, a pianist studying in Juilliard's graduate program. Jennifer had placed an ad on the college bulletin board looking for an accompanist for her first student recital and Kent had answered. He'd swept her off her feet at first, beguiling her with his knowledge of sonatas for cello and piano by obscure composers she'd never heard of, some of whom were living and were friendly with Kent. Kent epitomized everything that was hip and cool about New York; his hair was shaggy and he had a scruffy beard and favored skin tight T-shirts with cardigans layered over the top, and he told her that he was very sensitive. They'd shared a studio apartment on the Upper West Side, a bed, and even a toothbrush on occasion. Kent's grand piano took up almost one fourth of the total floor space and they'd eaten suppers Japanese style half underneath the piano, sitting cross legged on pillows around the coffee table.

Things started to turn sour when Jennifer got her job offer from the London Quartet. Kent accused her of betraying him by going behind his back to audition. He pouted and sulked, saying how much he needed her to be in New York with him, how selfish she was being. When that didn't work, he alternated tears with pleading her to stay. It was as if scales had fallen from her eyes. Jennifer realized that it had been all about Kent all along. She wasn't interested in playing second fiddle to an egotistical pianist. She wanted her own career and if her boyfriend couldn't be supportive of her ambitions, he was not the person she wanted to share her life with. She moved out and slept on a friend's couch while she finished up her studies and the final exam. Kent bombarded her with phone calls, which she didn't answer, and with text messages, which she deleted. He took to hanging around at Juilliard, trying to catch her when she came out of classes, which she found really creepy, so she took care to stick with the crowd so she couldn't be picked off. When Kent found out that she'd hired another accompanist for her final recital, he lambasted her in a series of obscene texts that had left her hands shaking as she read them on her cellphone. She'd been so relieved to be able to flee to London to start her career and leave over three thousand miles of the Atlantic Ocean between her and Kent.

While London was exciting, she missed being on the same continent as her Dad, and being able to text him or phone him whenever she needed some guidance or advice. She'd called him daily ever since leaving home to pursue her cello studies. The eight-hour time difference was a real challenge. She felt comforted to have Jacek as her ally, a man she could trust almost like a surrogate father, as she learned the ropes in her new job.

She opened her Beethoven part to the beginning of the Opus 74 quartet. The group focused their gaze on Gordon, who raised his head and shoulders to cue them to take a collective breath and simultaneously glide their bows along the strings. Jennifer loved that aspect of chamber music – being able to communicate without words but by gestures and breath alone. That part of joining the quartet had been easy to assimilate, as it came naturally. All you had to do was be aware of the slightest movement of your fellow players. The next hardest was to watch and listen to the others and make sure your bow stroke and vibrato matched theirs so that your sound blended rather than sticking out harshly. This was especially important when it came to matching the length of a note. People forgot, you didn't just have to start exactly together, you had to finish together as well. The most difficult part was getting used to the musical style of the group, how they interpreted the works with which she was already familiar, but had learned to play with other people. Since she was new it meant the group had to spend an inordinate amount of time (or so it seemed, when they would rather just play) talking about the music, explaining, or arguing, about the phrasing and interpretation and particularly about the balance between the instruments.

They had only gotten about twelve bars into the movement when Jacek called out 'Stop'. His keen ear had detected some raggedness in the sudden loud chord that punctuated the soft music. 'Jennifer, we all have double stopped chords here except for you. Can you delay your pedal note until Gordon reaches the top of his chord? And then, Gordon, I'm going to take my time with the viola entry that comes next, just so you know to wait for me.' They went back a little way in the music and tried again. Jennifer looked anxiously at Jacek to check if he was happy the second time around and his eyes smiled back at her. The introduction wound slowly up like a spring and it was a relief to be able to sit back and enjoy the jaunty Allegro that ensued. The cello part was easy and alternated between a simple baseline and duets with Jacek. Every time they had parallel passages, Jacek twisted towards her slightly as if he was inviting her to dance with his viola, and beamed encouragingly into her eyes. Gordon and Gunther had similar duets, but as she glanced up from her page at them she noticed the dynamic between them was different. Gunther's eyes were fixed on Gordon but there was no friendly smile. It was more a look of submission, like a dog anxiously watching its master, with Gunther following exactly in Gordon's footsteps, carrying the weight of Gordon's melody with his supporting notes. She was reminded of the words of the old carol *Good King Wenceslas* – 'In his master's steps he trod, where the slow lay dinted'.

They got to a passage where each player had scales building on each other. Jennifer raced down her scale while Gordon was climbing into the stratosphere and she arrived before he did. Gordon stopped and snorted. 'Steady now, I want to enjoy my high notes.'

'Don't you think that's a bit over-dramatic so early in the movement?' blurted Jennifer. 'I rather think we should accelerate through that scale and pull back afterwards.' Gunther quickly chimed in, agreeing with Jennifer. 'Gordon, don't be a prima donna. Your moment will come soon enough.'

Jennifer was pleased that Gunther had backed her on a musical point. She smiled at him and he twisted his lips wryly in return. They reached the part where plucked strings ripple up in arpeggios, starting with the cello and picked up by the viola and second violin, that gives the quartet its nickname 'The Harp'. Then, towards the end of the movement, Gordon launched into a thrilling obbligato passage, his bow flying over all four strings, at once virtuosic but at the same time making it look effortless. Jennifer couldn't help herself. 'Wow! Bravo Gordon! That was fantastic!'

Gordon smirked. All those hours of practice had paid off. It wasn't easy leading a string quartet. He'd taken a risk forming the group when he'd graduated from the Royal Academy. He could have played it safe and got a job with one of the major orchestras but he aspired to the limelight and he knew in his heart of hearts that he hadn't got what it took to become a soloist. Forming a quartet in which he could showcase his talent was the most obvious path, and he'd picked others who were solid and reliable, but above whom he could shine. Gordon was the one who called all the shots; he chose the repertoire, making sure the first violin parts were suitably showy, and he gave the others musical direction. When Jacek came up with a novel idea or interpretation, Gordon sometimes resisted but later would brag that it had really been his own idea.

Gordon subscribed to the 'work hard, play hard' mentality. Before a concert he would shut himself away and practice obsessively, but after performing he enjoyed nothing more than repairing to the nearest bar with a bevy of admiring fans whom he regaled with stories of his musical exploits. It wasn't unusual for Gordon to end up taking a woman back home with him to his upscale flat in Edgware and seducing her. He wasn't fussy about age but he liked his women wealthy and well dressed (dripping with pearls as Jacek memorably described one of them). But these dalliances were usually short-lived and like the proverbial rolling stone, Gordon swiftly moved on from one conquest to the next.

Gunther watched Jennifer intently as he played. He hoped that her arrival would shake things up a little in the quartet. Gordon had held sway for far too long and it was about time someone challenged him in his bossy ways, dictating to the others how they should play. After all, they'd all been contemporaries at the Academy with the same teacher and the same way of playing. Jennifer brought fresh ideas from Juilliard in New York and Gordon would do well to listen to her. It was one of the pluses they had discussed when deciding to offer her the position. And she was incredibly lovely to watch while she played. Her long tanned arms moved as gracefully as a ballerina's and she swayed her whole body as she moved in time with the music. Her hair glinted under the lights and her lips worked unconsciously as she played, alternately pouting at the trickier passages and smiling when she was enjoying the harmonies. As they rehearsed, Gunther relished the moments when he got to play a duo with Jennifer. He could tell she was listening for him and playing gently from underneath to support his line, matching but never exceeding his sound. From time to time he caught her eye. She never looked directly at him, but he could tell she was watching from the corner of her eye, and he gave her an encouraging nod.

They turned to the slow movement of the piece. Gunther cued in the lower strings as they built a soft cushion of sound for Gordon to use as a springboard as he entered with the eloquent melody. Gunther enjoyed being in control of the accompaniment. He glanced across at Jennifer and was piqued to notice that rather than watching him and following his lead, she was gazing at Gordon with a dreamy smile playing on her lips. He looked out of the corner of his eye at Gordon and realized that the first violin was looking into Jennifer's eyes, playing his sweet melody to her and her alone, serenading her as if he were some cheesy mariachi musician at a Mexican restaurant. What was Gordon playing at? This was no way to exploit Beethoven, cheapening the music by using it to his own ends to woo the newest member of the group. Gunther couldn't believe that Gordon was trying to muscle his way in on their colleague just the same way he did with all the cooing female fans after a concert. Amid his indignation he hated to admit to himself that he was a little jealous. If Jennifer was going to date anyone it should be him, Gunther. He knew how to treat a woman with respect. Distracted by his flash of insight into what Gordon was up to, he almost lost his place on the page but managed to gather his wits in time to make his entrance. He finished the rest of the movement mechanically, his mind on other things.

None of this had escaped Jacek. His eyes darted everywhere and he too had noticed Gordon's seductive serenade to Jennifer and Gunther's stumble. He rolled his eyes and chuckled sardonically to himself. Gordon was at it again, and Gunther had risen to the bait. The pair of them were so predictable, always competing, trying to score points against each other. Jacek liked Jennifer and hoped she had enough sense not to fall for Gordon's charms. The quartet didn't need a love triangle in its midst. He ran down his mental list of Gordon's previous conquests. It had started right out of college with a young woman majoring in piano who had accompanied Gordon in his solo recitals. Daphne, that was her name. She'd followed Gordon around like a faithful spaniel, she looked a little like one as well with her springy red hair and those big brown eyes, magnified by the horn-rimmed spectacles she wore – she had been very short sighted. Daphne had attended all their performances, sitting in the front row with complimentary tickets courtesy of Gordon, never failing to rise to her feet and applaud enthusiastically whether they'd played well or badly. He remembered the terrible scene when Daphne had burst backstage to find her beloved Gordon embracing a tall willowy blonde to whom he had recently also been giving complimentary tickets.

Then there was the dreadful dinner at which John's wife Susie had tried to set up Gunther on a blind date with her cousin Margaret. Gunther had been despondent after his German girlfriend Elfriede had left him for a radical environmentalist and Susie, newly married to John, was intent on playing matchmaker for her less fortunate friends. The whole quartet had gone together to Susie's favorite Italian restaurant, but Gordon's girlfriend at the time had been sick and could make it, and Gordon had so charmed Margaret over the breadsticks that by the time they reached the tiramisu (and three bottles of chianti later), Gordon and Margaret were 'sharing a taxi' home. Margaret soon realized her mistake and dumped Gordon within a week.

Over the years Gordon had firmly established his reputation among London musical circles as a serial womanizer, so much that he now tended to target younger women or those who were new to London. Jacek doubted that Jennifer had heard the rumors about Gordon. He vowed to keep an eye on her, perhaps whisper a word in her ear if he thought she might be at risk of falling for the lothario fiddler. She'd find out soon enough.

Gordon had been born with a silver spoon in his mouth and his parents had given him the best of everything – schools, teachers, instruments. They had even helped him buy his home, a half-timbered 1930's semi in Edgware. His natural confidence and drive had helped him succeed and as well as being first violin of the London Quartet, he had founded a chamber orchestra, the New London Sinfonietta, of which he was both concertmaster and conductor. With two good jobs, Gordon didn't need to take private students, and he made enough money to afford the finer things in life. He liked to be seen arriving in his classic British racing green Jaguar XJS, and he dressed to impress, from his Burberry raincoat to his polished Church's shoes. Jacek knew that beneath his vanity and ego, Gordon was actually quite fragile, a slave to his violin who practised obsessively for fear of the critics and bad reviews. He'd seen through the thin skin to the insecurity that lay below. He even felt a little sorry for Gordon, who could be so uptight at time that he didn't seem able to enjoy life as much as someone with so many material possessions might.

Jacek looked at Gunther. Poor Gunther, always the underdog, never succeeding no matter how hard he tried. Back in their student days, Jacek sensed an affinity with Gunther, since they were both foreign students and both minorities, viewed with unease in their home countries. As a Pole, Jacek had ingrained suspicion of anyone with a German accent but he soon realized that the assertive young Turk had grown up being excluded from mainstream society. Gays were similarly shunned in Poland, where the Catholic church held sway. Jacek thought back to the bitter-sweet memory of his own first love. He'd met Sigismund when they both served as altar boys at St. Barbara's church, where his mother attended Mass twice weekly. Blond haired and blue eyed, with roses blooming in his pale cheeks, Sigismund looked like a cherub in a baroque painting of heaven. Jacek had fallen head over heels in love. One morning as the boys were preparing the sacraments, bending over the wafers together, Jacek had brushed his lips on Sigismund's cheek. He'd waited with bated breath to see what would happen and still remembered his ecstasy when Sigismund had kissed him back. For several weeks' they had managed to keep their romance secret from the priest, but then one day he'd caught them embracing behind the altar and their secret was out. The priest had beaten them both with his leather belt and sent them home in disgrace. Jacek's mother had wept at the double shame of his dismissal and his unholy love for the other boy. He'd refused to go back to church after that.

Anyway, Jacek had always liked Gunther. He worked so hard, kept his nose clean and was painfully honest. Jacek tried to get Gunther to loosen up a bit, forget his worries, just enjoy the music for once instead of stressing and worrying about money all the time.

After they had finished working on the Beethoven, the quartet took a break. Jennifer set her cello aside and stretched her arms high above her head before bending into a series of lunges. She had made yoga stretches part of her practice in the hope that this would ward off any repetitive stress injuries from too much playing or sitting on one position. She reached in her purse and checked her cellphone for messages. Gunther took a cake of rosin from his case and applied it to his bow, stroking the hairs systematically like a meditation. Jacek pulled a chocolate bar from his pocket. He needed a sugar fix before they started work on the Shostakovich. Meanwhile Gordon filed his nails meticulously, pausing now and again to run a finger along their tips to test their smoothness. He tipped his head back and applied some eye drops – he wore contacts since he was too vain to wear glasses. Then he pulled a tin of breath mints from his leather music case and offered one to Jennifer before popping one in his own mouth. He looked at his wristwatch, an engraved antique that had belonged to his grandfather.

'We've only forty-five minutes left. Better move on to the Shostakovich before our time's up.'

Shostakovich's Eighth quartet, Opus 110, is dedicated in remembrance of the victims of fascism and war. Written in C minor, Beethoven's favorite key, in Dresden, East Germany in 1960, it opens with a mournful passacaglia started by the cello. The viola laments in the minor key while the first violin plays sweetly in the major key over the top. Then with a sudden attacca the savage second movement breaks out, alarms and sirens all over the place. The upper strings wail as the cello gets busy with bariolage. In the third movement Gordon played the ghostly fiddler dancing on the graves of the dead, while Gunther shivered and Jennifer and Jacek waltzed grotesquely "oom cha cha" together. The fourth movement which Shostakovich signs with his DSCH moniker is punctuated with gunshot-like rat-tat-tat chords over the heavy drone of bomber aircraft, and then moves into a sad Russian song 'Exhausted by the hardships of Prison' and ends as it began with echoes Lady Macbeth of Mtsensk's lament over the lover who has abandoned her.

Gunther played his part savagely, tearing into the violin as if he were pounding Gordon with his fists in a street brawl. He found Shostakovich's music very satisfying to play, it allowed him to work out and release his aggression and emotions, breaking away from the constraints of classical and romantic musical form. He knew all about the victims of fascism. The fascists were alive and well in Germany and he'd suffered at their hands. Their silent ostracism at high school, the graffiti and broken glass littering the streets where the Turkish community in Essen lived. The music of Shostakovich's ghetto with its echoes of Klezmer reminded him of the Turkish music of his youth, the violin and clarinet moaning and sobbing in minor keys.

'Steady now Gunther' called Gordon with his plummy British accent. 'I've a difficult passage coming up. I'm an octave above you.' Gunther gritted his teeth and imagined that his bow was heavy and his arms more muscular, so that his strokes became more labored and weighty. Meanwhile Jennifer and Jacek were getting into their waltz together, Jennifer stomping her Ugg boot on the heavy downbeat and Jacek the perfect foil, springing off her. Jacek's viola growled menacingly as his bow bit roughly into the strings. The piece ended solemnly with all four players on their lowest, open strings.

'Oh, that's so sad' burst out Jennifer. 'It's so clever the way he quotes his other works, the cello concerto, and Lady Macbeth, like that.'

Jacek had a lump in his throat so could only nod in agreement. Gunther began to pack his instrument away, carefully wiping off the rosin from the strings and the polished front of his Vuillaume, before wrapping it in a silk scarf and tucking it securely into the case. A knock sounded at the door and a head peered in.

'You finished in there? We've booked the room next'.

The London quartet finished packing up and hustled out into the hallway.

'Let's go for dinner at Giovanni's' suggested Jacek. 'I've been wanting to try it ever since they opened last month. It's not far from here, on the Edgware Road.

'Can I help you with the cello?' Gordon offered Jennifer, stretching out a hand. She laughed him off.

'I've been carrying this baby around since I was a little kid. I prefer to carry it myself. Thanks anyway.'

It was already dark, and the raw November air bit at their fingers. Gordon pulled a pair of leather gloves from his pocket, and Gunther miserably clutched the handle of his case tighter, his fingers already numb. Jennifer slung the strap of her cello case over her shoulder so that she could bury her hands in her coat pockets. She wore a knitted headband around her ears, looking for all the world as if she'd just left the ski slopes at Aspen.

They tumbled in through the restaurant door into a comforting fug in which the aromas of garlic and Mediterranean herbs swirled, instantly transporting them far away from the London gloom to sunnier climes. The dinner rush hadn't yet started, so they chose a table in the corner where they could pile the instruments against the walls, out of harm's way.

"Everyone OK with chianti?' Jacek asked.

Jennifer wrinkled her nose. 'I'd rather have a glass of prosecco, if you don't mind. I don't drink red wine unless I'm in Napa. I'm afraid my Dad's raised me to be a bit of a wine snob.' She pulled out her cellphone and opened up Facebook to check in. Jacek was already making a serious study of the menu. His facial expressions tickled Jennifer – he'd lift a quizzical eyebrow at one item, then smack his lips at the next, or just nod as he read, murmuring in approval.

'Shall I order appetizers for the table?' he asked.

'Just go ahead, you always do anyway' Gordon drawled lazily. Gunther frowned as he tried to remember how much cash he had in his wallet. The drinks arrived and he gulped greedily at his glass of red wine. He needed a drink after the stresses of the day.

'How did the audition go this morning?' asked Jacek.

Gunther made a moue and shrugged, trying to look nonchalant. 'Same as usual. It was fine.'

'You seemed a bit distracted today, that's all.'

Gunther colored, remembering his chilling interview with Heimlich. Jacek, although well intentioned, could be incredibly nosy, and Gunther didn't dare let slip his troubles with back taxes and vague threats from the German government. He changed the subject and turned to Jennifer.

'So how are you settling in? Found a place to live yet?' Jennifer had been staying at an AirBnB that she'd booked online, until she found her feet in London.

'I'm still learning how the Tube works' laughed Jennifer ruefully. 'Once I figure out the most efficient way to get around to all the places I need to go, I can narrow down what part of the city makes most sense. But first, I want to learn more about the history of the quartet, and how you guys got together. How did you pick the name?'

Gordon took a swig of his wine and leaned forward. 'It was my idea, of course. We all studied together at the Royal Academy of Music in the 1990's. Professional string quartets were quite unusual back then – people thought it would be difficult to get enough work to make a living. Quartets were just something you played for fun with members of the orchestra on your night off or a way of earning extra cash from wedding gigs when you were a student.' Gunther flushed again. He downplayed his extracurricular activities since he knew Gordon looked down on freelancers. But he needed any work he could get. Gordon continued 'There were very few professional quartets in London; first were the Amadeus, then the Lindsays, and now the Chilingirians. I had the idea of performing complete cycles of the great quartet composers' works. So, we started with all the Haydns and that gave me the idea for the name for the group. You know Haydn visited London in the 1790's, that's when he wrote his London Trios and London Symphonies. We even dressed up in long coats and powdered wigs, Haydn style. People loved the idea, and we've managed to attract and keep quite a following. We've done cycles of all the Beethovens too, and all the Shostakovich quartets.'

'And I'm the first new person in the group since you formed?'

'Yes, that's right. John, our original cellist has turned family man. He and his wife have their hands full with three kids at school now, so he's gone into teaching full time.'

'So, I take it none of the rest of you has a family?'

'No, we're all still young, free and single' bantered Gordon. 'I haven't met the right woman yet.' Jacek shook his head wryly – civil same sex unions were not allowed in Poland and gays faced discrimination and hate crimes from the majority Catholic population. Gunther downed his wine morosely and poured himself another glass. 'Gunther's a dark horse though. He always says he's working but for all we know he might have a harem tucked away somewhere, keeping him busy and spending all his money.'

Gunther scowled. 'Oh, leave him alone Gordon, can't you?' said Jacek. 'Enough of your teasing.'

Jennifer privately agreed. She thought Gordon's remarks were in poor taste. It was painfully obvious that Gunther didn't have a girlfriend. His shyness and awkwardness revealed a lack of experience with women, although he seemed quite genuine and respectful as a professional colleague. He looked a little sallow, despite his swarthy skin, and she guessed from the dullness of his eyes and the stress lines that surrounded them, that he worked long hours outside the quartet.

The antipasti arrived – crispy calamari, transparently thin slices of carpaccio and burrata cheese that oozed softly over the garlicky toasted slices of ciabatta bread when pricked with your fork. Jacek sighed contentedly as he chewed each dainty morsel.

Trying to steer the conversation away from his own personal problems once more, Gunther asked Jennifer about her family.

'My Dad's been hugely supportive of my career' she bubbled. 'He's a venture capitalist in Silicon Valley but even though he majored in Computer Science and Business, he's totally encouraged me to follow my passion for the cello. My brother and I grew up in San Jose, California –

he's working out some issues right now so he's still living with my parents. My Dad's a classical music fan – he took us to so many concerts growing up, that's where I first heard the cello and decided I wanted to play one.'

'Does your Dad play an instrument?' asked Jacek.

'He doesn't play, but he's a big collector of Beethoven memorabilia – he's always on the look-out for letters and other papers of Beethoven's that come up in auction. When I graduated from Juilliard he gave me a first edition of Beethoven's Opus 5 cello sonatas.'

Gunther opened his eyes wide but said nothing. Jennifer's father must be seriously rich. He wondered where she kept the cello sonata imprint but thought it would be rude to ask. The mention of Beethoven manuscripts pricked at his conscience. How ironic that he'd been asked to steal one for the German government, to learn on the same day that Jennifer actually had one in her possession. He had no clue how he would get the manuscript. He looked across the table at Jacek. Having a native Pole in the group would surely be a help but he couldn't let Jacek in on the secret.

The entrées arrived. Jennifer tucked into her caprese salad with gusto while Gunther picked halfheartedly at his spaghetti puttanesca, the cheapest thing he could find on the menu. He'd tried to fill up as much as possible on breadsticks and appetizers so he wouldn't go hungry. Gordon chewed on a steak and Jacek savored his osso bucco, one of his favorite Italian dishes and the one he used as his yardstick to assess a new Italian restaurant.

Once they had reached the cappuccino stage, the conversation moved on to their upcoming performance schedule. Gunther had arranged the European tour in January starting in Berlin, going on to Kraków in Poland. Now that he had an additional mission to accomplish he was anxious to hammer out the final details. Gunther had taken responsibility for organizing the German leg of the trip and Jacek was working on the arrangements in Poland. Gordon had written programme notes which the other two had translated; Gunther planned to get them printed when he arrived in Germany, a day before the others would get there. He would stay with a cousin who lived in Berlin, just as he had done so twenty years before when he was preparing to come to the Academy. He had a printer in mind – the same printer who had so expertly crafted his phony birth certificate and passport and slipped them under the counter in exchange for an envelope bulging with Euros.

'I still can't believe we got the Pierre Boulez Saal at the Barenboim-Said Akademie' said Gordon. 'You must have pulled some strings there, Gunther'. Gunther smiled. Sometimes, very rarely, coming from an ethnic minority could be helpful. 'D'you know how ticket sales are going?'

'Last I heard they were a little slow but the students will be back in January so hopefully sales will pick up then. There's not a lot else going on in January and we're listed on their website so we should pull in the local crowd as well as any winter tourists. Jacek, how about the Polish part? Have your contacts been able to help us with publicity? And how about accommodations?'

Jacek leaned back in his chair as he scooped the foam from his cappuccino cup with one finger and popped it in his mouth. 'Ah, you are going to love Kraków. I've arranged for us to play in Florianka Hall; it's a palace right outside the old city wall. The local people love classical music as much as

Berliners do; you should see our Polish audiences. Nothing like London ones. The women in their glamorous evening dresses, wrapped up in furs and elegant boots against the winter cold; before the concert there's such a buzz with everyone greeting one another and clapping their friends on the back, and kissing the ladies' hands. They call for encore after encore and afterwards everyone piles into the restaurants in old town and the toasts go on late into the night. Poles really know how to have a good time. We'll be staying just ten minutes' walk from there at a cozy little hotel just off the market square, so we won't have far to stagger back to our beds after a good hot dinner of braised goose washed down with vodka of any flavor you care to choose. I'm also planning some educational activities for you all while we're there.'

He raised an arch eyebrow and winked at Jennifer, who giggled, loosened up by the prosecco.

'Well, Jacek, it depends what kind of an education you have in mind. It sounds like you're already planning to show us some gastronomic delights and teach us something about vodka drinking.'

'Aha! My dear Jennifer, I fear you have found me out. And now that you mention it, I know a great vodka tasting bar where I would be more than happy to initiate you into one of Poland's most solemn rites – drinking! But seriously, there's something I'm sure even Gordon will want to see in Kraków, at the library, of all places.'

'Come on Jacek! Why would I want to spend my time in Kraków at the library?' scoffed Gordon. Surely if there's time for sightseeing you can come up with something a bit more exciting. Gunther held his breath. It couldn't be, could it? Was Jacek going where he thought?

Jacek was enjoying himself. He held up an admonishing finger and wagged it at Gordon.

'Now, now Maestro, trust me. Not many people know what the Jagiellonian Library in Kraków holds.'

'I don't even know how to spell that' quipped Gordon 'let alone what it is.'

'Well, would you be surprised if I told you that the library has Beethoven's original autograph manuscript of the very string quartet that we've been working on today? And I've arranged a private viewing just for us the day before the concert.'

He sat back on his hands, triumphant. Gordon for once was at a loss for words and Jennifer even gasped. Gunther tried his hardest to look surprised and let his mouth drop open in an O.

'Wow! That's so cool! My Dad would be so into that! How on earth did the manuscript wind up in Kraków? I wasn't aware Beethoven ever went there.'

'He didn't. It's a long story. In short, it's part of what's now called the Berlinka collection, rare books from the Berlin Library that were stored for safekeeping in Poland during the second world war and are still there. I pulled a few strings to get us in.'

Gunther's mind was racing. Yet another coincidence. Jacek was playing right into his hands – this was going to make his task so much easier. He'd have to make the most of the opportunity of getting an advanced look at the manuscript to check out the building and security arrangements and formulate his plans.

Jennifer piped up. 'I have a suggestion for something we could do later in the year. It would be a benefit concert in Napa, California in April for a charity I support called Strike Up. I'm on their

Board. We're campaigning to keep young first-time offenders out of prison.'

Gunther looked doubtful. 'It's a long way to go for a charity concert. What kind of fee would Strike Up be able to pay?'

Jennifer flushed. 'Well, we're a non-profit and it's supposed to be a fundraiser. I'd really like to give the opportunity to our group since it would give us good exposure in the States, but I was hoping that you'd all be willing to play for a discounted fee.' She added hastily 'I've got tons of contacts all over the Bay Area, through my teachers, and my Dad's connections. I'm sure I can arrange for us to tour out there and we'd have enough work to make the trip worth our while and comfortably pay for the flights and everything. Do say yes, please?'

Gunther still hesitated. Jennifer persisted, her voice getting a little louder and higher. Clearly, she was used to getting her own way, at least where her father was concerned

'Look, this matters to me. Since I so much want to make this happen, I'll waive my fee altogether. Then you don't have to, OK?' Gordon jumped in. 'Since it means so much to you, Jennifer, I can waive my fee as well. It would be great to get more gigs on the West Coast; we haven't had the opportunity to do much work there so far.' Gunther and Jacek looked moodily at each other – neither could afford to take a lower fee. After an awkward silence, Gordon said brightly 'Well, that's decided then, we'll do it, and overall it should work out at around half our usual fee.'

They settled the check and got up to leave. Gunther rubbed his eyes. It had been a long and stressful day. He was looking forward to getting home and spending some time alone to gather his thoughts. He took his Vuillaume from the stack of instruments by the wall, bundled himself up warmly in his coat and scarf and said his goodbyes. He scurried to the tube station, descended the steps and was gone. Gordon turned to Jennifer.

'The night is yet young. I'd love to hear more about your charity work. Can I buy you a drink?'

Jacek rolled his eyes. Trust Gordon not to miss a beat where a pretty young woman was concerned.

'Watch out for Gordon – he's dangerous' he joked, before heading off into the darkness. Jennifer laughed. She was confident she could take care of herself.

'Shall we?' asked Gordon. Mindful of her refusal to accept his offer to carry the cello before, he restrained himself from asking again and stood a respectful distance while she hoisted the unwieldy case on her back.

'Come this way. I know just the place.'

Jennifer followed him, striding along, her long legs easily keeping pace. They turned into an old-fashioned bar with stained glass set in the door and windows. Inside was all dark wood and Wilton carpets.

'It's just like an olde English pub!' exclaimed Jennifer with delight. 'Is it authentic, you know, really old?'

'I believe so. Old enough for Sherlock Holmes to have been a regular here.'

Jennifer looked at him and then slapped his shoulder. 'Go on, you're teasing me. Sherlock Holmes was fictional.'

'What can I get you?'

'I'll have a Scotch please, on the rocks.'

Gordon didn't know whether to be impressed or dismayed. The girl had good taste in liquor but she also had that dreadful American habit of killing the flavor of everything by serving it ice cold. He bought the drinks at the bar and turned around to see that Jennifer had found a high table by the wall. She sat on a stool, her cello standing next to her with her arm protectively draped around its neck. 'Meet my best friend and constant companion, Tessa' she joked, making a mock introduction of the cello to Gordon. He played along, making a courtly bow. 'Nice to meet you, Tessa' and pulled up a stool opposite Jennifer. They clinked glasses.

'Now, tell me more about this charity – what was its name, Strike Out?'

She giggled. 'Almost, Strike Up. Like Strike Up the Band. Strike Out is from baseball.' Gordon looked perplexed. 'Oh, I forgot, you Brits do cricket instead, don't you? Never mind.'

'So how did you get involved in the first place?'

Jennifer sighed and took a sip of her whisky.

'D'you remember I mentioned I have a brother? Jason is a couple of years older than me but he's never truly found his passion in life the way I have. When I was still in High School, Jason got into trouble with the law for underage drinking and possession of marijuana. We have the three strikes law in California and he had several warnings and would have ended up in jail if Daddy hadn't intervened. We managed to get a top lawyer and Jason got off without being sent to jail. He's truly not a bad person, and he didn't belong in jail. I've been interested in criminal justice ever since then. I dated a lawyer for a while and he told me about Strike Up. I wanted to help other kids like Jason stay out of jail and get back on the right track. I've been on the Board for a couple of years now and I'm in charge of fundraising. Thanks so much for your support today, by the way. I do appreciate it.'

Gordon leaned in for a kiss but Jennifer shrank back, dismayed that he'd misinterpreted her interest. 'No, no, no. Sorry Gordon, I didn't mean that. Let's keep it professional, OK?'

Gordon blinked and shifted back on his stool. He wasn't used to being rejected, but in a strange way it only spurred him on. He'd find another way to seduce Jennifer, but not tonight.

'Of course, I'm sorry. I just got a bit carried away. Nice to see someone who believes in a good cause.' He looked awkwardly at his watch, its face fogged and scratched with age. 'I'm so sorry, I'm going to have to run to catch the last train home. Will you be OK getting back to your B&B?'

Jennifer grasped at the chance to get away from Gordon's unwanted advances. She certainly didn't want him walking her home.

'Yes, I'll be fine. I'll hop in a taxi with the cello. Don't want to get it stuck in a turnstile this time of night!' She waited until Gordon had gone and then hailed a taxi. With her long blonde hair, she cast a striking figure and had no problem getting a cab to stop. She flung herself on the back seat, dragged the cello in after her and slammed the door shut. 'Whew, dodged a bullet there!' she congratulated herself, and gave the driver the address.

Chapter 9 - The plot hatches

The two soft chords at the end of the rollicking Coda that finished the Beethoven quartet took the audience by surprise. The London quartet froze for an instant, bows poised in the air, and there was a moment of silence broken by a guffaw a split second before the crowd broke into applause. Gordon leapt to his feet, grandiosely waving his bow at his colleagues for them to do the same. Jacek, holding both viola and bow in his left hand towards the audience, extended his right towards Jennifer to draw her up on her feet. She'd played very well in this, her first public performance with the group, and first live broadcast to boot. The London Quartet had played at the BBC Thursday lunchtime chamber music concert series at St. Luke's once before, and received a warm welcome this second time around. The space had surprisingly good acoustics, the polished wooden floor and wooden wall panels lending the sound life and warmth while the original rough brick walls soaked up the excessive echo that one might expect in a former church.

The applause continued and the quartet grinned and bowed. Even Gunther wore an uncustomary smile. As the audience started to drift out of the double doors, they headed back to the green room to pack up their instruments. The producer came up to congratulate them. He shook hands all around and patted Jennifer on the shoulder. 'Magnificent job, well done! Amazing how well your sound's blending already, while adding a certain *je-ne-sais-quoi* to the overall effect. It sounded wonderful through the headphones. You should check the listener comments on our website to see how it came across on the radio.'

Before the concert, while the hall was still empty, Gordon had arranged a photoshoot while they were all in concert dress, so that they'd have a group shot that included Jennifer as the group's newest member for publicity. The London Quartet had been using the same photo that had been taken when the group was formed. Gordon had insisted they look as 'professional as possible' and as a result the four had lined up, choking in their tight wing collars and bow ties with their instruments held stiffly in front of them for the black and white photo. Shag cuts and designer stubble had been fashionable at the time. The three remaining founders looked quite different fifteen years on. Gordon kept his hair longer on top but now neatly combed back and trimmed short at the nape of his neck. He'd been clean shaven ever since, to his horror, his beard had started growing in grey. Jacek shaved his head once his hairline started to recede although he had hung on to his stubble. His boyfriends joked that he had more hair on his chin than his head. Gunther's hair, although still messy, was streaked with grey and his face was thinner, with deep creases around his eyes. Gordon had to admit, much as he liked the youthful image of the original photo, that it was time for a redo.

Jennifer had broken with tradition to wear skin-tight black leather trousers and a flowing black silk blouse rather than a long dress, which led Jacek to break into a spontaneous whoop when she'd walked into the hall three hours previously for the sound check. Having always been an all-male ensemble, they'd never previously had the need to discuss concert attire, since it was a given that one wore black tie for formal evening concerts, and for less formal lunchtime concerts, all black, either a collared shirt and long black tie, or, if you were offering a contemporary programme or the weather was particularly cold, a turtleneck. The photographer's face lit up when he saw Jennifer. Having an attractive young woman in the group opened up all kinds of possibilities for a more contemporary, informal portrait. He played with the idea of having Jennifer as a dominatrix, with her male colleagues prostrate at her feet while she speared them with her stilettos and the sharp endpin of her cello. Jennifer collapsed in giggles at the suggestion but it had the effect of putting the quartet at their ease. In the end, he got some good candid shots of the group animatedly discussing a score, their instruments and bows in their hands as if they were in mid-rehearsal.

Now, after the concert and back in the green room, Gunther looked across to the table in the corner where he'd left his empty violin case and frowned. A piece of paper that hadn't been there when he left to go onstage lay on top of the case.

The dressing rooms were supposed to be kept locked for security when the performers weren't there, and it looked like someone had got inside. He was glad he'd kept his wallet in his inside jacket pocket and that he'd only left his emergency spare bow inside the case. He scurried across to look more closely at the paper. It was a paper napkin on which a note saying 'Call me' and a phone number were scrawled messily in red biro. The writer had been in such a hurry that the pen had torn the napkin slightly, like a scratch on the arm from a thorn when one is pruning roses. He wrinkled his forehead, perplexed. Who would want to send him such a cryptic note? He racked his brains to think. Had he recognized anyone in the audience? No, and if anyone got fan mail backstage it was invariably Gordon. Perhaps there was a trace of perfume lingering on it that might trigger a memory of who might have left the note. He lifted the napkin to his face and sniffed it. It smelt faintly of mothballs and tobacco. He started and clutched his fist, crumpling the soft tissue. Turning it over and spreading it out on the lid of his case with a shaking hand, he saw the printed logo of the Barbican Center coffee shop. Heimlich! Heimlich had been there. Gunther didn't recall seeing him in the audience, but then again, the man had few distinguishing features and it was difficult to remember his face. It was his voice that Gunther remembered, bland and chilling with his precise German accent. He'd remember that voice if he heard it again. He read the phone number – it looked like a mobile phone, he didn't recognize the area code. He stuffed the napkin in his pocket, and hurriedly packed away his violin, swaddling it in the silk cloth and tucking his good bow on top before securing the clasps. Grabbling the case, he ran to the dressing room door and looked up and down the narrow passageway to see if Heimlich was lurking there in wait. A young couple in their twenties were talking animatedly with Jennifer, who lounged against the wall, still holding her cello in one hand, gesticulating animatedly with her free one. There was no sign of Heimlich.

'What's up, Gunther?' asked Jacek, standing right behind him and speaking in his ear 'Are you expecting someone?' Gunther jumped.

'I…, I thought I heard voices in the hallway' he stammered the first excuse that came into his head.

'Ja, Jennifer's got a following already', chuckled Jacek. 'The girl is full of surprises – I think we're in for quite a ride!'

'I've got to go' mumbled Gunther, pushing his way through the door and heading for the exit. He was sweaty from playing on stage in his tuxedo and the stiff collar of his dress shirt choked his throat. He crossed the street and headed for the phone booths inside the Barbican lobby. After the lunchtime rush the place seemed deserted. He selected the farthest booth at the end of the row, and fumbled in his wallet for his phone card, and then punched in the numbers from the napkin with a trembling finger. The phone rang once and Gunther tensed himself. It rang again, two, three, four times, while his nerves jangled as loud as the ring tone. He was about to give up when he heard a click.

'Hallo?' he whispered. The other end of the line was silent. 'Hallo?'

'Ah. Mr. Erdogan. You got my message.'

It was Heimlich, all right. The flat, emotionless voice made his skin crawl.

'I enjoyed your concert. I see you have been hard at work, studying your Beethoven.'

'What do you want?'

'Now, now, Mr. Erdogan. We had a deal, remember. I said I would be in touch with you again. I thought it was time we got down to business and discussed the details. Have you thought some more about how you will get the manuscript for us?'

The success of the lunchtime concert and the unexpected bonus of having Jacek arrange access to the Jagiellonian library emboldened Gunther. He wasn't a nobody – his playing had just been broadcast live on the BBC to hundreds of thousands, maybe even a million listeners worldwide if you counted the BBC World Service and the internet livestream. He had connections, influence. Heimlich and his government cronies needed Gunther more than he needed them. He took a deep breath.

'OK Heimlich, I've been thinking about this. A Beethoven autograph manuscript is worth way more to any collector than some two thousand four hundred Euros. If I'm to take such a risk, I need to be adequately compensated. What if I'm injured, or worse, caught and have to face criminal proceedings?'

Heimlich chuckled softly. 'Hah! I see you've grown a backbone since we last met. Good for you. As it happens, I am authorized to negotiate with you. What price are you asking?'

Gunther ran a quick mental calculation of the remaining balance of the loan on his Vuillaume violin. He took his courage in both hands, and doubled the number. 'Two hundred thousand Euros.'

The line was silent. Gunther's heart pounded in his ears. His throat was too tight even to squeak, so he waited. He could hear Heimlich breathing at the other end. Gunther held his ground. The thought flashed into his mind that Heimlich hadn't gasped, so the number wasn't out of line. He'd heard of such manuscripts going at auction for over a million dollars. And he hadn't hung up either. Gunther cursed himself. He should have asked for more. He hurriedly broke the silence.

'And that isn't all. As well as two hundred thousand Euros, I need a break. A lucky break career-wise, that is. I want an invitation to play in the orchestra next September at Beethovenfest in Bonn.'

As a teenager, Gunther had the opportunity to attend the Beethovenfest as part of a youth music camp. He'd never forgotten the experience of hearing all of Beethoven's symphonies played in the space of four evenings at the concert hall where Beethoven himself had attended concerts as a young man. Gunther had watched the concertmaster of the festival orchestra in awe, aspiring to become like that player, all eyes of the other players watching him, his fellow violins intent on the tip of his bow, synchronizing their movements to his. He wasn't going to let this opportunity slip through his fingers. He waited. After ten seconds or so of silence, Heimlich sighed.

'Is that all?' he asked, in a slightly sarcastic tone.

'Yes, that is all. Two hundred thousand and the job at Beethovenfest.'

'You drive a hard bargain, Mr Erdogan. But I think we can accommodate your fee.'

Gunther moved the receiver away from his mouth, covered it with his sleeve and let out the breath he had been holding. He couldn't believe that Heimlich had accepted his demands. With that much money and the prestigious job, he'd be able to start afresh, clear his debts and begin to live life at last instead of just eking out a miserable existence. It was time for him to take control, to make sure he got all the help that he needed to succeed.

'OK, now we've got the business out of the way, let's talk details. I've arranged to get access to the Jagiellonian Library and see the Berlinka collection the day before our concert in Kraków. But I'll need any intelligence you have about the set-up there. What arrangements they have for security, for example, any surveillance you have on their staff and shifts. And I may need help in getting the manuscript in and out of the building and out of Poland without raising suspicion.'

'We can help with that. But I can't discuss those details now. You'll get the information and equipment you need closer to the time. Be sure to travel to Berlin a day or two before your concert there, and await further instructions. Once the manuscript is in your possession you are to bring it back to Berlin and then you will receive payment as agreed. Is it all clear?'

'Yes. I'll do as you say.'

'Very good.'

Heimlich hung up and Gunther heard the dial tone. He carefully placed the receiver back on the hook and then pumped his fist exultant in the air. This was it! If he played his cards right, all his problems would be over. He couldn't believe his good fortune. For the first time in his life things seem to be going his way.

Gunther decided a mini celebration was in order. He had no other engagements that day – he was usually too tired after a performance, too emotionally drained even to teach. His life had suddenly assumed an air of intrigue, of glamor. He was going to swipe a national treasure from under the noses of the Poles! He would be as cunning as the Pink Panther planning a diamond heist, as suave as James Bond. He took the escalator up to the swanky cocktail bar and ordered a vodka martini, shaken not stirred. He took it over to the balcony and looked down through the glass walls to the park below. A shaft of light from the setting sun cut through the December gloom, bathing the buildings opposite in an orange glow. Life was looking up.

He sat alone at his table for a while, savoring the aromatic fumes of his drink and the salty tang of the olive, which he chewed pensively. The bar was starting to fill with the after-office crowd, so he gathered up his things and headed for home. He decided to take the bus; he couldn't face the steaming, raucous crowds and the crush on the tube. He climbed up to the upper deck and leaned his forehead on the window, cradling his violin case on his lap. The bus swayed and lurched in the rush-hour traffic and as Gunther's eyelids drooped, the street lights and illuminated windows of the homes twinkled like stars in a faraway galaxy. The bus dropped him right outside the music store. The store was closed by now and the lights were turned off. He took out his key and let himself in the side door, wearily climbing the stairs to his flat. He dumped his case on the floor and headed for the bathroom, stripping off his tuxedo jacket as he walked. Time for a shower and to get into more comfortable clothes.

Gunther sat down in front of the mirror and rested his head in his hands. He looked up and critically assessed the image before him. His forehead above the beetling eyebrows was crisscrossed with furrows among the acne scars, and the eyes scowling back at him were bloodshot. He looked awful. The task Heimlich had set him danced, tantalizingly just beyond his reach. It couldn't be impossible. He had to find a way to pull it off in order to dig his way out of his debts and unpaid taxes. He pounded his fist on the dressing table, angry at himself for playing second fiddle to Gordon all these years. If only he'd had the courage to break away from the quartet when he was younger and had more fire. He'd worked diligently all these years – for what? What did he have to show for it apart from a fine violin that brought it with crippling debt.

Gunther's thoughts turned to Jennifer. He appreciated her musicianship, and he admired her all the more for refusing Gordon's crude and clumsy advances. Faithless Gordon was unworthy of her sunny Californian innocence. He'd chewed up so many women and spat them out over the fifteen years they'd been working together, leaving a trail of broken hearts in his wake. Jennifer was different. Despite her youth she was both intelligent and streetwise. And stunningly beautiful...she'd taken his breath away when she'd materialized that afternoon in those tight leather leggings. Gunther had always been attracted to serious, smart women, but he had to be honest with himself, his tongue had been hanging out like a panting dog on an August afternoon at the sight of her that afternoon. She was both intriguing and an open book. She'd spoken freely of her family while they had been rehearsing. It was plain to see that she worshipped her father and that their bond was a close one. In Gunther's limited experience of women, that type was often attracted to men that they viewed as surrogates for their father. Age was certainly on his side, if not the wealth that she casually hinted at. He wondered what he could do to pique her interest in him on a personal, rather than purely professional level. Unfortunately, he wasn't in a position financially, at least not yet, to contribute to her charity, the one for young offenders. And his time was very limited too, due to his workload, so offering to show her the sights of London probably wasn't feasible either.

He thought what else Jennifer had mentioned, any other angle he might use to build a closer relationship with her. A crazy thought flickered in his mind, like a mosquito. He mentally squashed it before it could take shape, but it buzzed annoyingly in his head, growing in a crescendo that eventually he couldn't ignore. Jennifer's father was an avid Beethoven collector – and Gunther was planning the most audacious heist of the century, to steal a Beethoven autograph score. What if, instead of delivering it to the German government, Gunther were to offer the manuscript to Edgar Rose? If he were to strike up a friendship with Jennifer's father, to perform a service that left Rose forever in his debt, would the circle of his daughter's affection expand to encompass Gunther? Of course, Jennifer must never know about the deal, or the provenance of the document. He knew that with her youthful idealism, he'd lose any hope of ever winning her heart if she learned of the theft and his role in it. But how above-board was Rose? Gunther had no idea of his ethics, but you could bet that most self-made men have trodden on a few others to get there. Rose was sure to have a few guilty secrets of his own. Would he even entertain the idea of adding a priceless manuscript to his collection by dubious means, or would he promptly hand Gunther over to the authorities? Would desire and greed overcome any moral objections he might have to acquiring the string quartet? Gunther would need to find a way to approach him, sound him out. Of course, the price would need to be higher, to balance the increased risk that Gunther was taking on in this enterprise.

And then there was the small matter of what to do about Herr Heimlich, how to get out of his obligation and his tax debts.

Gunther yawned. He looked at his alarm clock and was amazed to see the lateness of the hour. Now the seed of this new idea was firmly planted in his brain, he resolved let it germinate for a few days, while he mulled it over and figured out a way he might get it to work.

Chapter 10

Berlin, January – Monday

As instructed by Heimlich, Gunther arrived in Berlin a day before his colleagues, saying that he had personal business in Germany to attend to. No-one turned a hair since the others were all preoccupied with their own affairs. Jennifer was flying in direct from San Francisco, after spending New Year with her family in California. Gordon had a concert with the New London Sinfonietta that evening, so would be leaving London first thing in the morning for the quartet's rehearsals in Berlin. Jacek had been busy in Kraków, finalizing arrangements for their visit and tirelessly promoting the concert.

Heimlich was waiting at the airport when Gunther arrived. He picked up Gunther's suitcase without asking, seized his elbow and propelled him firmly outside, where a dark grey Mercedes limousine waited at the curb. The pavement was slick with frozen snow and the air reeked of kerosene. Gunther climbed carefully in to the back seat, glad to get out of the cold, and slid along to make room for Heimlich to sit next to him. Heimlich closed the door with a heavy thunk, hermetically sealing them inside. He rapped on the dividing window and the driver moved off. Heimlich remained silent and Gunther, in no mood for idle chatter, looked out of the window. It was a while since he'd been in Berlin, and they were driving though a part of the city he hadn't been to before. On the left-hand side, anonymous grey buildings loomed, with rows of tiny windows peering blindly from the concrete façade. On the right-hand side lay waste ground, fenced off with barbed wire, the weedy grass poking brown and shriveled through the dirty ridges of compacted snow thrown off the road by the snow ploughs.

They stopped outside a nondescript building and the driver hopped out and came around to open the door. Heimlich looked quickly about and then pulled Gunther inside the street door, his violin clutched firmly in his other hand.

'You can leave your suitcase with the driver' said Heimlich. 'He'll be back to collect you later. Come, this way.'

Heimlich led him into a small old-fashioned elevator, the type that had a metal lattice safety door that you had to pull across and latch securely before the elevator would move. Heimlich punched the button for the tenth floor. The elevator stopped and he led the way down a gloomy corridor, harshly lit with fluorescent strip lights. Their footsteps echoed on the linoleum floors. The place had an institutional smell of musty paper and floor polish.

Heimlich opened the door at the end of the hallway and waved Gunther inside. 'Welcome to my office' he said, in an ironic tone that was anything but welcoming. He held out a hand for Gunther's coat and hat, which he placed on a coat stand behind the door, and motioned for him to take a seat. Gunther sat cautiously down in the chair in front of the desk and set his violin at his feet. A large, oblong case sat on top of the desk. Heimlich moved around behind the desk, and leaned over the case, snapping it open so that its crushed brown velvet lined interior yawned towards Gunther.

'Welcome to your new violin case. I hope this fits. Would you try it for size, please?'

Gunther obligingly took out his Vuillaume and laid it in the recess. It fitted perfectly. The case was of a much higher quality than his own.

'Very good' said Heimlich. 'Now look here.' He reached into the lid of the case, lying open flat on the desk, and pressed down simultaneously on the two clips that held the bows in place. A soft click, almost imperceptible, sounded, and the panel sprang up, with the bows still attached, revealing a compartment underneath. Inside the compartment lay a bound volume, looking like an old photograph album.

'See this? This is an exact replica of the manuscript that we've had made. You are to substitute this copy for the original and then replace the original in the secret compartment. You will appear to be a professional musician, carrying his instrument with him at all times. In this way, you will be able to bring the manuscript undetected back to Berlin.

'What about the X-rays at the airport? Won't they see there's something else in the case?'

'The outer shell is shielded with lead. They won't be able to see a thing. If they ask, it's a pocket for carrying your music.

Next, Heimlich fired up the monitor on his desk and swiveled the screen to face Gunther.

'Listen very carefully. I'm going to show you the lay-out of the library and everything we know about the staffing there. I can't give you a copy so you will have to memorize. But musicians are used to memorizing, ja?' Heimlich pulled up a schematic floor plan on the screen and zoomed in to an area in the center of the building. Taking up a pencil, he tapped on the screen. 'This is the room where the Berlinka collection is stored. To access it you will need to go through two locked doors. There are two entrances to the building, the front entrance on Mickiewiczka Avenue, and the visitors' entrance where the registration desk is located at the back on Oleandry Street. But there are also fire exits – he tapped at various points around the perimeter of the building – that you could use to get out quickly if needed. All the doors and windows are alarmed, and there are video cameras at the entrances to the building and in all the reading rooms.' He reached in the desk drawer and pulled out a key fob with what looked like an emergency car key. 'This should come in handy. The key is a master key that should operate all the doors in the library. Our operative managed to obtain one from the cleaners. The remote control emits a radio frequency signal that is tuned to jam the video cameras. If you press the button like this' he demonstrated and a red LED illuminated 'the interference will black out the video cameras. I'd advise you to keep your eyes open and look for the cameras and use the jammer judiciously so that your path through the museum is not obvious to their security staff. There are four security officers on duty in any one shift; two at the visitor entrance, one at the main entrance and one patrolling inside the building. The first shift starts at seven thirty before the library opens and finishes at two thirty, and the second shift works from two thirty to nine thirty, through closing time which is at nine. There is no night shift. On Saturdays, the library is open from nine to four, with a single security shift, but it's closed on Sundays. Got it?'

Gunther's mind worked furiously. It looked like the best time to slip in un-noticed would be around two thirty when the shift changed, or on the Saturday afternoon when the library closed early.

He took a long hard look at the computer screen, trying to fix all the details in his mind. As Heimlich had remarked, he had trained himself to memorize music, in part by visualizing the notes on the page and also by following the flow of the melody. He traced the route from the back entrance to the manuscript room with his finger, and then back out again via the nearest fire exit, trying to commit it to memory. Finally, he looked up from the monitor to Heimlich. 'Yes, I've got it.'

'That's all then. Call me if you need anything else. Otherwise I'll wait to hear from you once the manuscript is in your possession. Any questions?'

Gunther pondered a moment, hesitated, and then spoke up. 'There is one thing. I may need supplies but I'm short of cash. I'll need an advance, to make sure I can get what I need.'

'I thought so. How much?'

'Two thousand four hundred Euros.'

Heimlich laughed. 'And get away scot free? I'm going to need some collateral.'

Gunther looked pained. 'I told you, I don't have any cash'.

'Ja, but you have a spare violin bow? I'll take that in exchange for the cash. You can have it back, plus the balance, on delivery of the manuscript.'

Gunther didn't like it, but he had no other option. He'd have to keep his fingers crossed that there were no mishaps with his good bow. At least it had plenty of hair. Worst case, he'd have to borrow one of Gordon's bows if his own broke.

'Don't forget your new case. You can leave your old one here.'

Gunther was only too glad to accept the new deluxe model in exchange for his battered old one, which he'd had since his father bought him his first violin. He unpacked the contents of his old case – a cake of rosin, his spare concert strings, several pencil stubs and a handful of photos, and transferred them all to the sleek brown velvet one together with his violin and his better bow, as well as the key fob, which he tucked carefully in the compartment. He was amazed to find that even with the manuscript and the lead lining it was only slightly heavier than the older case. He left his second bow in the old case and handed it to Heimlich, who counted out notes from a roll in his inside coat pocket and handed them to Gunther. Heimlich led him back to the elevator and out of the building. The grey Mercedes was waiting, steam puffing from its tailpipe. Heimlich opened the door for Gunther and rested a hand on his arm.

'Good luck' then he closed the door and waved the driver off. Gunther gave him the address of his cousin's apartment and some twenty minutes later the driver dropped him outside. Gunther waited until the car had disappeared into the traffic before climbing the front steps and ringing the bell to his cousin Yusuf's apartment. Yusuf greeted him with a bear hug, grabbed his suitcase and dragged in up the stairs to the second floor. The apartment was surprisingly spacious inside, with large windows that looked down on the busy street below, framed with elaborate gold silk drapes looped up with tasseled cords. Gunther slipped off his shoes and set his violin case down in the hallway. The warmth of the living room enveloped him and the soft silk rug with its intricate tree of life design caressed his feet. Yusuf took Gunther's coat and disappeared into the bedroom to drop his case and coat on the bed, while urging Gunther to make himself comfortable on the overstuffed couch. Gunther sighed in contentment. He'd risen very early that morning and taken the tube out to the airport while it was still pitch-black outside, watching the sunrise as the plane had taken off, and then his whole afternoon had been taken up by his briefing with Heimlich. He lay back on the couch and tucked his feet underneath him, wiggling his toes as he enjoyed the heat emanating from the gently hissing radiators.

He could hear Yusuf rattling around in the kitchen. Presently Yusuf emerged, beaming, carrying a large tray which he set down on the coffee table. It was heaped with meze – stuffed vine leaves and marinated red peppers, sardines in oil and bean salad. Yusuf pulled up a stool for himself, poured two glasses of raki, and handed one to Gunther. 'Şerefe! Prost! Here's to your concert!'

The familiar aromas of garlic and olive oil reminded Gunther of home and his mother's cooking, and a lump rose in his throat. He missed his family and the relatively carefree days of his youth. He raised his glass to Yusuf and thanked him for his hospitality. Then without needing to be asked he grabbed a plate and piled it high. He was ravenous.

When his belly was full, he reclined, warm and sleepy on the couch as he relived the old days with his cousin. They had grown up living in the same apartment building in Essen, and being the same age, had been as close, if not closer, as brothers. When Gunther had left home to study in London, Yusuf had made his way to Berlin and got a job at the Philip Morris tobacco factory. He'd done well and had been promoted to manager.

'How's Otto? I haven't heard from him recently.'

Otto Erdogan was Gunther's younger brother. Gunther pulled a face.

'I haven't heard from him either, but that's not necessarily so bad. There was a time when he only called me when he needed money and I barely make enough to pay my bills, let alone get Otto out of trouble.'

Yusuf shook his head. 'I know Auntie – your mother – worries about him. You and I were the good ones, we worked hard at school, we obeyed our parents, we moved away to build better lives. It's a shame he fell in with that crowd.'

'Yes, I feel bad. Last time I was in Essen, it must have been three years ago now, I had words with him – I told him he must change his ways, he must stop using drugs, get a steady job, honor our parents. I have no idea if he listened to me, but he's stopped pestering me for money, at least.'

'Do you plan to go home, see your parents in Essen on this trip?'

Gunther sighed. 'I don't really have time. And every time I do visit, mother gets so excited – she invites her friends over and boasts about her famous son and how talented he is, and I wish I could become invisible, and then she gets upset with me and there are tears. I'm just getting by; I wish I could do something that would justify her pride in me.'

Yusuf nodded in sympathy and then stood up and yawned. 'What am I thinking? You must be tired. Here, let me show you your room, and the bathroom. I'm sure you'll be needing your sleep.'

Gunther slid off the couch and stumbled after his cousin, taking his new violin case to bed with him. Once he'd bathed and changed, he closed the bedroom door and sat on the bed. He opened up the case, pressed the hidden catch in the lid and took out the replica of the Beethoven manuscript, laying it carefully on the bed beside him.

From its cover, plain pasteboard covered in utilitarian brown buckram, this could have been any score from a music library anywhere in the world. But as he carefully peeled back the cover, Beethoven's signature on the frontispiece leapt out at him, setting this score apart as unique. Gunther marveled at the quality of the forgery. The pages were yellowed, with darker brown mottling around the margins that spoke of their age, the corners rounded with centuries of handling. He stared at the autograph, fixated by the sight of Beethoven's handwriting. The signature was underlined no fewer than four times, and the dedication beneath it 'Franz Joseph Maximilian Fürst von Lobkowitz' with the Fürst emphatically underlined and another four lines scored beneath that. Gunther by now knew the music by heart but was transfixed by the sign of its creator. As Gunther idly paged through the piece, the germ of an idea formed in his mind. What if he were to have another copy made of the title page for himself to keep for inspiration? Or, even better, could he pull off some kind of bait and switch, offering Jennifer's father the title page but then substituting a copy so that he could keep the original. The thought made him giddy. He knew just the person for the job – the printer from whom he planned to collect the concert programmes the following morning, and who had forged his birth certificate and passport. Surely it wouldn't take long to forge just one page. He should have enough time in Berlin to be able to pick it up before he left for Kraków.

Chapter 11

Tuesday

In the morning, Gunther gulped down his coffee and a roll, and left the apartment with Yusuf. The cousins parted company at the tram stop, Yusuf waiting in line while Gunther walked to the print shop, carrying the fake manuscript in his violin case. He arrived as the proprietor was unlocking the door. The shop was small and cramped, stacks of papers and antiquated brass machinery piled up around the edges to make space for a gigantic new Xerox printer that occupied most of the floor space in front of the counter. The room reeked of machine oil and the sickly-sweet smell of paper. It was chilly inside, as the furnace had been turned down overnight. Gunther introduced himself and explained that he'd come to pick up the programmes. The proprietor's eyes widened in recognition as he invited Gunther to step to the back room with him, where the finished copies were stored. He handed the stack of programmes to Gunther, who inspected them. The German translation looked good; he'd have to take it on faith that the Polish was a faithful rendition of Jacek's draft. He shifted from one foot to the other, unsure how to bring up his new request. The proprietor looked keenly at him.

'Don't I know you from somewhere?'

Gunther was grateful for the opening.

'Yes, I'm impressed that you remember. You did some special work for me twenty years ago, before I went to college in London.'

The proprietor grinned, showing his nicotine stained teeth.

'I've a good memory for faces. It goes with the eye for detail.'

'I may have another special job for you. Are you still in that line of business?'

'It depends.' He looked enquiringly at Gunther.

'I need copies – two exact copies – of a page of a manuscript. And I need them by tomorrow evening. Can you do it?'

'Can you show me?'

Gunther looked behind him and pulled the connecting door closed. He turned around and fiddled with the hidden catch so the printer wouldn't see how he did it, extracted the score and handed it over.

'It's just the front page, the one with the signature.' He opened the cover and pointed.

The printer pursed his lips and raised his eyebrows. He rubbed the paper with his finger and then put the finger to his lips and tasted it.

'Hmm' he muttered, appreciatively. 'This is fine work. Where did you get it?'

'I can't say. Can you do it? Just the one page, two copies?'

The printer eyed him shrewdly. 'What if I can? What's it worth?'

'Five hundred Euro, cash.'

The printer laughed scornfully. 'My rates have gone up in the last twenty years. One thousand for the two copies.'

Gunther scowled. He'd hoped to be able to keep more of his cash advance for other expenses, but the forger seemed adamant. 'Absolute secrecy, and you'll have them ready tomorrow, by close of business?'

'Of course. My word is my bond.'

The two shook hands. The printer wrapped the stack of programmes in brown paper and slid them into a plastic bag. Gunther laid his hand on the manuscript, as if to bid it farewell, reluctant to let it out of his possession. It was time to go, to set up for the rehearsal with the other Londoners that morning.

The Presto movement began as a scurrying parody of the famous da da da dum opening of Beethoven's fifth symphony. Gunther and Jacek's notes ran in parallel, while Jennifer mocked them in a cheeky echo. The whole group played in unison for a few bars and then blew bubbles in turn, and then paired up so that the two violins were together, answered by the violin and cello. Jennifer descended, quieter and quieter, until she burst forth in the *piu presto quasi prestissimo* section, taking the three men by surprise. Jacek missed his entry and they had to stop and go back to the *prestissimo*. Beethoven wrote this section as a parody of the plodding lessons in counterpoint he received as a young man and as Gordon took over the tune the other three strings played the *cantus firmus* in canon. Soon they paired off, upper strings versus lower strings, until they threw on the brakes on an impossibly high held chord. Then the first theme returned. Jennifer exploded into the second *prestissimo* and once again Jacek lost his place and had to stop. The *presto* returned for a third time and now it was Jacek who yelled at Gunther in frustration when he missed the sudden *piano* marking. The tension spilled over into their playing and Jennifer's triple *piano* scales sounded rushed and anxious. Gordon told her to stop rushing as the upper strings were having difficulty coming in together.

Jennifer contradicted Gordon. She had studied this piece at Juilliard and her professor was a Beethoven expert. She explained, her cheeks burning, that several scholars had confirmed the metronome marking and cited several recordings from other quartets. The reviews of their BBC lunchtime concert had been very favorable overall, complimenting her playing. However, the review in Strad Magazine had been critical of the London Quartet's interpretation of the Presto movement, describing it as staid and conventional. Jennifer had kicked herself on reading the write-up. The reviewer was quite right, and she'd wanted to take it at a faster tempo, but she had deferred to Gordon at the time, not wanting to rock the boat as the newcomer to the group. She determined to stand her ground on musical interpretation in the future, not let Gordon walk all over her. In the few months, they had been working together she was starting to wonder whether, for all his charm and attempts at womanizing, Gordon might actually be a closet misogynist. Even though she was as tall as him, taller when she was wearing her concert heels (she privately called them her drop-dead stilettos), he had a way of talking down to her patronizingly that she never heard him use with Gunther or Jacek.

Gunther, gratified that at last someone was standing up to Gordon, came to her defense.

'Gordon, you have to follow Jennifer's lead here. She's right. We've fallen into a rut and we sound boring. You just have to listen, that's all. All those hours of practising – you must surely be able to play it up to tempo.'

'Who are you to talk about listening, Gunther? You've been playing out of tune for the whole movement, or couldn't you tell?'

'Let's play the third recap again – my way' said Jennifer and launched into the passage without waiting for the violins to ready themselves. Gordon stared at her coldly making no attempt to play, and in his scramble to come in on cue, and his frustration with Gordon, Gunther whacked the bow clumsily on the string, which snapped with a loud crack.

'Shit!' Gunther swung his violin down from his chin to inspect the damage. His A string had gone, his best concert string no less, that he'd just put on in the run-up to their performance. He'd have to find a violin shop the next day to buy a replacement as he only had his cheap practice strings with him. He forced himself to gently lay his violin down in his new case and then paced up and down, his face in his hands.

'Fuck. Fuck. Fuck.'

'Come on, Gunther, no point crying over a broken string, just get on and change it, will you?' drawled Gordon.

'Fuck you Gordon' screamed Gunther. He slammed the case closed, snatched up his music from the stand and his coat from the chair, and stormed out of the room. Jennifer and Jacek looked at each other, perplexed.

'What was that all about?' wondered Jennifer, out loud.

'I'll go after him' sighed Jacek. He dashed to the door, viola still dangling from his left hand, and called after Gunther, who kept walking. 'Wait, Gunther, wait!' He ran down the hallway and caught up with Gunther, reaching for his shoulder. 'Hey, what's the matter?'

Gunther stopped walking, and looked down at his shoes, shaking his head. He was already embarrassed at losing his cool like that. He knew that he'd overreacted. He mumbled 'Gordon's a shit'.

Jacek chuckled. 'Tell me something I don't know. Of course he's a shit. He's been a shit since his first day at the Academy. But we both knew that when we joined up. It could be worse. He could be an asshole.'

Despite himself, Gunther had to laugh. If it weren't for Jacek's warped sense of humor the London Quartet would have split up years ago.

'Come on, what is it, honestly?'

Gunther reluctantly spat it out. 'That was my concert A string. I don't have a good spare and I wasn't planning on having to take time out to go string shopping in Berlin.'

Jacek persisted. 'If you make Gordon feel guilty enough you can borrow one of his for now. Are you sure that's all? You haven't been your usual life-of-the-party self recently.'

Gunther had to laugh again. Jacek was ridiculous. 'The only party I ever get to go to is me and a pot noodle in my bed-sit. I've just got a lot on my plate, money stuff, you know.' He indicated his violin.

'Is that a new case? I haven't seen it before – looks expensive.'

Gunther reddened. 'Yeah, I just picked it up this morning. I splurged – that's why I can't really afford a new string right now.'

'Can I lure you back to finishing our rehearsal? I can offer you a seductive wiggle of my ass, or alternatively a stiff drink afterwards, whichever you prefer.'

It was impossible to stay cross with Jacek for long. Gunther made a moue and slapped him hard on the behind. 'Get along with you, viola seductress. You can keep your ass wiggles for someone else but I'll take you up on the offer of a drink.'

Jacek slapped him on the back and then, twining his arm around Gunther's shoulder, led him back to the studio. He pushed open the door. Gordon and Jennifer looked up expectantly and their faces relaxed when they saw Gunther behind Jacek.

'Behold, the prodigal son!' beamed Jacek. 'Gordon, you owe Gunther an apology and a loan of your finest spare A string. Jennifer, you owe us both your patience and forbearance while Gunther changes his string and I fortify myself from my hip flask.'

Ten minutes later, the quartet was back at work. Gunther felt a little sheepish after his outburst and Gordon a little sulky, so neither spoke much and they were able to quickly get through the rest of the movements without incident. They finished around four in the afternoon. Jacek had arranged for dinner at a beer hall that evening, but with several hours to kill, they dispersed and went their own ways.

Gunther rushed to a violin shop that he knew stocked the brand of strings that he used, calculating that he had enough time to get there before they closed for the day. To his great relief they had the right string in stock. He paid from the wad of Euros that Heimlich had given him, which was shrinking rapidly. Gunther cursed inwardly. He should have asked for a larger advance. At this rate, he'd have none left by the time he arrived to Kraków. He took the tram back to Yusuf's apartment to rest. He'd developed a stress headache and all he wanted to do was take an aspirin and lie down for a couple of hours before dinner.

The other members of the quartet were all staying at the same hotel, which Jacek had selected close to the Barenboim-Saad Akademie. Jacek made his excuses. He had some errands to run. Gordon and Jennifer shrugged. 'Want to share a taxi back to the hotel?' asked Gordon. 'We could take in some of the sights of Berlin before dark on the way.' Jennifer eagerly agreed. She wanted to soak up as much European culture as possible while she was there. Gordon led the way to the nearest taxi rank and soon they were driving up Unter den Linden oohing and aahing at the historical buildings and the magnificent museum buildings on the island. They stopped by the Brandenburg Gate while Gordon obligingly took charge of Jennifer's smartphone to photograph her posing with her cello,

which she promptly posted to Instagram and
Twitter, before they even climbed back into the taxi.
They arrived at the hotel in high spirits and retired
immediately to the bar. Emboldened by having
made Gordon play the Presto her way at the
afternoon rehearsal and inspired by all the history
and culture as well as the hipness of Berlin, Jennifer
challenged Gordon to a drinking contest in the hotel
bar. They would take it in turns to quiz each other
on obscure musical questions and the loser would
have to down a shot of schnapps.

Despite his joking with Gunther, Jacek had a
more serious purpose in mind for his afternoon. He
had long wanted to visit Berlin's renowned
Holocaust memorial, and had set aside the precious
free hours that afternoon for the purpose. The
memorial occupied a whole block of the city. From
the outside, it looked like a simple array of concrete
blocks, but as he wandered in between them, the
pavement dipped down and undulated, and he found
himself lost in a concrete jungle. He'd round one
corner after another and peer down the canyon
between the tall blocks, occasionally seeing the
figure of another visitor flitting just out of sight.
The setting sun cast long shadows down the

alleyways that crisscrossed the memorial at right
angles, deep shadows in which one could imagine
long dead ghosts lingered. He felt like a rat in a
maze, claustrophobic and a little panicky about
being able to retrace his steps out of this city of the
dead. He found the entrance to the visitor center and
descended the stairs to the underground exhibition
hall where the stories of the families wiped out in
the Holocaust were starkly and simply told. Black
and white photographs of the lost and disappeared
stared, hollow-cheeked from the walls and
fragments of their letters to loved ones lined the
floor like epitaphs on tombstones. Around the
ceiling were painted lists and statistics of the
number of Jews exterminated by the Nazis. One and
a half million Polish Jews. Many times more killed
than Jews from any other country. The numbers
were staggering when you thought about it. Jacek's
mouth tasted sour. He loved so much about Berlin,
not least the flamboyant culture of its gay bars but
its undercurrents disturbed him. Berlin made him
feel queasy, whether it was survivor guilt or the
nausea coming from a hangover after a night of
overindulgence, and he longed to get back to the
comforting familiarity of Poland. For now, the

creature comforts of the hotel and the dinner he'd planned would have to do. Jacek hurried back to the hotel and took a hot shower. The water almost scalded his shoulders, but the heat felt good in a Catholic self-flagellating kind of way, purging away the awkwardness of the rehearsal and the somber funereal atmosphere of the Holocaust Memorial. He took a new razor from his bag, lathered his face and took a satisfyingly close shave. His chin felt as fresh and raw as a teenager's. He hopped into a clean pair of jeans and a skinny black turtleneck and pouted at himself in the mirror, feeling sexy, and then took the elevator down to the lobby, where he'd arranged to meet the quartet to walk over to the beer hall.

Gunther was already there, sitting on one of the couches that were artfully scattered around the lobby. He looked a little pale, but smiled and waved when he spotted Jacek.

'I managed to get a new string and a nap. I'm feeling a little better – and you owe me that drink.'

Jacek beamed. 'Ready to go out on the town? Have you seen the others?' Gunther shrugged and shook his head. At the very same moment they heard a familiar peal of laughter, and spinning around, were treated to the sight of Jennifer strutting out of the bar, a somewhat worse for wear Gordon stumbling after her.

'I win!' crowed Jennifer. 'Mr James is going to have to brush up on his Arvo Pärt and Thomas Adès before he can get the better of me!'

Gordon spotted Jacek and Gunther, and raising his hand in mock defeat, called out to them. 'Save me! She's merciless, I tell you!'

Jacek put his hands on his hips and roared with laughter.

'Gordon, Gordon, we've only just started. The night is young. Come, follow me!'

The quartet made quite a spectacle as Jacek led them in procession to the beer hall – the slender Pole mincing proudly as he led the way, the tall blonde Californian girl striding along beside him, the short swarthy Turk trotting behind and the Englishman staggering along in the rear calling 'Wait for me!' They found a space at one of the long tables, and in a conciliatory gesture, Gordon offered to buy the first round of beer. Soon all was forgiven and forgotten, and the four tucked into bratwurst, sauerkraut and potatoes with relish. With discreet gestures, Jacek made sure the waiter kept their glasses filled until all four were quite as drunk as Gordon.

'Time for a drinking song!' cried Gordon 'Does anyone know a good one?' The quartet looked at one another and shook their heads. After a moment's silence, Jennifer slammed her fist on the wooden table, making the glasses shiver. 'What, Madame Cellist?' slurred Gordon.

'I know, we can sing Scherzo of our Beethoven quartet!' she shouted, 'Da da da dum!'

'Yes, yes' cried Gunther, so enthusiastically that he almost fell off the bench. Jacek caught him and hauled him upright. Gordon pulled himself up as straight as he could.

'All right, I'll count us in.'

'Nooo' shrieked Jennifer. 'My tempo, not yours'. She promptly dissolved in a fit of giggles.

'All right Miss Bossy Boots, take it away.'

Jennifer led the singing with much merriment, as the four howled out their parts, switching octaves where necessary to fit their vocal ranges. The Berliners at the neighboring tables pointed and laughed, and swayed in time with the singing, beating their glasses on the tables. As the beer garden began to empty, Jacek discreetly beckoned for the bill and asked the waiter to call a taxi for his comrades in arms. Having seen them safely off, he hopped on a tram, exhilarated and excitedly anticipating dancing until the wee hours at his favorite nightclub.

and wishing the cups were larger, and piled her plate high with crusty bread rolls and Swiss cheese. Unlike Gordon, she preferred fresh air and exercise away from her cello on the day of the concert so that she could arrive on the stage relaxed and refreshed. She intended to go for a run in the Tiergarten, the large park by the Brandenburg Gate that they had driven through on the previous afternoon.

Gunther ate a hurried breakfast with Yusuf, before his cousin had to leave for work. Any anxiety he might have had about the performance that evening was far outweighed by his worries about how he would pull off the substitution of the manuscript at the Jagiellonian library. He sat cross-legged on the bed, still huddled in Yusuf's spare dressing gown which was made of a beautiful quilted silky fabric and which, like all Yusuf's things, smelt comfortingly of tobacco, formulating his plan.

Based on the information Heimlich had given him, his best opportunity would be on the late Saturday afternoon before their concert. He would need to wait until the office staff went home for the day and then manage to elude both the guards and

Chapter 12
Wednesday

Gordon woke the next morning with a pounding head and a queasy stomach. He shuffled to the window and winced at the daylight, grateful for once for the grey skies and pouring rain that softened the glare. He shuffled to the bathroom, took some Alka Seltzer, peered at his reflection in the mirror and groaned. His skin was mottled and his eyes were bloodshot slots in his puffy face. The thought that he would have to perform that night made him retch and he spent a few miserable minutes hunched over the toilet reviewing the previous evening before splashing his face with water and staggering back to bed. He poured a glass of water and set it on the nightstand before pulling the sheets up over his head and going back to sleep.

Gordon had a routine that he practiced religiously on performance days which involved whole body stretching based on the Alexander technique he'd learned at the Academy. Next, he would unpack his violin and tune it with even more care and precision than usual, and then warm up by playing on open strings, focusing on producing an even bow speed and tone. Then came numerous scales in many configurations, and only then would he open the music to be performed. Even then he restricted himself to only working on certain passages that he'd marked on his part. He wanted to keep his stamina for the performance. Then came the ritual rosining of his bow, just the right amount, not too little, not too much and the cleaning of his violin, wiping the strings with alcohol and polishing up the varnish. Finally, he would run a steaming bath – it had to be a bath, not a shower, which had caused them some trouble in the past when Jacek hadn't checked the bathing facilities at the hotel they'd stayed at) – he would pour in a splash of his favorite Penhaligon's Endymion bath oil, and would lie back and relax there for thirty minutes with his eyes closed. Over the years he'd become quite superstitious about this routine and became very

tetchy if any part of it had to be modified, point where he would ascribe any slips or aspe his performance that were less than perfect to defect in his concert-day preparations. He was particular about mealtimes on the day of a cor refusing to eat anything in the four hours bef performance, less it made him gassy or sleep he would try to time his lunch (or breakfast, lunchtime concert) and would limit himself to n potatoes and a piece of fruit.

Jacek had slipped back into the hotel at thre the morning, exhilarated after dancing the ni away with some of Berlin's finest young men. planned on sleeping in and venturing out for a f lunch before meeting Gunther at the Barenboi Said Akademie at four o'clock as they had planne to start setting up for the concert.

Jennifer bounced out of bed at eight, her usu hour, performed her daily yoga stretches (ten Su Salutations) and then wandered downstairs in he yoga pants, a thick fluffy sweater pulled over th top, her hair wound into a messy bun, for a leisurely breakfast in the hotel restaurant. She looked around, but there was no sight of either Gordon nor Jacek. She sipped her coffee, enjoying the rich dark roast

the security cameras to get to the locked room in the center of the building to retrieve the manuscripts. Even with the jammer that would be hard to do. And then, once he had made the switch, he'd have to leave by the closest fire exit and disappear. He shook his head in frustration. It seemed like an impossible task. Gunther took out his violin and tested the new string that he'd put on the night before. It seemed to have held its tune. He placed the instrument under his chin and started to play the prelude to the third Bach Partita for solo violin, soft and slow. Playing Bach was like a meditation – it cleared his mind and cleansed his soul and he found it often helped him when he was stuck in his thinking, to find a way forward. He lost himself in the music, allowing the muscle memory and the harmonic progressions wash over him. When he had finished, he laid the Vuillaume down on the bed and smiled to himself. The instrument was sounding more beautiful than ever, and he was at the dawn of a new and better stage in his life, he could just feel it in his fingers.

He went to take a shower, and as he walked back from the bathroom, barefoot, he once again remarked on Yusuf's silk rugs. Now, if I only had a flying carpet, Gunther laughed to himself, I could sail into that library and back with ease, floating above the guards and out of sight of the cameras. Still without a solution, he decided to wait until he'd had the chance to visit the library himself with Jacek and the quartet. He'd feign a longstanding interest in the detailed workings of libraries and would make sure they got a full tour of the whole facility. Meanwhile he'd keep his eyes peeled for cameras so he could note their locations and keep looking for ideas – perhaps he could pinch a staff pass or watch as the librarian typed in the entry code to a keypad by the locked rooms, as well as look for hiding places, so that he could finalize his plan there and then.

Gunther checked his watch. It was already two o' clock. Timing that afternoon was very tight since he now had to pick up the fake manuscript and the two new forged frontispieces before meeting Jacek at the Akademie at four, and then preparing for the concert. He deliberated and then dressed in his concert clothes, just in case time got away from him later, and there was no opportunity to change. He let himself out of Yusuf's flat and walked over to the printer's shop. The bell jangled as he pushed the door open, and the printer emerged from the back room, a pair of reading glasses perched on his nose. He squinted over the top off the lenses at Gunther.

'You're too early. They aren't ready yet.'

Gunther felt the knot in his stomach tighten and his throat constricted.

'How long?' he checked his watch again.

'Give me half an hour.'

He left the store and paced around the block outside. The heavy grey clouds had lifted a little, and weak sunbeams slanted from the watery veins of blue sky above the western horizon. The pavement was drying in patches around the lingering puddles. It was four o'clock. Jacek would be at the Akademie already. He re-entered the store, and impatiently rang the bell again.

The printer emerged. 'OK, OK, I've just finished. Come through.'

In his haste to round it, Gunther banged his knee on the counter. He ground his teeth in pain. He'd have a bruise later, for sure. He climbed over the piles of paper and followed the proprietor. There, on a desk under bright lamp, lay the open volume and next to it, the two copies. He bent over the table to inspect them closely.

'Careful there! The second one is still slightly damp. You don't want to smudge it.'

Gunther looked back and forth between the three copies. They looked identical as far as he could tell. He picked up the dry copy by the edge, between his finger and thumb, feeling the weight and texture of the paper. The forger had done a good job – he couldn't tell the difference.

'You satisfied? The money?'

Gunther handed him the notes, rolled ready in his fist. He hadn't much time. He fidgeted and clicked his tongue as he watched the printer carefully wrap the forged sheets in tissue and tuck them inside the volume to keep them flat. He grabbed the bundle and thrust it inside his case, thanked the printer again and then ran out of the door. He looked both ways for a taxi but, not seeing one, ran to the tram stop and leapt on, breathing heavily from the exertion. By the time he jumped off at the Akademie stop, it was after five. He rushed inside to find Jacek, sitting in the empty auditorium, fuming.

'Where the hell have you been, Gunther? I waited twenty minutes for you with the manager, and when you didn't show up, we just had to do the best we could without you. He had another meeting to get to after ours. If I've missed anything, it's your fault. You were supposed to be in charge of logistics for this one.'

Gunther had his story prepared. 'I'm so sorry, the tram I was on broke down and blocked the line, so I had a long walk to get to another stop. But you were able to sort out payment? You got the check for our fee?' he asked anxiously.

Jacek pouted. 'What do you take me for? Yes, of course. But you put me in a difficult situation; I had to take his word for it on the terms you'd negotiated. Next time, leave earlier!'

'How about ticket sales? How did we do?'

Jacek shrugged. 'So-so. They're at about 60% at the moment, but they told me they get quite a few walk-ins. But we'll have a decent sized audience in any case.'

Gunther stood up and walked around the concert hall, inspecting the set-up. The hall was so new that you could still smell the sawdust and varnish from the polished birch wood walls and floor. The stage was set in the round, with banked seats rising on all sides. He took out his violin and played a few notes into the space. The acoustic was as warm as he would expect with all the wooden surfaces, but crisp and precise. Jacek watched him and nodded in approval.

'Yes, I tried it too. Lovely, isn't it! I just hope it doesn't change too much when the audience is here.'

Jacek showed Gunther the green room, and as they headed back to the hall for their warm up, they heard voices and footsteps approaching. Jennifer and Gordon had arrived. They checked the positioning of their chairs and stands, and the lighting, which the technician had set up earlier with Jacek, and then played a few notes to assess the balance. All seemed good.

An hour later, they walked out on stage to enthusiastic applause. Gunther looked quickly over the audience, to see if he could spot Yusuf, to whom he'd given a free ticket. Yes, there he was, grinning and wildly waving from a spot where he had direct line of sight to Gunther. Gunther grinned back and inclined his head slightly to Yusuf. The rest of the audience was an interesting mixture of grey-haired patrons, the women with rather dated bouffant hairdos, the men with white beards and patterned silk scarves draped over their jackets, and young students in jeans and sweaters with long, scruffy hair, some of the young women wearing headscarves, Muslim style. Many of the students were olive skinned like him, and he guessed they must be enrolled in the Akademie, which specialized in East-West relations and in giving opportunities to young musicians from the Middle East.

This was now their second performance of the Beethoven and Shostakovich program and the quartet was beginning to coalesce and settle around the sound and ideas of its newest member. Gordon had to admit that Jennifer's faster tempo in the Presto gave the movement added sparkle and pizzazz. The last soft chord of the piece was interrupted this time by shouts and clapping before the sound died away to nothing. Some of the students leaped to their feet, raising their hands over their heads as they applauded, and even the elderly audience members nodded and smiled appreciatively as the quartet bowed again and again. Eventually the cheers died away and the quartet hastened back to the green room to celebrate another successful concert. Yusuf came backstage to find Gunther and clapped him on the back, congratulating his cousin and marveling at the sound he made compared with the sometimes-painful notes Yusuf had to endure when listening to Gunther practising as a kid.

The quartet had booked an early morning flight to Kraków, so only had time for a quick drink and light snacks in the hotel bar before heading back to their respective digs to pack and sleep. Gunther waited until he was back in the privacy of his room to check on the fake frontispieces. He opened the volume and carefully removed the tissue-wrapped pages. To his relief they both looked identical, the pages were pressed flat and smooth with no telltale ripples from the water-based ink the printer had used craft them, and no bleeding or smudges from their hurried drying. He unrolled the wad of banknotes in his pocket and counted them. After paying the printer for the programmes and the extra work, plus the dinner and drinks from last night, he was down to just over one thousand. He hoped that he didn't encounter any more unforeseen expenses before the deed was done and the original manuscript was safely back in Germany.

Chapter 13

Kraków, Thursday

Gunther was waiting at the gate at Tegel airport when the rest of the quartet arrived, just prior to boarding.

'Security gave us a tough time with the instruments' panted Jennifer, her cheeks flushed. 'They made me take my cello out of its case and sent both through the X-ray twice! I thought we weren't going to make the flight. I just hope I don't have any problems with the flight attendants when I bring the cello on board. Flying with a cello is such a hassle – you wouldn't believe the number of times they've tried to stop me boarding even though I paid extra for the cello to have its seat. And then it can be almost impossible to squeeze it in to some of these smaller planes for short hops.'

Gunther thanked his lucky stars that he'd come early, heeding Jacek's admonition the day before to be on time. His violin had gone through the X-ray with its secret safely concealed in the shielded compartment. The guard had asked him to open his case after it passed through the machine, but as soon as he saw the instrument he'd waved Gunther through. He hoped this was a good omen, that his luck would hold.

They landed in Kraków to a fresh snowfall. Gunther gazed out of the airplane window as they taxied to the gate, mesmerized by the unmarked whiteness on the ground, from the unnatural quiet inside the hermetically sealed cabin. Directly in front of him the top of Jennifer's cello case rose above the seat back. She rested her hand protectively around its neck, steadying it in case of bumps. Once outside the terminal, Jacek was in his element, directing traffic, calling excitedly in his mother tongue to the taxi drivers. He secured them a minivan big enough to accommodate all four players, their instruments and luggage, and spent a few minutes conversing with the driver.

'What did you say to him?' asked Jennifer, curious.

'I've asked him to take the scenic route. I suspected you might like to see some of the sights.'

Jennifer settled back in her seat and looked eagerly out of the window. They drove through the countryside, its gently undulating hills blanketed in snow, the branches of the fir trees drooping under the weight. 'Over there' Jacek pointed, and the group looked down into a valley where large imposing gates marked the entrance to a complex of long, low buildings. 'Auschwitz' said Jacek. It was right here, just outside Kraków.' Jennifer shuddered. The place looked so bare and forlorn. The van rolled on and soon they came to the bridge over the wide river, with church steeples rising above the city walls on the far side. 'The Vistula River' said Jacek proudly. 'This is Kraków!' Once they had crossed the bridge, the streets narrowed and the van's wheels thrummed over the cobblestones and tramlines. Jacek pointed out the castle and the various churches and other monuments as they passed, giving a rapid commentary on everything they saw. The van pulled up outside the hotel and Jennifer cried out in excitement as a horse drawn carriage passed them, the coach open to the air, its driver wearing a heavy coat with ornate gold braid and buttons, and the horse with its mane and tail braided with a headdress and trappings of red and white ribbons and feathers.

'That's just for the tourists' scoffed Jacek. 'You'll see, I'm going to show you the real Poland.' As soon as the driver opened the sliding door to the van, the cold bit at their faces and fingers. They stepped out, careful not to slip on the icy pavement, and carried their luggage inside the hotel. Jacek checked the time on his phone. 'I have a few errands to run. Take a couple of hours to relax and settle in and then meet me in my room at one o'clock. I have a surprise planned for you. Oh, and by the way, bring a big appetite with you!' He winked.

At the appointed hour, the rest of the quartet trooped up to Jacek's room on the top floor. As they neared the door they heard voices talking animatedly and the clinking of glasses. It sounded like Jacek had company. Gunther reached out and rapped tentatively at the door, which flung outwards, revealing Jacek, beaming broadly. 'Come in, come in! You're just in time for the party! Welcome to Poland!' Somehow Jacek had talked the hotel into giving him the penthouse suite. He'd turned the credenza into a buffet, laden with artfully arranged platters of food. Gunther, always hungry, went to take a closer look. There were several kinds of smoked fish, wafer thin slices fanned out on the plate with dark rye bread and three kinds of caviar – glossy grey, black and red bubbles. Another dish with marinated herrings, their silver skin glistening under the drizzled sour cream sauce that garnished them. Dishes of pickled cucumbers, capsicum peppers and tiny pearl onions. Ham, salami and bologna sausage thinly sliced and rolled into cigar shapes. Two different pâtés, sliced and garnished with glazed orange slices. And at the end of the buffet, a couple of bottles of prosecco and several more of vodka.

'Help yourselves! Eat!' cried Jacek, expansively to the whole room. 'You must try the smoked trout and eel – they're local specialties. And some vodka so we can toast the London Quartet!'

The quartet needed no further invitation – breakfast in Berlin seemed an infinity ago. They piled their plates high and munched as Jacek's friends plied them with questions. Jacek had invited several contacts from the local Symphony

Orchestra, as well as the hotel manager and the staff from Florianka Hall, urging them to each bring a guest to meet his colleagues, with the hope of spreading the word and swelling the audience for their concert. Gordon set down his plate of food and held court, enjoying being the center of attention. He was soon deep in conversation with two violinists from the Symphony who wanted to ask his opinion on some bowings in the Beethoven quartet.

Jacek, from the far corner of the room, spotted a young man standing alone next to the drinks, silhouetted against the bright sunlight that poured in through the window. He appeared to be barely out of his teens, clean shaven with tousled glossy black curls. He twirled a half full shot glass in his hand, looking down at it as the crystal facets flashed and sparkled with rainbow colors. Thinking the young man must be shy, Jacek approached him kindly. The guest looked up and to Jacek's great surprise his eyes met a shrewd pair that danced with knowledge beyond his years and a wry smile. Jacek laughed and stuck out his hand. He recognized a kindred spirit. 'I'm Jacek. What's your name?'

'Krzysztof. Magdalena brought me – I'm her little brother.' He pointed out one of the women who worked in the Florianka ticket office.

'Nice to meet you, Krzysztof. Now don't tell me, you've been quietly sizing us all up from your corner, haven't you? You can't fool me, that's exactly what I like to do at parties. And since I've found you out, now you have to tell me about everyone in the room.'

Krzysztof raised his eyebrows. 'What's it worth, Jacek? Surely you don't expect me to divulge all my secrets for nothing?'

'How about a spoonful of caviar? Will that do?'

Krzysztof put his head on one side. 'Hmmm – no. What else can you offer me?'

'A free ticket to our concert?'

'Already got one from Magdalena.'

'How about a private viola serenade?'

'Now you're talking. OK. Here comes the dirt.' He glanced at Gordon, still deep in conversation with the symphony players. 'Him. Huge ego, easily flattered. Metrosexual by the look of him – expensive but traditional clothes. Keeps eyeing up the women.' Jacek laughed out loud at Krzysztof's audacity and then pinched his lips together. 'Am I right?'

'Oh, more than you could ever know. Go on.'

Krzysztof turned his attention to Jennifer. 'American, obviously. Ruthlessly ambitious. Quite the honeypot, looks like most of the men in the room are salivating over her, including both your colleagues. But I don't think either of them has managed to get a leg over yet. Mr. Metrosexual already acts like she's his and he's assuming it's just a matter of time, and Mr. Puppy dog in the corner keeps gazing at her with big brown eyes, knowing she's completely out of his league.'

'And what about me?' asked Jacek, softly, already knowing the answer.

'I think you're more interested in me than you are in her'

'I'd like to get to know you better' murmured Jacek. 'Can we spend more time together while I'm in town?'

In response, Krzysztof took Jacek's left hand with his, flipped it over to expose his wrist, and pulling a biro from his pocket, scribbled a phone number on Jacek's wrist.

'There you go! Now you can't lose it. Anyway, I should let you get back to your guests.'

Jacek wallowed in a warm glow that could be attributed to more than just the vodka. He couldn't help the goofy smile that spread across his lips. Meanwhile the hotel manager was monopolizing Jennifer, seeking her opinion of every aspect of his hotel compared with others she had stayed at in America and Europe. Flattered by his attention, she answered very seriously, as he took notes on a pad. One of the older women from Florianka Hall, Barbara, tall and thin with her grey hair wound tightly and pinned into a severe bun, was quizzing Gunther about the string quartet repertoire while he cast anguished looks at Jennifer, trying to catch her eye so she could rescue him from this inquisition.

In fact, his savior turned out to be Jacek, who walked up just as Barbara was in the middle of a long lecture on the topic of Beethoven's Opus 74 quartet, explaining to Gunther how it came to be Kraków. Jacek, having watched Gunther squirm for long enough, broke into the conversation.

'Yes Barbara, I've arranged a private viewing for the quartet of the manuscripts tomorrow at the Jagiellonian Library tomorrow. We will see the original score that we'll be performing at Florianka Hall. Imagine that! Have you ever visited the Berlinka Collection?'

Barbara turned eagerly to Jacek, happy to have found a receptive audience. 'Well, it's a long story…' she launched in to a complicated account in which she described how she had by chance met a musicologist who was in Kraków to study the collection when he came to a concert at Florianka Hall – she simpered and blushed like a sixteen-year-old girl as she reminisced – and how he had taken her to see the manuscripts. It was the most unusual date she had ever been on. He had shown her the sketchbooks of Beethoven's that he was studying; he'd pointed out the fragments of music that he was deciphering, trying to piece together the compositional process that Beethoven had used. He'd even sung snatches of music to her to illustrate a point here or there. And then she blushed again, leaned forward and whispered that the professor had kissed her behind the book stacks before he took her home.

'And then?' asked Jacek, intrigued. Barbara's face fell. She'd tried to call him a few times, even written to him at the University, but he'd never responded. She found out later by making discreet enquiries that he was married. Jacek squeezed her arm. 'Never trust a musicologist, Barbara. They can be sly. You're much better off dating a performing musician. We wear our hearts on our sleeves. What you see is what you get.'

The guests began to drift out. Gunther took the opportunity to liberate himself from Barbara and backed through the door, bowing in thanks, both hands pressed together, to Jacek for both the party and saving him. Jennifer followed Gunther's lead, extricating herself from the hotel manager and his notepad and calling her adieus from the doorway. Jacek cleared his throat and Gordon looked around, realized the room was emptying and invited the symphony players to join him in the bar downstairs. Only Krzysztof remained, sitting quietly on the couch, his arm extended along the back.

'You're still here' said Jacek.

'I thought you promised me a viola serenade.'

'What would you like me to play? Any requests?'

'Come closer. I'll whisper it to you.'

Jacek sat next to Krzysztof on the couch and leaned closer. He noticed the asymmetric kink in

Krzysztof's nose, and the lushness of his lips. Krzysztof's breath was hot in his ear and the scent of his cologne tantalized him. 'Kiss me'. Jacek could do nothing but obey. He kissed him full on the lips and everything melted away. They moved apart. Jacek forgot to breathe. Krzysztof stood up and tenderly stroked his cheek with a finger. 'Call me. Soon.' He took his coat from the hook on the door and left.

Jacek remained on the couch, unable to move. He realized he was still holding his breath and let out a noisy gasp. He hadn't felt this way in a long time. He touched his hand to his lips and his cheek where Krzysztof's finger had traced, and stared at it in wonder. Then he came to his senses, reached for his cellphone, flipped his hand over so he could read the number written on his wrist, and typed it into the phone. Krzysztof picked up right away.

'Hi, it's me, Jacek.'

Krzysztof laughed, a deep musical laugh. 'You didn't waste any time!'

'You told me to call you soon. When can I see you again?'

'How about breakfast?'

'Just tell me when and where.'

Krzysztof worked at a bakery in the old town. He gave Jacek directions. 'See you at nine. I start work at six, I'll be able to take a break by then.'

Jacek hung up. His heart flipped with joy. Tomorrow morning couldn't come soon enough.

Chapter 14

Friday

Jacek got to the bakery at eight forty-five, so that he could check it out and not waste a precious moment of time together with Krzyzstof. He lingered outside the window, enjoying the display of breads and pastries. There were trays of glazed gingerbread hearts and doughnuts, baked cheesecakes and braided loaves of bread. He pulled open the door and a bell jangled overhead. The warm yeasty aroma enveloped him in a soft embrace. He approached the counter and asked for Krzysztof. The serving girl stuck her head through the vinyl strip curtain into the bakery behind the store and yelled his name. Krzysztof appeared, wrapped in white overalls, his dark curls tucked into a hair net under a white cap, wiping his floury hands on his apron. He grinned at Jacek and invited him to sit down at one of the small tables and wait. Jacek's heart was pounding. He sat where he was told and jiggled his heels impatiently until Krzysztof joined him, carrying a red plastic tray with croissants and two steaming cups of coffee.

'Go on, try one.'

Jacek bit into the pastry, crisp and buttery. He took a swig of coffee to wash it down.

'Mmm, mmm' he spluttered with his mouth full. 'Delicious.'

Krzysztof gazed at his with his clear grey eyes fringed with long lustrous lashes. The white baker's cap only accentuated his beauty.

'So, how is my viola player doing today?'

'Well, I didn't sleep a wink. Visions disturbed me all night. And now I am enjoying my breakfast in good company. And the cause of all of this is sitting right in front of me.'

Krzysztof smiled benevolently. 'Pleased to be of assistance. And your plans for the rest of the day?'

'I'm taking the quartet to the Jagiellonian library this morning. But then I'm free for the rest of the day' he ended on a rising note.

Krzysztof took the hint. 'I get off work at three. I'll come by your hotel at four.'

They sat together sipping coffee and crumbling their croissants, quietly enjoying each other's company. Krzysztof stood reluctantly. 'I'm afraid my break is over. I need to get back to work. See you at four.'

Jacek wiped his hands and face on a paper napkin and rose to leave, giving Krzysztof a quick hug and grazing the other's cheeks with his own. He wandered happily out of the bakery, and only then checked his watch. He needed to get back to the hotel to meet the others for the library tour.

His three colleagues were waiting in the hotel lobby when he arrived, champing at the bit to see the Beethoven manuscript. Jennifer was bundled up in what looked like a ski jacket and ski hat, and Gunther had a canvas bag slung over his shoulder. Gordon had wound a cashmere scarf around his neck and up to his ears and slouched with his hands in his coat pockets. Jacek led the way through the snowy streets past the tram stops where students waited, huddled in the cold.

Gunther recognized the library building from his virtual tour on Heimlich's desktop. They turned right down the alleyway toward the visitor entrance. The side street was empty, compared with

Mickiewiczka Avenue. Jacek led them inside and spoke to the receptionist.

'One of the librarians is coming to fetch us. You can leave your coats here.' Jennifer, who was now sweating lightly from the walk in her bulky jacket, gratefully pulled it off and gave it to the cloakroom attendant. Gordon followed suit. Gunther hugged his bag closely. He'd already slipped out to the town that morning to buy some supplies – a new smartphone, something he'd never been able to afford before but essential for taking pictures inside the library that he could examine later, a laser measure so that he could accurately assess distances, some sticky tape and a notebook and pen. He would need to keep it with him as he cased the library during the tour.

The librarian arrived and introduced herself as Wanda. She looked unlike any librarian Gunther had ever encountered, with a mane of white-blond hair, stiletto heels and short tweed skirt. Almost like some sexual fantasy librarian in a computer role-playing game. Jacek walked in front next to Wanda, who gave a running commentary on the architecture and history of the library as they followed. Jennifer came next, eager and full of questions, closely

pursued by Gordon, who was rather obviously
leering at Wanda's bottom as she walked in her
tight skirt and heels. Gunther lingered at the back of
the group so that he'd have more time to take
photos and notes without Wanda noticing. The
building they were in had been constructed in the
1930's in contemporary Art Deco style. The walls
were decorated with round-cornered marble panels
in mustard yellow, ferrous green and oxblood
colors, and the place had an institutional feel that
fell somewhere between a mental hospital and a
subway station of the era.

Jacek and Wanda had clearly planned the tour in
advance, showcasing the library reading rooms and
systems before the grand finale of the Beethoven
viewing. Gunther was secretly delighted to have as
much time as possible to look around, despite
Gordon's yawning protests. The main reading room
had a large space with desks for students in the
middle, and bookshelves all around the edge, with
two galleries that wrapped around the walls, one
above the other. The ceiling was set with glass tiles,
to let inside what natural light the dull Polish winter
skies afforded. A mural depicting a battle,
presumably one that was significant to Polish

history, graced the far wall. Wanda took them to the circulation desk and showed them the robotic system that delivered books requested by the scholars.

'The robot is our pride and joy. The system was only recently installed. Let me show you how it works.' She selected a book from the desk. 'This one. The user has finished with it, and it has to be returned to the correct shelf. See, here we have the list of all the storage areas within the library. The ticket inside the book identifies the location and then I look up the code and punch it into the control panel.' She punched in three digits. The robotic cradle swung into place, a red light flashing at the top. It was large enough to hold a stack of books, perhaps as many as a dozen encyclopedic volumes. Wanda placed a book inside the cradle, pressed the red light which turned green, and the cradle swung upwards and rolled along the cable at ceiling height, where it disappeared through a hole in the wall. The quartet watched, fascinated. 'The whole library has been wired so I can send the book anywhere' Wanda explained proudly.

Gunther had seen television commercials for automobile companies that showed robots assembling cars, but he'd never observed a real live robotic system at close quarters. The mechanical sounds – the swish and gentle pop of the hydraulic switches and the quiet whirring of the cradle as it moved along the wires – and the sight of the cradle swinging to and fro on its journey were mesmerizing. It seemed more like magic than engineering. Then the penny dropped and he let out an involuntary gasp. Here was the magic carpet he had idly wished for the previous evening while the silk rug in Yusuf's hallway caressed his bare feet. He studied the wall behind the cables, looking for the security cameras. Sure enough, they were directed at the circulation desk. The robot worked anonymously and un-observed in the background, out of sight of the camera. This could be the means by which he could access and enter the manuscript room unseen, and how he could smuggle out his quarry. He needed to find out as much as he could from Wanda about how to operate the thing. He realized that his gasp had been audible and that Wanda was smiling at him. He had to explain himself.

'It's amazing, Wanda. I've never seen anything like it – this must be state of the art technology.

Please do tell us more about how it works.' Wanda beamed. She needed no further invitation to show off her new system. Gunther moved closer so that he could see the control panel clearly and watch what she did. 'So how would I find the code for, say, the manuscript room?' Wanda obligingly showed him the log book and pointed out the code, 124. Gunther repeated it over and over so he wouldn't forget.

Jennifer, also intrigued, asked her 'How do you know when the book has arrived?' Grateful for the distraction, Gunther turned away slightly so Wanda couldn't see what he was doing, and jotted down the number in his notebook, while Wanda explained the lights that illuminated when the book reached its destination. 'If you listen closely, you can hear the hydraulics switching and the cable stops vibrating as the cradle comes to rest.'

'Does it ever get stuck?' asked Gunther?

Wanda laughed. 'Oh no, when it was installed the engineers were careful to cut openings large enough to allow the cradle through even when it is fully loaded with books. They calculated for the sagging of the cable when the cradle is loaded to twice its rated capacity.' 'And what is that?' 'Oh, it is rated to thirty kilos. I think they calculated for a sixty kilo load. But I don't think it's ever been tested with more than about twenty books at a time.' Gunther started making mental calculations of his own. He weighed sixty-five kilos. He looked at the cable and the cradle. Would it bear his weight? He reached out and tugged at the cable. It held firm and taut.

'Please, don't touch the cable' frowned Wanda.

'Sorry.' The cable left a dusty streak of oil across his palm. He pulled his handkerchief from his trouser pocket and wiped his hand clean.

'How reliable is the robotic system? Does it ever break down?'

'Yes' laughed Wanda 'Sometimes it gets confused if you enter codes too quickly. But then we just press zero to reset the system, and start over.'

Gordon, who had been fidgeting and looking at his watch, piped up plaintively. 'I think we've seen enough robots for now. I'd really like to see the manuscripts.'

'Yes, of course. Follow me, this way please.'

Wanda led the way up a short flight of stairs towards the center of the building. Gunther looked around for landmarks, trying to lay a mental breadcrumb trail to remind his of the way. It was hard to remember the layout from the floor plans that Heimlich had shown him. As they walked he glanced up from time to time to trace the path of the cables along the ceiling. As Wanda had explained, there were holes cut high up in the wall above the doorways, through which the cradle could pass on its route from room to room. On the pretext of tying his shoelace, he took his laser measure to check the dimensions of the opening and whether it was big enough for a small man to squeeze through carried by the cradle. He noted the position of the security cameras from the corner of his eye, trying not to look directly at the cameras for fear the security guards might notice him. The cameras were laid out very predictably above each doorway, but always pointing at the floor and not at the cables that ran above. He fingered the jamming device in his pocket. Unfortunately, he had no way of testing whether it worked here. Perhaps he could try using it when they were back at the registration desk, if the guard stationed there had a monitor so that he could snatch a glance at the screen.

As Heimlich had described, they passed through two locked doors. In each case, Wanda punched in a code on the keypad to the right of the door waited a moment for the latch to release and then held the door open as they passed through. Gunther watched her hand closely. Not wanting to chip her flawless French manicure, Wanda pressed the keys with her long nails slowly and carefully. The code was easy to decipher, making a straight line down the right-hand edge and then the bottom left corner, 3697, the same for both doors. Gunther scribbled it down in his notebook. She stopped with her hand on the door knob to the right, turned and smiled at the quartet. 'Here we are.' She opened the door and reached inside to flick on the light switch.

They entered the room. A large table stood in the middle and on the far side a bank of book shelves with locked glass doors rose to the ceiling. Wanda reached for the key chain clipped to her belt along with her staff security pass, unlocked the door and reached for a volume on one of the upper shelves. She carried it reverently over to the table and set it down. 'Here it is, gentlemen and lady. Beethoven's autograph score for his string quartet opus 74.' The four crowded around to look. Wanda slid a finger under the cover and lightly lifted it. Beethoven's signature was scrawled across the front page. Gunther leaned over to look. After the hours he'd spent poring over his forged copy, the page was startlingly familiar, like seeing his own face in the mirror. Jennifer leaned over behind him. He smelt her warm scent, like nutmeg, and a wisp of her hair fell forward and tickled the back of his neck. He held his breath.

'Oh my God! My Dad would be so excited to see this. Is it OK to take photos?' Wanda assured Jennifer it was fine. She pulled her iPhone from her jeans pocket and put her hand on Gunther's shoulder so that he would move aside and let her photograph the page. As she touched him, an electric thrill of excitement coursed down his arm. He hadn't anticipated the heady combination of being so close to something of Beethoven's as well as so close to winning Jennifer's favor. Everything seemed to be going his way, so long as he didn't screw up. Jennifer was unwittingly playing right into his hands.

Wanda obligingly turned the pages one by one for the quartet as they read the score together, exclaiming over a marking here, a note there, a doodle in the margin. While Beethoven's writing was remarkably clear, it was evident from the verve and energy of the notes, the slanting stems and the curl at the end of the strokes made by an impatient flick of the pen, how he had dashed them down on the page. In other places, Beethoven had made edits, some in the same brown ink, as the original, perhaps when he'd had a sudden change of mind, or a flash of inspiration into how to perfect a phrase. Other edits were calmer and more considered, painstakingly drawn in the tiny space left on the paper in blue-grey lead pencil. In other spots, he had scrawled instructions to his publisher that were difficult to decipher from the archaic German, however his dynamic markings, piano and forte, instructions for players to be followed long after Beethoven was gone were neatly inscribed and unambiguous.

Jacek exclaimed at one point. 'Look, he's added a fingering in the viola part here!'

Jennifer peered at the page. 'Oh yes, so he has. How funny! I wonder if he played it with his friends and the marking was for him? You know he played the viola but I'm not sure he was that good at it.' She pointed at the opposite page. 'Look at these crescendo markings. He's very precise about where they start and finish. But here, are these shorter markings crescendi or just accents?'

Gordon leaned in to take a closer look, resting his hand on Jennifer's waist as he did. Gunther gritted his teeth and nudged closer on her other side. 'I've always thought they were accents, but I suppose you could play them like mini crescendi, delaying the accent by adding a kick to the end of the note.'

They worked their way through the full score, making note of places where Beethoven had made edits, seeking insight into his compositional process. Gordon had also brought a notebook in which he made detailed notes on the points he'd observed, while Jennifer snapped photo after photo on her phone. After an hour, Wanda announced that their time was almost over. 'Please excuse me, but I have other duties that I need to get to. I will have to escort you back to the registration desk.' Gunther watched as she replaced the volume on the shelf. He noted the size and shape of the volume and the brown buckram cover, so that he would be able to quickly recognize it when he returned.

They arrived back at the entrance just in time for the changing of the guard. While the others lined up at the coat check to retrieve their things, Gunther slipped behind the security desk. As he'd expected, the monitor with an array of views from the video cameras was just below the counter. He reached in his pocket and pressed the jammer. One of the squares in the array snowed out. He released the jammer and to his relief, the picture of his standing at the desk with his back to the nearest camera sprang back into view. So, the jammer worked. He'd just have to be careful to use it judiciously. He walked back to join the others and collected his coat.

Once outside, they squinted in the winter sunshine reflecting from the snow. Gordon was in a hurry to get back to the hotel, anxious to consolidate his observations from the manuscript into his part and to practice for the concert. Jacek slipped away, seeking solitude as he prepared himself for his evening with Krzysztof.

Jennifer lingered behind. Exhilarated at seeing the manuscript at close quarters, she was on a high almost like an overdose of caffeine. She felt restless; she wanted to be able to discuss the experience, and relive the high points. And after spending the morning indoors she wanted to feel the sun on her face, inhale the crisp air and walk, run, laugh. Gunther was only too happy to oblige. It was rare for him to get Jennifer on her own, and her youth and vivacity were intoxicating. 'Would you like to explore the old town? I can show you Florianka Hall if you like.'

'Oh yes! Let's make the most of the sunshine while it lasts.' In her exuberance, Jennifer's foot skidded on the ice. Gunther grabbed her arm to steady her. She smiled down at him and linked her arm through his.

'Thanks! I don't need a sprained ankle or wrist before our concert.'

Jennifer chattered happily as they walked. Gunther wasn't really listening, he was in his own reverie. Today was the stuff of his dreams. They walked through the park, pausing to look at the sculptures interspersed along the paths, and then he led the way through the narrow streets that opened out into the main square. Restaurants and bars lined the edges of the square, some diners still lingering at the end of a late lunch. Some brave souls sat at the open-air cafés, the tables and chairs enclosed in transparent plastic tents with heaters overhead to keep the cold at bay. The Christmas decorations were still up, pine garlands tied in festive swags along the ridge poles of the tents. The medieval cloth hall straddled the center of the square, its brick arches now filled in by the glass shop windows. At the far end stood St. Mary's church with its imposing bell tower. The clock hands stood at almost three. Gunther pulled Jennifer over to watch it strike the hour. The minute hand clicked around and the bell rang one, two three times. Before the peal had died away, a trumpet fanfare sounded from the top of the tower.

'Look!' said Jennifer, pointing up. Gunther could see the trumpeter standing at the open window, the bell of his trumpet lifted to sound through the vent. The sun flashed from the glass as the trumpeter closed the window and then the same fanfare sounded, slightly muted as the trumpeter played it again from the second side of the tower. He repeated his tune four times, one from each side of the tower. 'Just like the muezzin, only more martial' thought Gunther, harking back to his childhood when his uncles had taken him to the mosque. In Essen, they'd had to make do with a recorded call to prayer. The Kraków trumpeters had been marking every hour this way for centuries. Gunther couldn't help wondering if they got bored, playing the same fanfare over and over.

They walked over to Florianka Hall. Barbara was at the ticket office, and obligingly took Gunther and Jennifer up to see the recital hall. Jennifer stood on the stage and sang a few notes to test the acoustic to her satisfaction, and then snapped some more photos.

'My Dad will love getting these so he can imagine us playing here. I'm going to text with him this evening when we get back to the hotel. It's still too early for California.'

Gunther didn't want the magical afternoon to end and suggested to Jennifer that they walk through the market in the cloth hall to look for souvenirs. They wandered slowly through the arcade, browsing the various stalls. There were wooden toys, crystal glasses, miniature icons painted on gilded wood and warm knitted bobble hats, some trimmed with fur pom-poms. Jennifer stopped at a stall selling amber jewelry. The pieces varied from tiny earrings and dainty rings mounted on silver wires to massive pendants and strings of chunky beads, in hues that ranged from honey to mahogany, clear, striated and opaque. Jennifer suddenly squealed. 'Look, look! It's a cello!' With a gloved hand, she reached out and touched the brooch, a single smooth piece of amber, curved and waisted like a cello with silver wire for strings. The stall owner took it down for her so she could inspect it more closely. The amber was exactly the color of the varnish on her own cello, and the attention to detail was impressive, with tiny pegs made of wire and even the 'F' holes carved in the front of the amber.

'How much?'

'One hundred Euros.'

'I'll take it.' Jennifer pulled out her wallet and thrust her American Express card into the stall owner's hand. The woman glanced at the hand and shook her head.

'Sorry no American Express.'

Jennifer's face fell.

'It's the only credit card I have. Are you sure you can't take it?'

The woman shook her head again firmly, no.

Gunther looked at Jennifer's face. Her eyes and mouth were full of disappointment. Without giving it a second thought, he reached in his pocket for the roll of Euros, peeled off a hundred Euro bill and handed it to the saleswoman.

'I'll get it for you.'

Jennifer protested 'Oh Gunther, I can't let you do that.'

'I insist. I can see how much you want it.'

Jennifer relented. 'Yes, I do. That's so sweet of you. But I'll pay you back.'

'No, no. Consider it a welcome gift to the quartet.'

She hesitated a moment and then agreed 'Thank you so much, Gunther, it's beautiful'. The saleswoman wrapped the brooch in tissue and tucked it into a little box, then slipped it in a bag and handed it to Jennifer.

Gunther wondered if he'd been too rash. He really couldn't afford the gift, but the soft look in Jennifer's eyes as she'd thanked him had been worth it. He could tell by the excitement in her voice and the way she couldn't take her eyes off the jewel that she'd set her heart on having it. He fervently hoped that he was working his way into her heart as well. Anyway, if all went well then soon he wouldn't have to worry about money any more.

Chapter 15 – Longing

Adagio ma non troppo

The lower three strings prepare a soft bed to comfort the first violin as he sings his song of loss and yearning. He is joined first by the second violin and then the cello, and lastly the viola as their voices swell together in sadness. The cello soothes the upper strings with a low pedal A flat and the second violin has the last word before the key shifts to A flat minor. The cello cries out in an impassioned sigh, echoed by the second violin and viola, which is repeated more hopefully before the theme returns, this time beautifully accompanied by rising triplets that cascade through the three lower parts, as the first violin plays a florid variation of the theme over the top. The triplets come together in rhythmic unison and then it's the viola's turn. He plays a murmuring accompaniment that spins like a top underneath the first violin who repeats his lament this time very simply and unadorned. The cello joins in with the tune in her lowest register and the second violin takes over the murmuring so that the viola can join in with the cello in thirds.

The voices drop to a whisper as they croak out the lament together, quiet and still. The sadness is like a lump in the throats of the instruments. Suddenly they break out into a loud, deep, gruff sigh and then meander back to the tune. The first violin is playing the tune low now, while the second violin spins a delicate filigree above him. The first violin takes over the filigree and the cello echoes the tune in staccato notes off the beat. The inner voices pick up the chugging rhythm and hand the tune back and forth between themselves together and the first violin while the cello pedals A flats. The instruments answer each other with rising doublets that echo the pizzicato of the first movement, and the cello sings a final phrase to bring the movement to a peaceful close as the group tiptoes quietly away.

Jacek had made his way to a vodka bar in the old town, close by the US Embassy. He'd selected a flight of four different vodkas – raspberry, plum, mint and lemon – and had climbed the sloping wooden staircase to the cramped upper room, which was more of a loft where one had to stoop to avoid banging one's head on the exposed beams. He picked a seat that afforded a bird-eye view over the bar below and sipped his vodka contemplatively. He was overwhelmed with emotions of as many different flavors as his vodka. Seeing Beethoven's manuscripts at close quarters had been a surprisingly emotional experience. He felt a deeper connection to the composer and some insight into his compositional process. Seeing the fingering on the viola part had given him a new sense of the humanity of the man he'd always revered as a genius. It seemed that Beethoven had struggled to play the viola too.

He decided to try an experiment – he would seek to pair each of the drinks in the neat row of shot glasses in front of him to one of his emotions. A match for his new sense of Beethoven – that was easy - plum, for the richness of the fruit and its dark magenta color, like the blood that ran though his veins. He continued his analysis. The next emotion – love – swirled through him at the thought of seeing Krzysztof again. He'd never experienced such intensity of feeling, the obsession with another

person. He felt giddy with anticipation. But how
would he compare the essence of love to a flavor of
vodka? He picked up the mint glass and took a sip.
The menthol vapors numbed his tongue and rose in
his nose like incense, cleansing, purifying,
freshening. Perhaps. He tried the lemon, acerbic,
cutting yet sweet, like his sweetheart's wit. He
couldn't decide which of the two better represented
Krzysztof. The third emotion that moved him was a
swelling of patriotism. He felt happy that these
manuscripts, these treasures had come to rest in
Poland, his spiritual home. He'd fled the country
many years before in fear of censure by the church,
feeling unwanted and unwelcome. But now his
heart flamed with love for his country and one
fellow countryman in particular. He raised the last
glass, the raspberry vodka, with a stretch of the
imagination, the color of the Polish flag, the taste of
berries and green leaves evoking memories of
childhood countryside summers, of picnics and jam
making. His heart was bursting with happiness, it
was almost too much to bear. He drained the last
drop of liquor, and, maudlin and swaying gently on
his feet, he carefully descended the stairs, tipped the
bartender and went out into the street.

It was already dark and the bells of St. Mary's church were tolling for mass. On a whim, Jacek allowed himself to be carried along by the rivulets of worshippers converging on the church, swept through the massive oak doors and inside, where he made his way to the front pew and sat before the Veit Stoss altar, its carved panels stretching high above him, the stained-glass windows behind it ascending to the gilded vaults of the ceiling. His fingers and toes began to throb from the cold and he tucked his hands inside his coat to warm them. Inside, his heart flamed, fired by the vodka and his emotions. He hadn't been to mass since the priest had thrown him out of St. Barbara's all those years ago, and he couldn't bring himself to watch the preparation of sacraments, to risk seeing a tow-headed altar boy that would remind him of his first kiss with Sigismund. That would be one emotion too many, he would shatter into a thousand pieces. Instead he gazed at the altar, listening to the familiar words being chanted while contemplating the masterpiece before him.

Every Polish child learned in school the story of the Veit Stoss altar – how it had been dismantled and packed up for safety in the thirties when war broke out, but discovered and taken by the Nazis, and then how it had been rediscovered in the ruins of the Nuremberg castle in Bavaria and returned to Poland in 1946 where it was rebuilt and restored. The altar represented Polish culture and national pride. Jacek reflected on the history of his country, thankful that this treasure had survived through five centuries of violence and wars. He looked up at the images of Mary, glowing luminous in her golden robes, her face always serene, even in death. He wondered about all the other artworks that were looted or destroyed by the Nazis. He felt a new sense of ambivalence on the dispute between Poland and Germany over ownership of the Beethoven manuscripts. On the one hand, sitting before the altar, he empathized with the deep sense of loss of the German people for this piece of their cultural history. On the other hand, the memory of the Holocaust Memorial in Berlin was still raw and it was hard to imagine how Germany could ever make adequate reparations for murder and looting on such a colossal scale. On a personal level, he was also conflicted by the incompatibility of his Catholic faith with his being gay. Homosexuality was still barely legal in Poland, largely due to the disapproval of the church, and he'd been afraid to come out until he left Poland to attend the Royal Academy in London, for fear of discrimination in his home country. Until now he'd always felt like a stranger in his own homeland, but with Krzysztof he felt strangely completed.

When the people began to file up to kneel at the altar to receive communion, Jacek was surprised to find himself following, as naturally as he had done as a boy. He received the sacraments and a sense of peace descended on him, calming his turbulent emotions. His hands and feet no longer felt cold. He returned to his seat and bowed his head, savoring the moment. When the service ended, he slipped out and made his way with a light step back to the hotel. He stopped by the desk to check for messages, and no sooner had he turned around than Krzysztof burst through the revolving doors, bringing with him an icy blast. His cheeks were pink as roses from the walk. Jacek welcomed him with an embrace then stepped back and exclaimed 'Mint! Mint it is!'. Krzysztof pealed with laughter. 'I have no idea what you are talking about!'

'Come on up and I'll explain.'

With that, the two disappeared into the elevator.

Chapter 16 – Liberation
Saturday

Gunther woke with a start, experiencing the disorienting moment of the frequent traveler when you aren't sure where in the world you've arrived. He'd slept well and the sunlight was already streaming through the chinks in the curtains. He lay with his head on the pillow and blinked as his mind turned over the possibilities. Ah yes, he was in Kraków, and today was the day of the concert – and the grand theft. His stomach clenched suddenly and he ran to the bathroom, only just making it in time to hurl into the toilet. He groaned wretchedly. His anxiety often got the better of him on days when he had an important performance or meeting and today he would have to give the performance of his life. He filled the teakettle and while the water boiled, hobbled to his suitcase, rummaging until he found the ziploc bag in which he'd packed the ginger teabags that helped soothe his stomach, and then sat hunched in an armchair waiting for the tea to brew.

Gunther had every reason to feel confident. He'd worked out his plan to the last detail, he had all the equipment he needed, and most of all, he was buoyed up by having had the opportunity to spend one-on-one time to get closer to Jennifer the previous day. He decided to take it easy in the morning, eat a light lunch and then prepare to head for the library with his violin. He'd vacillated on whether to take the instrument or just the empty case, with the fake manuscript concealed inside it with him, but in the end decided to bring both. If he was challenged, opening an empty case would immediately cast suspicion. Also, he was loath to leave his precious Vuillaume naked and vulnerable to being damaged or stolen by the housekeeping staff at the hotel, but his main reason for bringing the violin was a practical one, in case he was delayed and had to rush directly to the concert. For the same reason, he planned to wear the black trousers and turtleneck that he used for contemporary performances. Unfortunately, it made him look rather too much like a cat burglar, but he couldn't think of an alternative, if he hadn't time to change. Gunther planned to hide in the museum after it closed at four and timing would be rather tight as the quartet was due to perform at eight the same evening. He hoped it wouldn't take him more than a couple of hours to get in and out, which would give him enough time to get back to the hotel, freshen up and walk over to Florianka Hall, cool as a cucumber, for the concert. He took the two forgeries of the frontispiece that he'd had made, still wrapped in tissue, and placed them in the safe in his hotel room. He'd need those later.

Gunther went down to the hotel restaurant just before noon, hoping it was too early for the others to eat lunch. He didn't want to bump into any of his colleagues and risk awkward questions or being delayed. His stomach still felt tender but he knew he had to eat something to maintain his blood sugar, and keep him going through the evening. His next meal wouldn't be until after the concert. He ordered some borscht and rye bread, and sipped the delicate broth, crumbling the bread into the bowl. Around one o'clock, he headed over to the library, taking his violin with him, the duplicate manuscript hidden inside the case. The woman at the library registration desk smiled at him and greeted him in heavily accented English 'Welcome back! Weren't you here with the string quartet yesterday?' Gunther froze. He hadn't counted on being recognized, but there was no point in pretending otherwise. He forced himself to respond, trying to sound as friendly as he could. 'Yes, I'd like to use the reading room.'

'Yes, of course!'

He checked his coat at the cloakroom and was about to walk away when the attendant stopped him.

'I'm sorry, Sir, but you can't take your case in there. It's too big. You'll have to leave it here with your coat.'

'I prefer to keep my instrument with me. It's valuable.'

The woman was adamant. 'I am sorry, it's the rule. You can't take it in. It will be safe here, I'll be here until we close at four.'

Gunther complied reluctantly. He climbed the few shallow steps and headed in the direction of the reading room. Only a few students sat reading at the desks or wandered between the bookshelves – Gunther imagined most of them had better things to do than study on a sunny Saturday afternoon. He tagged along nonchalantly behind the students, using them to shield him from view of the video cameras, as he walked from room to room, surreptitiously trying doors, exploring the building, finding locations of bathrooms and fire exits. Given the weight limitations of the robotic cradle, he wanted to minimize the distance it would have to carry him, so he wanted to find the closest control station to the manuscript room as his point of entry. His explorations took him down into the basement, where the larger bookshelves were located. The bookstacks were packed densely together, set on a track with winders at the end of each stack that allowed the user to open a gap large enough to slip between them to retrieve a book. Gunther shuddered. He didn't like tight spaces and the thought of getting stuck and crushed between the stacks made him nauseous. He stood by the basement circulation desk and took some measurements of its distances from the desk to the outer walls of the building with his laser reader. By his calculations, he was standing only a short distance and one level down from the manuscript room. An empty cradle sat on the docking station, next to a robotic control panel identical to the one Wanda had demonstrated to them in the main reading room. And at the far end of the stacks was a fire exit that led directly out into the alley. He'd found his entry point. He retraced his steps to the reading room, climbing the stairs to the gallery, and found an unoccupied desk where he could sit and look out over the readers below. The room was so quiet that he could hear his own breathing, which sounded unnaturally loud, above the almost imperceptible scratching of pencils on paper and, intermittently, the dry rustle of a page being turned. He became aware of the ticking of a clock, and twisted his neck to look behind him to see where it was coming from. It was just past three. He realized he was holding his breath. He tried to focus on the task ahead, while not wanting to lose track of time. The clock seemed to be playing tricks on him – surely time couldn't possibly be passing that slowly.

Finally, at 3:45, an announcement that the library was closing came across the public-address system. Gunther made his way back to the cloak room to collect his violin and coat, trying to keep within the thickest part of the throng making its way towards the exit. He walked towards the door but then, as if suddenly changing his mind, spun around on his heel and approached the guard, asking 'Toilet?' The guard pointed to the hallway behind the desk and clicked his tongue, telling Gunther to hurry up. Gunther hustled to the bathroom carrying his coat and violin with him. He locked himself in the farthest stall and prepared to wait, hoping that no-one would come looking for him. If he heard footsteps, he would climb up on the toilet lid, with his violin, to stay out of view.

Gunther waited for fifteen minutes. No-one came. He waited another five minutes, and hearing no sound, he slipped on his gloves and with his coat over one arm and the violin case in the other, tiptoed out of the bathroom, heading down to the basement.

He reached the circulation desk and set down his coat and case, removing the fake manuscript and securing it with his belt under his sweater to keep his hands free. He tucked the key fob with the jammer inside his right glove and stuffed his flashlight into his pocket – the light was fading fast and it would be dark in the manuscript room as it was in the interior of the building. He stashed his coat and violin case out of sight beneath the desk.

He moved around to the control pad and, being careful to keep his gloves on to avoid leaving prints, he punched in the code for the manuscript room, 124. Right on cue, the gondola swung down to the book loading bay. Gunther steadied it with his left hand as he climbed inside. He couldn't help being reminded of the school skiing trip he'd been on in his teens, climbing on to a chair lift that swayed wildly as it swept him up the mountain. He gritted his teeth. Now for the moment of truth, would the system be able to bear his weight? The cable jerked and he could feel the gears straining but sure enough, the gondola began to rise and he began his magical flight upwards. He sat as still as he could, resisting the temptation to lean over and crane down to look at the floor, lest he upset the balance. Instead he raised his eyes and fixed them on the opening near the ceiling, making sure he was ready to duck his head or pull in his feet if needed to squeeze through the hole.

The cable ran over a pulley at the top of the ceiling before disappearing into the vent. Gunther braced himself for the bump, trying to dampen the swinging that ensued as the cradle navigated the pulley. A cold breath of air coming from the vent puffed cobwebs into his face making him draw a sharp breath in surprise. The thick dust in the vent choked him but he dared not cough, fearing the noise might attract attention. His skin crawled as the spider silk clung to his face, but he dared not take his hands off the cradle to wipe it away, for fear he might lose his grip and fall. He reached the top of the vent and the cradle shot up to the ceiling of the corridor he'd walked through the day before. He was getting close. The cradle circumnavigated another pulley and carried him off towards the locked room. Gunther suddenly realized that even though he'd pulled them us as high as he could, his feet might be dangling low enough to be visible on the cameras, so he squeezed his right hand around the jammer to knock out the cameras in the vicinity and avoid detection.

He sailed through the last hole in the wall and the gondola dropped down into the docking station in the manuscript room. He couldn't believe the crazy ride had worked. He climbed down and massaged his fingers, stiff from gripping the gondola. He'd better work fast and get out of there as soon as he could. He flicked on his flashlight and moved over to the glass-fronted bookshelves. The manuscript was still where Wanda had placed it the previous day. To his surprise, despite all the security measures in the library, the key to the glass case sat in the lock. He opened the door and slid out the volume, taking it over to the table to inspect it more closely in the beam of the flashlight. Yes, that was the one, the original copy of Beethoven's quartet. He turned the pages with his gloved hand. The volume fell open at the fourth movement.

Allegretto con Variazioni. The first violin states the simple theme, and then the cello plays the first variation in loud staccato arpeggios, followed by the first violin, each accompanied by his neighbor. The second variation has the viola playing sweetly in triplet rhythm while the other accompany with smooth chords. The third variation – ah bliss, this is the place where Gunther and Jennifer take on the theme, marching loudly in sixteenth notes in harmonic thirds.

Gunther was transported momentarily to their last rehearsal and savored the moment of unity with Jennifer. He closed the score and checked his watch. He needed to get out of the library and get ready for the performance. He pulled the forged manuscript from under his jersey. He'd better not mix them up now! It really was difficult to tell them apart. He set the forgery on the table and belted the original to his chest, rolling his sweater down protectively to keep it snug. He hardly had time to marvel that he was carrying something Beethoven once held, right over his heart. He replaced the forgery on the bookshelf, and closed and locked the door. It was time to fly his magic carpet back down to the basement.

Gunther stopped in his tracks, as his heart turned to ice. In his nervousness, he'd forgotten to look up the code that would direct the robotic cradle back to the basement. Shit! He ran over to the control panel, looking for the manual, and thumbed frantically down the list. Shit! It was all in Polish. He tried to calm himself, to read each line. Even though their spelling was bizarre, sometimes you could guess what Polish words meant if you read them out loud, if they were cognates. He mouthed his way down the list searching for anything that sounded vaguely like 'keller', the German word for cellar. He could hardly breathe and his eyes were starting to blur with desperate tears and the sweat pouring down his forehead. He'd come this far, he couldn't fail now. Nothing. He weighed his options.

He had to get down to the basement. He'd left his violin there and he had to hide the manuscript in the case to get it out of the library. With the manuscript belted under his thin black wool sweater he looked like he was wearing a bullet-proof vest. Even a cursory search would reveal it. It was too dangerous to punch a random number into the control panel and hope the gondola would take him part of the way. The cable ran too high, too close to the ceiling for him to jump down safely without injuring himself. There was nothing for it – he'd have to walk out through the corridor, find his way back to the basement and jam the cameras as he went. Thank goodness, he'd memorized the code for the keypads on the doors – down the right-hand side and to the bottom left corner, 3697.

He swept his flashlight around the room to make sure he'd left everything in order, then took a breath and opened the door into the hallway, pressing the jammer he clutched in his sweaty right palm. He walked along the wall on which the cameras were mounted, reasoning that they wouldn't be able to capture him at such a sharp angle, and made his way through the two locked doors, swiftly typing in the code at each. Once he reached the stairs to the basement, he started to run, fear and panic rising. He grabbed his case from under the desk, threw it on top and fumbled with the clasps to open the compartment and slide the manuscript under his bows. Gunther snapped the locks shut, then struggled into his coat, trying and failing to button it with his gloves on. He was about to rush for the fire exit when he remembered one last thing. He needed to reset the robot to get it out of the manuscript room, where it would betray his presence, so that he could cover his tracks and no-one could tell where the cradle had last been. He shone his flashlight on the control panel and to his great relief he saw a three-digit number written on a label on the front. He punched in the number and heard the compressed air of the valves pop as the robot swung into motion. He hid his face in his hands as he waited for it to reappear, by now in anguish. The robot seemed to take longer than the last movement of a Schubert string quartet when played with all repeats. At last, the gondola descended into sight and settled gracefully in its docking station. Gunther exhaled and pressed zero to reset the system, and then not wanting to spend a minute longer, ran to the fire exit, pressed the bar and slipped out into the alley. He heard the fire alarm begin its clanging behind him and willed himself not to run, but to keep walking until he was lost in the shadows of the building opposite. He turned down the first side street he could find, thankful that the snow on the streets was frozen solid so his shoes left no mark.

Once he was back on the main street, Gunther relaxed his pace. A warm glow enveloped him like a hot shower. He'd done it! He'd pulled it off! He savored the first moment of the rest of his life, feeling as if he were six feet tall and invincible. Oh, how he would play that evening, coaxing the finest sound from his Vuillaume, which would soon be his forever, not collateral for the bank. And Jennifer would fall in love with him and they would live happily ever after. He scooped a handful of snow in his gloved hand and tossed it in the air, laughing. It sparkled down on him like fairy dust, some landing on his tongue, fresh and pure. The church clock struck six. He even had time to get back to the hotel, freshen up and change into black tie before meeting the others at six thirty as they'd planned, to walk over together to Florianka Hall.

Chapter 17 – Performance

Gordon was the last of the London quartet to make it down to the lobby. He'd spent the afternoon practicing obsessively in his room and as a result had ended up with a headache. His tetchiness couldn't have contrasted more with the mood of his colleagues. Jennifer chattered excitedly about the tour she'd taken of Wawel castle, exclaiming over the tapestries and the Da Vinci painting of 'Lady with an Ermine' that she'd seen there. Jacek was giddy with his infatuation over Krzysztof. He couldn't stop smiling. And as for Gunther, he was uncharacteristically ebullient, with a new spring in his step. He'd dithered over what to do with the manuscript, hesitant about leaving it unattended in the hotel but equally concerned about leaving it backstage at the concert. He'd decided in the end to bring it with him. Now that it was in his possession he didn't want to let it out of his sight. His entire future depended on delivering it safely to Berlin the next day.

In keeping with the historical setting of Florianka Hall, the quartet had decided on formal dress, the men in tuxedos with black bow ties, and Jennifer in a floor length black velvet gown whose hem trailed on the floor, as she swept up the stairs. They reached the green room and readied themselves to play. Gordon popped a couple of aspirin in his mouth, swallowing them dry, and then flexed his fingers and started playing scales. Jacek tuned his viola and then lifted it to his shoulder and, caressing it with his cheek, waltzed slowly around the green room playing the theme from the movie *Schindler's List*. Jennifer shrugged off her coat and as she turned around, Gunther saw the amber brooch he'd given her pinned to her right shoulder. She saw him looking, smiled and patted it, her left hand reaching across her heart. He turned back around and lifted his Vuillaume from the case, his hand lingering on the lid as he removed his performing bow, caressing the panel that concealed the manuscript. He closed his eyes and inhaled long and slow, seeking to draw inspiration from the pages that Beethoven had created, through his fingers and into his soul for the performance. He smelt the sweet scent of yellowed paper, echoes of the pine forest from the resin on his bow and lingering traces of candlewax and wine.

'Well, shall we?' asked Gordon. Gunther opened his eyes and looked up at the clock on the wall. The hands pointed to just after eight. He pushed the door open. The babble of conversation from the hall assailed them. Jacek swung his viola down and followed Gordon down the corridor, his instrument and bow dangling from his fingers. Jennifer went next, gathering her long skirt up in one hand so that she wouldn't trip on the hem, her cello and bow clutched in the other. She wobbled on her high heels and Gunther reached out to grab her arm to steady her. She turned back and smiled at him, her teeth as bright as a flash bulb. Gunther was momentarily dazzled. He stepped through the door, looked back over his shoulder to check his case was closed and secure, and then shut the door behind them.

The rumbling of the audience got louder as they neared the stage door, and as Gordon stepped into the limelight they burst into applause. The quartet took their places on the stage. Gunther looked around the hall. It was even more beautiful at night time. Chandeliers with crystal drops shivering on gilded stems glittered around the walls, their light amplified by reflection in the tall silvered mirrors that stretched from floor ceiling at the far end of the hall. The polished marble panels on the wall glowed softly, their cream and honey tones lending warmth to the reflected light, and the elaborate plaster moldings of the cornice and ceiling looked like decorations on a wedding cake. The hall was packed - every seat was taken. The audience members were dressed to the nines; the men in suits, the women in evening dresses or tailored woolen skirts and elegant leather boots. He lifted his bow to the string to check his tuning. The acoustic was as warm as the light, even with a full audience. His Vuillaume had never sounded sweeter.

Jacek scanned the audience, checking to see where Krzysztof was sitting. He spotted him immediately in the front row and their eyes locked for a moment. Krzysztof blew him a kiss and Jacek almost blushed. Good old Magdalena. She must have reserved her brother a seat. Gordon cleared his throat and sat up straight, raising his violin to his shoulder. The others followed suit. Gordon looked from one to the other, catching their eyes to be sure they were ready, and then with an inward breath, an imperceptible nod, and a graceful drop of his right wrist to lower his bow onto the string, he cued them to begin.

Gunther felt like a new man. He moved with confidence, as if playing the violin were the easiest thing in the world. He scarcely looked at the music; he had internalized Beethoven's music so much that he no longer needed to read the notes on the page since they were embedded in his soul. Instead, he played in ecstasy, closing his eyes from time to time to savor a choice moment, or turning and playing to his colleagues when they had parallel lines to play. At times, he looked directly into Jennifer's eyes, as she played alongside him or answered his phrase, and was rewarded by her steady, intelligent gaze, reading his musical intention, just as if they were dance partners, dancing cheek to cheek. Her cello brooch flashed under the stage lights as she moved, winking at him in complicity.

Gunther lost all sense of time. He couldn't tell if the music lasted for eternity or if it passed by in an instant. The Shostakovich ended with a plaintive whisper from Jacek's viola and after a moment of stillness, the audience erupted in cheers. Gunther snapped out of his reverie and blinked under the lights. He stumbled to his feet, a little dazed, and then grabbed Jennifer's hand and swung it in the air, exuberant. Jacek waved his own hand and beamed to Krzyzstof, while Gordon clasped the neck of his violin with both hands and bowed a little stiffly. The audience began to stream out of the hall and the musicians were caught in the crowd. The women from the box office jostled around Jacek, congratulating him and showering him with hugs and kisses. Gunther spotted Wanda, the librarian from the Jagiellonian who had shown them the Beethoven manuscript. She made a beeline in his direction.

'Wonderful, wonderful playing' she gushed. 'It was a joy to watch you put your heart and soul into the Beethoven. The way you looked at each other, the expression on your faces. It was beautiful to watch. I hope that seeing the manuscript gave you inspiration.'

Gunther was genuinely touched. He'd never had a member of the audience pay him a compliment like that before. He touched his heart and bowed slightly. 'Yes, of course. How could one not be moved in the presence of such greatness?'

Wanda's remark reminded him that the manuscript was still sitting unattended, hidden inside his case in the green room. He began to feel a little anxious, with all the people milling about, lest anyone should go in there and start poking around. He pushed his way through the crowd in the direction of the green room, murmuring 'Excuse me. Excuse me', while shaking hands and allowing his back to be slapped congenially by his new admirers. At last, he made it to the door, and turning the handle, slipped inside. He breathed a sigh of relief. His case was just where he'd left it. He lifted it up to test the weight. Was it still slightly heavier with its concealed load? He opened it up and furtively slipped a finger under the panel in the lid. He rubbed the texture of the buckram cover. Good. All was well. The door opened and suddenly the noise and chaos from the hallway swept into the room as Jacek, Gordon and Jennifer returned to pack away their instruments and pick up their coats.

'Let's all go and celebrate!' cried Jacek. 'Who's in the mood for singing? I've made us a reservation at the Klezmer House in Kazimierz.'

'Me! I'm starving!' cried Jennifer 'Let's go!' The crowd was dissipating, the stragglers waiting patiently in line at the coat check to retrieve their outer layers. The quartet burst out on to the street, their breath puffing in clouds in the chilly night air. Krzysztof flagged down a couple of taxis. Gordon opened the door of the first one and took Jennifer's cello from her, laying it inside across the seat. He put an arm around her waist as he helped her in to the cab and then slid in after her. Gunther ground his teeth. Gordon could be a smooth operator. He piled into the second cab with Jacek and Krzyzstof. Despite the hour (it was almost ten) the streets of Kraków were hopping, with crowds of concertgoers and diners promenading, warmly wrapped in furs and hats. The buildings of the old Jewish quarter crowded the streets, rising tall and blind, their small windows concealing secrets. The taxi dropped them outside the Klezmer House. From the outside it looked dark, but Jacek led the way around the side, where light, music and the sound of merrymaking spilled from the door. The waiter showed them to the back room where the klezmer band was playing, and found them a table. Gordon pulled out a seat for Jennifer next to him. Gunther glowered at Gordon and picked the seat opposite her, setting his violin on the seat next to him. Jacek and Krzyzstof took the adjacent table for two. The music was in full swing, a trio on clarinet, violin and double bass, and the other diners clapped along with the accelerating beat. The restaurant was very homey – chintz curtains dressed the small leaded-pane windows, and an ornate lamp with a stained-glass shade trimmed with silk fringes stood on a baby grand piano in the corner. The faded wallpaper and patterned carpet underfoot completed the old-fashioned 'just like your grandmother's living room' décor. Jacek ordered a round of vodka while they consulted the menu.

Once the shots were poured, he tapped his fork on his glass.

'Lady and gentlemen, I would like to make a toast to our outstanding success tonight. To the London Quartet!' He raised his glass and the others followed suit, clinking with each other then downing the drink. The mouthful warmed Gunther's gullet as it went down, leaving delicious vapors swirling in his throat. He made the next toast.

'To Beethoven, to genius, to inspiration!' They drank again.

Now it was Gordon's turn. He turned to Jennifer and lifted his glass appreciatively to her.

'To our newest member, beautiful woman and cellist extraordinaire – Jennifer!'

Jennifer rolled her eyes but accepted the compliment as she tapped Gordon's glass and tossed down the rest of her drink. Jacek beckoned for the waiter to refill their glasses.

'OK, I get to answer that.' She paused a moment, screwing up her face to think. 'OK. I got it.' She held her glass aloft. 'To all of you for welcoming me so graciously into the group, and to future successes!'

They all cheered, and Gordon reached out and patted her hand on the table. Jacek spoke up. 'I want to make one more toast.' He held his glass out to Krzyzstof. Its facets sparkled in the light of the candle that sat in the center of the table between them. 'To you – to us' he said softly. Gunther, seeing the look in Jacek's face as he softly beheld his new love, whooped in delight. 'To you both' he toasted as he rammed his glass into Jacek's, sloshing a few drops on the table in his enthusiasm.

The waiter, who had been hovering discreetly at the back of the room, returned to take their order. As they waited, the band struck up into 'Hava Nagila'. Gunther, his inhibitions freed by the vodka, couldn't help leaping to his feet. He seized his violin from the seat next to him and started to dance around the room from table to table, playing in thirds with the violinist of the klezmer band. Jennifer and Jacek began to clap and stomp their feet and the other diners joined in, singing lustily. The song sped up and Gunther with it, until he was fiddling crazily, his bow popping and crackling like a firebrand as he played. Jennifer jumped to her feet and cheered him on 'Go Gunther. Woo!' Gordon looked up at her, long golden hair shimmering in the lamplight, her cheeks flushed with alcohol and excitement as she egged Gunther on, and he followed her lead, trying to slip his arm around her waist and pull her closer to him. Jennifer pulled away abruptly and turned to him, her eyes glittering angrily.

'Give it a rest, Gordon. I've told you I'm not interested.'

Gordon dropped his arm, sulkily, and stood next to her, watching Gunther. He couldn't fathom what had gotten into his second violinist, usually so unremarkable that people often forgot he was there. After fifteen years working together, Gordon had become used to pitying Gunther in a condescending way, taking for granted that he'd always be there playing second fiddle. Gunther was short and ugly, nondescript, he would never amount to much or rise to challenge Gordon's supremacy. He constantly worried about money and was always rushing off to some lowly gig or to teach yet another student. Gunther's role in the quartet was to provide a foil for Gordon to showcase his own brilliance. Yet here was Gunther, life and soul of the party, commanding the attention of everyone in the room. Hell, even the klezmer band were cheering Gunther on, although he'd stolen their limelight. Gordon had sensed something different about Gunther during the concert. He couldn't quite put his finger on it; something or someone seemed to have instilled a new air of confidence in Gunther and he'd cast his cares to the winds. He glanced at Jennifer again. The silver strings on the cello brooch pinned to her shoulder glinted in the lamplight as she raised her hands high and applauded Gunther, who was now bowing to the room and grinning, as the klezmer clarinetist clapped him on the shoulder and the violinist swung Gunther's hand high in the air. Could Gunther and Jennifer...? He looked between the two in disbelief. Maybe he, Gordon was losing his touch. Anyway, Jennifer had made her lack of interest in him clear enough, twice now. He'd be better off shifting his attentions elsewhere.

Gunther returned to the table, beaming and rubbing his hands in anticipation of dinner. The plates arrived and the quartet tucked in – nothing could be better to satisfy appetites after a concert on a cold winter's night than Jewish comfort food. When they had eaten their fill and paid the check, Gunther pushed back his chair. He needed to use the washroom before they left. The band had finished and the other diners were leaving too. As he washed his hands, he looked up at the mirror at himself. His face glistened with sweat and satisfaction and his hair curled wildly, tousled by his crazy dance around the restaurant. He slicked it back with his fingers. He felt ten years younger. He went back into the dining room to find the others but the table was empty – and his violin case was nowhere to be seen.

A wave of panic hit him in the gut. He checked under the table. It wasn't there. He ran around the room. Nothing. Gunther groaned. How stupid he'd been to leave it unattended. He'd allowed himself to get carried away, he'd drunk too much and become careless. Everyone in the room had watched him play, he'd practically invited an opportunistic thief to rob him of not only his precious Vuillaume but also the priceless manuscript concealed above it. He stood in the center of the dining room paralyzed, not knowing what to do. He could hardly breathe and he badly wanted to cry. Then he heard Jennifer calling his name. She came striding into the room, holding up her long skirts.

'There you are, Gunther. We wondered where you'd gotten to. The taxi's waiting.'

'My violin…' was all he could choke out.

'Yes, we've got it with us in the cab. You didn't think we'd leave it here unattended while you were in the bathroom, do you? We've been waiting outside for you.'

Gunther could have kissed Jennifer. He followed her out to the street. The street lights had gone out and the stars hung low in the night sky.

'Come on, here's our taxi. See, your violin's right here, next to my cello. I sent Gordon on with Jacek.' She pulled a face. 'Gordon's such a lech. I didn't want him trying it on in the cab. I feel safe with you.'

Gunther leaned in and inspected his case, peeking inside just to reassure himself that the violin was there. He sighed in relief.

'That was quite a scare. Thank you for taking care of it. I don't know what I'd do if I lost it.'

Jennifer patted his arm. 'Of course, that's what friends are for. Come on, let's go. It's very late and I'm tired.' They slid into the back seat of the cab, and as soon as they slammed the door and moved off, she fell asleep with her head resting on Gunther's shoulder. When they reached the hotel, he shook her gently to wake her, and walked with her to the elevator, wishing her goodnight as she got out on her floor.

Gunther wasn't tired at all; he was still riding on the wave of pent-up energy released when he'd escaped from the library with the manuscript in his possession. He sat on the bed and removed his tuxedo jacket and tie so that he could relax. He sniffed the shoulder of the jacket where Jennifer had rested her head in the taxi. The smell of her perfume – that trace of nutmeg that reminded him of childhood junkets and gingerbread – conjured the memory of her smile as she'd stood to applaud him at the restaurant. The thought of her friendship, the words she'd spoken, her irritation with Gordon, warmed him. He lifted his violin case on to the bed next to him and reverently took out the manuscript. He'd been too busy with the concert to give it much thought, and now was his first opportunity to take a closer look. Gunther caressed the buckram cover with his fingertips and opened the manuscript to the front page. He felt very possessive of his prize. It would have been nice to spend more than one short night with the document, knowing that it was his and his alone, with time to peruse it and get more intimately acquainted with it. However, he was due to meet Heimlich at the Berlin Philharmonie the next day to hand it over and receive the balance of his payment. He had one last piece of business to take care of before he went to bed.

Gunther went into his bathroom and took a fresh razor blade from his wash bag. Then he went to the safe and retrieved the forgeries he'd had made. He took a deep breath, and with a trembling hand, he sliced out the front page from the original volume, as close as he could to the binding. He drew the blade slowly and surely down the page, and pulled gently to release it from the volume. Next, taking a tube of glue that the printer had given him for the purpose, he squeezed a bead onto a tissue, which he then carefully wiped along the cut edge of the forgery. Then he inserted the replacement page into the binding, pulling it level with the others, and closed the cover, squinting along the edge to make sure the new page lined up. The printer had done an excellent job – the edge of the sheet was exactly the same shade of brown as the original. It struck Gunther that he might have trouble telling the original page from the second forgery that he'd had made. He took his Dover Score of the Beethoven quartets and flipped through the pages to find a Post-it note he'd used as a book mark. He stuck the Post-it on the back of the second forgery, wrapped it together with the original in the tissue paper and then tucked both in his suitcase, between the lining, which unzipped, and the shell of the case. He piled his clothes back on top. There. The loose pages were secured. He didn't want to risk them falling out of his violin case when he handed over the bound volume to Heimlich. Gunther took one last look at the score and then wrapped it in the plastic laundry bag he'd taken from the closet and placed it back in the compartment in his violin case. Finally, he undressed and got into the bed. He fell asleep as soon as his head hit the pillow.

After breakfast, the quartet parted company. Jacek waved the other three off as they shared a taxi to the airport. He planned to stay behind an extra day with Krzysztof. Gordon and Jennifer were headed back to London and Gunther had told them he had some further business to attend to in Berlin. He took a taxi straight from Tegel Airport to the Philharmonie. By now it was lunchtime and the noonday sun bounced cheerfully from the yellow tiles on the exterior, as a steady stream of people bustled past the bare trees in and out of the building. Gunther left his suitcase at the coat check, and carrying only his violin, headed upstairs. As instructed, he had dressed smartly in black so that he'd appear to be a performer. He reached the sixth floor where a small balcony overlooked the foyer. Heimlich was waiting for him, leaning against the wall, so that he couldn't be seen from below, Gunther's old violin case and a black leather briefcase at his feet. Gunther joined him by the wall, snapped open his violin case and handed over the plastic-wrapped package. Heimlich eagerly pulled out the score and thumbed through the pages. Gunther held his breath as he examined the manuscript, hoping that the substituted frontispiece would stay glued in place, trying his hardest to look nonchalant. Heimlich was hard to read. It was impossible to tell what he was thinking. After what seemed like an age, he closed the book with a weighty thud. Gunther took his courage in both hands.

'I've fulfilled my side of the bargain. Now I want my payment.'

Heimlich hesitated for a moment, and looked him up and down. Gunther stuck out his chin, defiantly and waited.

'Yes. Yes, of course.' He picked up his briefcase and opened it, taking out a wad of cash which he handed to Gunther. Gunther counted it hastily. It was all there. One hundred and ninety-seven thousand, six hundred Euros. He stuffed in his coat pocket and looked up at Heimlich.

'And my bow – the one I left with you?'

Heimlich handed him his old case. Gunther fumbled with the clasps to check that his bow was still inside.

'And the Beethoven Festival? That was part of the deal.'

'Yes, that too.' He pulled a business card from a compartment in the lid of his briefcase and handed it to Gunther who read the name printed on it – Nike Wagner, Artistic Director, Beethoven Fest. 'Call her. She'll be expecting you.' Heimlich wrapped the score back in the laundry bag and placed it in his briefcase. He shook Gunther's hand and smiled. 'Thank you, Herr Erdogan. Your country appreciates your service. Consider your taxes paid up in full. Goodbye.'

He waved his hand towards the stairs in a gesture of dismissal. Gunther stumbled away and walked as fast as he could without running, without looking back, his old case tucked under his arm and the new one in his hand. He hoped never to see Heimlich again. He put his right hand in his pocket and fingered the notes. He'd better deposit the cash right away. Two hundred thousand Euro was a lot of money. What if the bank teller became suspicious? Well, it was a lot of money to him but you'd have to pay a lot more for a fine Italian instrument. He'd say he'd just sold a violin. That was it, that should be credible, especially since he was carrying two instrument cases with him. But he couldn't take his suitcase – that might look like he was laundering money, about to flee the country. A violin dealer wouldn't have a suitcase with him. He practiced what he would say a couple of times, until his voice stopped wavering, and sounded clear and confident. A branch of Deutsche Bank, at which he kept his Euro account, lay just a few blocks away. He walked quickly there, repeating over and over what he would say, and sure enough, the teller took the money in a matter-of-fact business-like manner and handed him a receipt.

Gunther walked out of the bank feeling like a free man. The sun blazed down on his hatless head and he could scarcely stop himself from skipping down the street. He returned to the Philharmonie to retrieve his suitcase and hailed a taxi from the rank back to the airport. Soon the loan on his Vuillaume would be paid off and he would turn a new page in his life.

Chapter 18 – Deliverance

Gunther alighted from the bus at his home stop in Kilburn to be greeted by grey skies and a light drizzle of rain. He'd never been so relieved to get home to his small and dingy flat. Concert tours took it out of you at the best of times, and the added stress of the heist had taken its toll. After the euphoria had faded, Gunther realized he was dog tired. He just wanted to sit down on his own couch, brew some good strong Turkish coffee and eat some beans on toast on a tray in front of the television. He fumbled in his pocket for the street door key and wearily climbed the narrow stairs, wrestling with his suitcase and instruments. The store owner had left his mail in a sprawling heap on the door mat. Gunther sidestepped the pile as he opened his front door and dropped his bags inside. He'd deal with the mail later.

He unpacked the suitcase, carefully removing the bottle of plum vodka that he'd picked up in the Kraków Duty Free and placing it on the kitchen counter before dumping his clothes in the laundry basket. He unzipped the lining of the empty case and drew out the tissue wrapped pages, laying them on the kitchen table to admire them. The forgery still had the Post-it note on its back to distinguish it from the original. He should find a nice piece of cardboard backing and a protective film to keep them clean and flat. Gunther gazed meditatively at Beethoven's signature. Somehow just looking at it gave him strength, making him feel like a winner. He groped in his trouser pocket for the business card that Heimlich had given him. The corners were a little creased now. He flattened it out and placed it on the table next to the manuscript. Nike Wagner. He would call her first thing in the morning to discuss his participation in the Beethovenfest orchestra. He went into the bathroom to wash his face, and looked in the mirror. His reflection looked different now. The change was hard to define – perhaps he was standing taller, and certainly the worry lines around his eyes were less. The face that looked back at him had some new quality about it –

confidence, hope? Whatever it was, he looked and felt young again.

He put the coffee on to boil, took a loaf of bread out of the freezer and popped a slice in the toaster, and opened a can of beans. He'd go shopping and stock up the fridge in the morning. While the beans were heating on the stove, he went to pick up the mail. As usual, most of it was junk mail, plus a couple of bills. By force of habit, he set those aside to deal with later, and then laughed at himself. New, bold Gunther didn't have to worry about finding the cash to pay his bills any more. The last letter was printed with the London Symphony Orchestra logo. He rubbed the envelope in his fingers. They used expensive stationery – the paper was bright white and had a slight texture to it. The audition seemed so long ago, although it had only been three weeks or so. He knew what the envelope would contain. One more in a long line of rejections. But then again, he wondered. The Beethoven manuscript seemed to have reversed his long run of bad luck. Would its power extend to influence the outcome of the audition? With shaking hands, he tore it open and unfolded the sheet inside.

'Dear Mr. Erdogan,

Thank you for auditioning to join the London Symphony Orchestra. The panel was very impressed with your playing and we would like to extend to you an offer of employment in the second violin section. Our terms and conditions are detailed on the enclosed sheet. We do hope that you will decide to join us.'

Gunther couldn't believe his eyes. He snatched up the paper and danced around his kitchen table, waving it and whooping with delight. After all these years – success! The sound of the beans boiling over and fizzing on the stovetop brought him back to reality and he quickly turned off the gas and sat back down at the table, turning the letter over in his hands wonderingly. At last he'd netted a well-paid job, that guaranteed him regular work. He could drop the dreadful wedding quartet gigs, and maybe even weed out his worst students. He read the terms and conditions. He couldn't believe his luck. He'd get paid sick leave, and the orchestra even offered a pension. Of course, he'd have to work out scheduling with the quartet but that should be possible and, worst case, the orchestra had a list of subs who could step in if a regular player had a conflicting engagement. He couldn't wait to tell the other members of the quartet.

As he ate his beans on toast and sipped his coffee, Gunther glanced idly at Beethoven's autograph. He'd had the copies made so that he could sell one to Jennifer's father, Beethovenmane and collector Ed Rose, with the dual purpose of making more money and winning the girl. But now he hesitated. He'd come to know Jennifer better during their wonderful afternoon exploring Kraków together. She'd said they were friends and she trusted him, to the point where she'd waited behind for him with the taxi so she wouldn't have to suffer Gordon's unwanted advances. Was he the kind of guy to go behind her back, to deceive her and her father so that he could make a quick buck? He just didn't know. He had no idea how he would even go about it, how he could set up the deal without her finding out and getting suspicious. They would be going to Napa in April to play for the charity benefit, so he had plenty of time to think about it before then. He stashed the autographs back in his violin case and hid it in the wardrobe before falling into bed.

Gunther rolled out of bed the following morning with a new sense of purpose. Despite the stresses and strains of the recent tour he felt energized and rejuvenated. His head was clear, his mind alert, and as he stretched he noticed he didn't have the usual stiffness in his shoulders and back from sitting on airplanes and schlepping heavy bags around that usually plagued him for several days after a tour. As he brewed his morning coffee and made some toast he caught himself whistling the tune from Wagner's Bridal Chorus from Lohengrin, one of the pieces the Nightingale Quartet was frequently asked to play for wedding gigs. He'd left Nike Wagner's card on the table last night as a reminder to himself to call her.

'Now's better than never' he told himself, breezily, and gulping down the last mouthful of scalding coffee, he picked up the phone and dialed the number.

'Hallo, Nike Wagner'

'Hallo, this is Gunther Erdogan, violinist from the London Quartet. I'm calling to enquire about the orchestra at Beethovenfest this fall.' He left the sentence hanging like a question.

'Ah yes, Herr Erdogan. I've heard good things about you from friends in high places. They insisted I invite you to come and play with our orchestra in Bonn this summer. As it happens, we do have an opening in the second violin section. Might you be interested in applying?'

Gunther tried to sound composed, but inside he was cheering wildly. 'Yes, very interested. Can you tell me more about the application process?'

'Certainly. If you can send me your curriculum vitae and a video or recording of your playing we can use that. There is also a formal application form; if you can give me your email address I will send it to you.'

'And how long will it take you to reach a decision?'

Nike laughed drily at the other end of the phone. 'My contacts assure me that you can "deliver the goods" as they put it. While I can't make any commitments, I can assure you the process will be very quick in your case, once we receive the required information.'

'Thank you, I can't thank you enough' said Gunther hastily.

'You're welcome. I look forward to working with you, Gunther.' There was a click as she hung up.

Chapter 19 – New Beginnings

The quartet regrouped several weeks later to start rehearsals back at the Royal Academy for their next programme. Gunther strode into the room with a spring in his step. Jacek was already there, setting up the chairs and music stands. He looked up as Gunther entered, and did a double take. Gunther was wearing a smart pair of black jeans that Jacek didn't remember seeing before and he'd had a haircut, but most remarkably, he bore no trace of his former hangdog expression.

'Hi Gunther. What's up?'

Gunther couldn't wait to brag about his new jobs. 'Guess what, I finally made it into the LSO. Just had my first rehearsal yesterday. And I've been accepted into the Beethovenfest orchestra for the festival in Bonn in September.'

'Really? That's wonderful. Well done!' Jacek jumped up and shook him vigorously by the hand. Gordon and Jennifer arrived at the door to see Jacek embracing Gunther warmly.

'What's up?' asked Jennifer.

'Gunther only got into the LSO, and the Bonn Beethoven Festival orchestra, that's all!'

'Oh, wow! Clever you!' exclaimed Jennifer. Even Gordon was grudgingly impressed.

'I hope that doesn't mean you'll be leaving us.'

'No, no' said Gunther, quickly 'Not any time soon. The LSO is fine with players having other gigs, of course we'll try to avoid conflicts but I've negotiated to get a leave of absence if there are any scheduling conflicts. They have subs who can cover.'

'Oh, good' said Jennifer, with relief. 'So, you can still make our California trip for the benefit in April?' Her hazel eyes were turned on him, pleading, and his heart leapt.

'Of course, Jennifer. I wouldn't miss it. It will be my first trip to the States.'

She beamed back at him and before he knew what he was doing he blurted out 'And of course, now I've got my new job, I can afford to waive my fee too, for your charity do.'

Jennifer spontaneously threw her arms around him and kissed his cheek. He felt himself getting hot under the collar and in his peripheral vision he thought he saw Gordon roll his eyes and mutter under his breath 'Creep'.

'Actually, I could really use your help in planning the tour, Gunther. I haven't organized concerts before and I'm worried I'll miss something important. Would you be able to give me a hand? I can give you all the contacts if you can help me with the negotiations and the arrangements.'

Cogs began to turn in Gunther's brain. If he could be the one to discuss the business end of the concert arrangements with Jennifer's father, he'd have an entrée into discussing another certain delicate business. 'No problem, Jennifer. I'd be happy to help.'

'Thanks so much – that's a weight off my mind. And, I have some news to share as well. I'm going to be quite busy in the next couple of months – I've got a recording contract with Hyperion to record a DVD of all five Beethoven sonatas for cello and piano. And I'm going to play from the first edition that my Dad gave me when I graduated. They were very interested in that, they think it can be highlighted as a unique feature of the recording.'

'That's fantastic!' gushed Gordon. 'Way to go Jennifer. How did you manage to pull that off?'

'They approached me after our lunchtime concert at the Barbican, the one that the BBC broadcast. The producer said he loved my fresh approach to interpreting Beethoven's music so I told him the story about the first edition I have of the sonatas.' She put her head on one side coyly. 'He said he thought I had "visual impact" as well.'

Gordon couldn't help but sneer. 'I thought you said you wanted to be taken seriously as a professional, not trade on your looks.'

'Hey, I told you the main reason was my musicianship. So what if being photogenic helps' she snapped back.

Gordon backpedaled 'Come on, I was only teasing. That's great, honestly. Well done you,'

Jacek spoke up. 'Well, if we are all making announcements, I have some news too.' The others stopped talking and looked at him expectantly. He blushed and looked at the floor. 'Krzyzstof will be coming to Napa with me in April.'

Jennifer let out a catcall. 'Way to go Jacek!' She hugged him too. 'So, Gordon, now it's your turn. You must have some news to share too, like the rest of us.'

Gordon stared back at her cool as a cucumber. 'Only that the London Quartet is now resuming rehearsals for its next concert series. Come on everyone, we're wasting valuable rehearsal time. Let's get to work.'

Jennifer gave Gunther the list of her contacts for concerts in California. She'd already done some of the groundwork, introducing the quartet, sending their bios and the new group photo, and proposing dates during a two-week period following the charity event. He set to work, researching flights and hotels and working out what they would need to charge to cover their expenses. He plucked up the courage late one evening, to call Ed Rose to discuss details of the charity concert. Ed had agreed to serve as the quartet's local contact for arrangements in Napa. Jennifer had advised him when to call.

'Dad's eight hours behind London time. He starts work early – he's always having "power breakfast meetings" but he's usually free around nine thirty in the evening London time – that's when he's eating lunch at his desk.'

With trepidation, Gunther dialed the number Jennifer had given him. It rang only once before Ed answered.

'Hello, this is Gunther Erdogan, from the London String Quartet. Your daughter, Jennifer gave me your number. I hope it's OK to call.'

'Hi Gunther. Yes, now's fine. Jen told me you'd call. I've been expecting you.'

Rose sounded just as Gunther had imagined – he spoke in a deep voice with the ease that comes from confidence. He wondered if Jennifer got her height and blonde hair from her father.

'Yes, I'm helping her with the logistical details for our concert tour. We're very excited about coming.'

'And I'm excited to be launching your tour from our winery. We're so proud of Jen and what she's accomplished.'

'She's already added a new dimension to the quartet. We're lucky to have her, especially now she's got her new recording contract. I understand she'll be playing the music you gave her when she graduated.'

'That's right. You know, I never had the chance to learn an instrument growing up. I was the first one in my family to go to college and I had to work to pay my way through Stanford. I worked damn hard to get where I am; I wanted my kids to have all the opportunities I didn't get. A fine instrument, lessons from the best teachers, Juilliard, you name it. She's earned it.'

'Yes sir. Now, about the concert.'

'You don't need to call me Sir, Gunther. Ed is just fine. Now, what do you need to know?'

With fifteen years of experience under his belt, Gunther knew exactly what to ask. He checked off the key points on his fingers as he spoke, covering space, lighting, sound, timing. When he came to the fee he explained that the Quartet had agreed to perform for the charity at a significant discount to their usual rate. 'We discussed it and we'd like to donate a substantial portion of our services to the cause.' He named an amount and paused.

'That sounds very reasonable. That's generous of you guys. I'm sure Jen will be grateful for every dollar the benefit raises. Did she give you any of the background on the organization?'

'She mentioned it had something to do with her brother' said Gunther cautiously. He didn't want to say anything out of line.

'Yeah, it's strange how two kids, brother and sister, can turn out so different. Her brother's been a challenge to us, I can tell you. I wish he had Jen's drive. Anyway Gunther, I must go, my next meeting's coming up, but it's been great talking to you. Don't hesitate to call if there's anything else you need to discuss.' He hung up.

Gunther sat back in his chair at the kitchen table. That had gone better than he expected. He didn't move in the kind of circles that Ed did but the American had put him at his ease. He'd been surprised to learn that Jennifer's father hadn't been born wealthy and had started out poor, like Gunther. But Ed had been friendly and approachable. Perhaps on their next call Gunther could draw Ed out to talk a little about his collection of Beethoven memorabilia. Maybe he could suggest some kind of Beethoven exhibit as part of the benefit, to complement the music.

The following morning, while Gunther was finishing his breakfast, his phone rang. It was

Jennifer, slightly breathless, explaining that she had just got back from taking a run.

'So, you talked to my Dad yesterday.'

'Yes, we discussed the arrangements for the concert.'

'I know, I spoke to him later. He said he enjoyed talking with you.'

Gunther beamed. So, the feeling had been mutual.

'I had an idea after he hung up that I'd like to bounce off you first. How do you think he'd react to having some kind of Beethoven display at the event? Maybe some pictures of memorabilia from his collection? Or your new CD, if its available, with a picture of your first edition score?'

'I think he'd love it – that's a great idea! Do you want me to ask him?'

'No, it's fine, I'll call him back this evening and see what he thinks.'

'Good, good. I must run – literally. Let me know if there's anything I can do to help.'

Gunther looked at the piece of unfinished toast on his plate, now stone cold and unappetizing. He slathered it with a generous dollop of fig jam before cramming it into his mouth. His conscience teetered on the brink. He had the perfect opening to bring up the autograph at his next call with Ed, but would he have the courage to do so? Everything was going so well that he was loath to risk spoiling it, but could he truly afford to pass up such a golden opportunity? He weighed up the options. He'd paid off the bank loan on the Vuillaume and spent several thousand of the Euros paying off other debts and replacing various items around the flat that were totally worn out. He had over eighty thousand left, but how long would that last him? His first paycheck from the LSO had been a little smaller than he was expecting; on examining the paystub he was dismayed to see all the deductions for taxes and other fringe benefits. As a freelancer, he was used to taking home gross earnings, often in cash, and reckoning his taxes later. He wasn't used to paying them at source and now he was making more money his tax rate was higher too. He absolutely didn't want to have to go back to playing wedding gigs to make ends meet. He shuddered at the memory of all those past bridezillas, the ones who couldn't decide what music they wanted until two days before the wedding and then demanded some pop song he'd never heard, let alone had music for.

Then there were the ones who were chronically late, who kept the quartet sitting there for an hour or more beyond the contracted time. And worst of all, the ones who 'forgot' to bring the agreed-upon payment on the day, whom he had to chase up for months afterwards to get paid. With his Symphony job, he just didn't have the time to be messed around like that. It was just too tempting. He had the autograph right there, he'd had the foresight and invested a hard-earned thousand Euros and more in the copies, let alone taken a huge risk to get it.

The big unknown was how Ed Rose would react to his offer. He didn't know how 'above board' Ed was, whether he would want to have anything to do with something that he'd quickly figure out had come into Gunther's possession by questionable means. He also didn't have any sense of how much Ed might want the autograph, how much he'd be willing to pay to get it for his collection. Gunther would just have to proceed cautiously and play it by ear, relying on his instincts.

He thought about how to broach the subject of the autograph through his Symphony rehearsal that morning. He was so preoccupied that he forgot to turn the page for his stand partner, who had to reach across and flip it over herself while hissing angrily at him. Gunther shook himself and tried to concentrate. He couldn't afford to make mistakes, not while he was still new to the orchestra. He taught several private lessons after school back at his flat, and listened impatiently to his students playing their exercises, almost pushing the last one out of the door so that he could prepare himself for his conversation with Rose. At last nine thirty came.

'Hi, Ed, it's Gunther. Sorry to bother you again, but I had an idea for the benefit.'

Ed listened, and then responded thoughtfully. 'That's an interesting concept. I'll have to think about it, what might be most appropriate from the collection.'

Gunther jumped in with both feet. 'Tell me more about the collection Ed. How did you get started?'

Ed took the bait. 'When Jen turned ten, I went to her first recital, at her teacher's home, and she performed this piece, the Sonatine by Beethoven. I'd never really paid that much attention to classical music but that piece just got me. I couldn't get it out of my head, I'd find myself humming the tune when I was driving in the car. So, I started listening to more Beethoven – his symphonies, and then his piano concerti, and then I discovered his chamber music. The guy was a genius. His music spoke to me, it was always about something bigger, something eternal, you know? And then a friend told me about the Ira Brilliant Center for Beethoven Studies at San Jose State University and I just had to drive down there and take a look.' Gunther had never heard of Ira Brilliant but he could sense that Ed was in full flow and listened quietly as he continued. 'So, I found out that Ira had collected all these first editions of Beethoven's music. It was mind-blowing. I got in touch with him directly – he lived in Scottsdale, Arizona – and asked if we could meet. That turned out to be the most inspirational meeting of my life. Brilliant told me the story of how he'd amassed his collection. He was very generous, he shared with me all his tips on which auctions and which dealers to follow. I got hooked. I started building my own collection of Beethoven first editions. Back then you could get the more common ones for a couple hundred bucks. I paid a lot more than that for the one I gave Jen as a graduation gift. Then again, it was also an early twenty first birthday gift, a two-fer. July tenth,

1995, that's my girl's birthday – best day of my life.'

Gunther congratulated Ed politely and then asked 'So is your collection first editions only or are you interested in other Beethoven memorabilia?'

'Sure I am! Pride of my collection right now is an original printed invitation to Beethoven's funeral in 1827. And you might be interested to know I have a first edition of the quartet your group has been performing, opus 74, the Harp. But what I'd really like to get is an original autograph by Beethoven. I've been looking at the auctions but nothing's come up in my price range.'

Gunther's heartbeat quickened. What could be a more blatant invitation than that? He took a deep breath.

'What if I told you I might be able to lay my hands on a Beethoven autograph. Would you be interested?'

Although Rose was eight thousand miles away, Gunther could hear the sudden piquing of Ed's attention in his voice over the telephone line.

'You bet, if the price is right.'

'It would need to be handled with great discretion. There are certain parties whom I would not want to know that you had gained possession of the article.'

Ed's voice sharpened. 'I'm curious, why are you offering this to me? If it's something of value I may not be in a position to be the highest bidder.'

Gunther paused. 'I want it to go to someone who will truly appreciate it. And you've been a huge help in getting the London Quartet to America. We've never had the opportunity before. And I like you.' He finished, lamely.

'OK, so can you tell me more? What is it?'

'You swear to keep it secret, you'll tell no-one? Not even your daughter?'

'Well, now I'm really curious. Yes, of course I'll keep it secret. Spit it out!'

'What would you say if I told you I had the autograph frontispiece of Beethoven's Opus 74 string quartet?'

He heard the audible gasp at the other end of the line. 'Seriously? But Jen said you'd just seen the score when you were in Kraków. Is there more than one version? How on earth did you come by it?'

'I can't divulge my contact. But it's the genuine article.'

'How can you be sure? Would you be open to having an expert verify its authenticity?'

'That would depend, if he could be relied upon to be discreet. And I'd have to stay anonymous.'

'What price are you asking?'

Gunther weighed his options. On the open market, he knew Beethoven autographs could go for fifty thousand dollars, a hundred thousand dollars for a page of one of Beethoven's sketchbooks. But Rose had indicated these were out of his price range. However, a first edition could go from a thousand to twenty thousand dollars. He needed enough to make it worth his while, to take the risk, but he also wanted Rose to feel indebted to him, and indirectly, Jennifer, although she must never find out how or why. He swallowed hard.

'Thirty thousand US dollars.'

Rose was silent. Gunther cursed himself. He'd been too greedy. He waited for Rose to speak. After what seemed like ten measures' rest, Rose answered 'Would you accept twenty-five thousand, in cash, subject to verification by an expert of my choosing?'

Gunther forced himself to wait, and then trying to make is voice as calm and matter-of-fact as possible, he responded 'Ed, we have a deal. Have your expert lined up in April when we come to Napa and I'll bring it with me for him to examine.'

'Sure thing! Can't wait to see it!'

'Don't forget, not a word to Jennifer.'

'Sure, sure. Thanks, Gunther. Talk to you soon.'

Chapter 20

Napa, California – April

Gunther craned his neck to look out of the window as the plane descended over San Francisco. He felt as excited as a little kid, on his first visit to the United States. He'd exhausted all the entertainment possibilities on the ten-and-a-half-hour flight from London to San Francisco – after three movies his headphones were digging into his ears, and he'd finished the in-flight magazine and even attempted the crossword. The skin on his hands was taut and dry and his shoes were uncomfortably tight. He watched the flight tracker impatiently, keen to reach the destination. Next to him, Krzysztof slept, his head lolling on one side, his lips parted and slick with saliva. No wonder Krzysztof was tired out – he and Jacek, who had the aisle seat, had spent the whole flight alternately laughing and joking, playing video games together on Jacek's iPad, and chatting with the cabin crew. Gunther had tried to ignore them, hunkering down with his noise-cancelling headphones and staring at the screen, or out of the window. He'd grudgingly given up the bulkhead seat next to Jennifer to Gordon, who didn't travel well and was always complaining that his legs were too long to fit into an economy seat and that he couldn't sleep on planes. It was a small sacrifice to make compared to having to listen to Gordon's whining. Jennifer's cello was strapped into the bulkhead seat by the window. At least the cello couldn't recline, Gunther thought. Gordon was practically lying in Jacek's lap, who sat directly behind him.

The captain announced the start of the descent. Beneath them rolled rugged hills, their crinkled crags coated yellow and green. Scarcely a road or a house could be seen. As they dropped, the hills fell away to a broad valley ringed around by mountains. Now he saw the rows of houses on the dense grid of streets that hugged the floor of the valley and rose in terraces up the lower slopes. As they approached the Bay, the shallow water gleamed in unexpected colors – red, orange, bottle green. He'd read about that in the airline magazine – the unusual coloring was due to algae. He squinted far ahead, in front of the plane to see the clustered skyscrapers of the city in the distance.

It took a couple of hours before the quartet assembled on the other side of security, by the time they'd navigated the immigration lines. The officials had selected Gunther for a special interview – he guessed because of his Turkish last name – and he'd been grilled for twenty minutes on exactly where he would be going and what he would be doing while in the United States, while they scrutinized his P visa. They'd even made him take out his violin and play something to prove that he was a legitimate professional musician. Thankfully they hadn't wanted to search his violin case, in which he'd secreted both the original and the copy of the autographed frontispiece, in identical envelopes, the forgery still marked with the Post-it note. He'd never been so relieved to emerge from the interview room into baggage claim, where the others were waiting anxiously for him.

They entered the arrivals hall. Jennifer looked up and down and then shrieked 'Dad' and waved wildly to a tall man in a sports jacket standing to one side. Ed had offered to come and pick them up at the airport. Gunther looked at him with interest – so this was Ed Rose, the man himself. He was tanned with a full head of well-groomed hair, and grinning with a perfect set of dazzling teeth.

Gordon lengthened his stride and shook Ed's hand, introducing himself. Jennifer introduced the other three to her father. Ed shook Gunther's hand with a firm grip, looking him directly in the eye, sizing him up.

The quartet followed Ed to his van, with Krzysztof hanging back a little, feeling out of place, and settled in for the two-hour ride to Napa. As they left the city, the landscape changed back to the rolling green hills that Gunther had seen from the plane. They arrived in wine country as the sun was setting, casting long shadows down the rows of vines that were just starting to bud and burst into leaf. Ed turned into a driveway marked by tall gates, the iron wrought into delicate vines. The tires crunched on the gravel as they wound up the driveway through the row of vines that wound parallel to the contour of the gentle slope all the way to the winery.

The winery building looked like an old stone barn that had been airlifted directly from Tuscany. The slanting sun cast a rosy glow on the stones and accentuated the red cedar frame of the large arched window at the front. Ed swung the car around to the side and pulled up outside a house built in ranch style, long and low, with stonework and cedar beams that complemented the main winery building. Two figures stood in the open doorway – a woman in her fifties, tanned and wearing sunglasses, her greying blond hair tied back in a ponytail. Beside her scowled a skinny younger man in a tight black t-shirt and jeans. Jennifer jumped from the car and ran over to hug them both.

'Mom! Jason! Good to see you!'

The quartet alighted from the van, stretching their legs and retrieving their bags and instruments from the trunk. Mrs. Rose greeted them 'Welcome to our Napa home. Come on in – we've been so looking forward to meeting you all.'

Ed, noticing the look of wonderment on Gunther's face, laughed and took him by the arm.

'Welcome to the American Dream, Gunther. It's every venture capitalist's dream to be able to buy a winery up here. I guess I got lucky.'

Inside the hall was spacious, with dark wood floors and tall white walls that stretched up the full height of the house, with a gallery running around at the top of the stairs. To Gunther's eye it was sparsely, but expensively furnished, the big and heavy pieces made of dark wood and leather. A large abstract painting with blocks of garish red and yellow colors hung on the wall opposite the front door, and centered below the staircase was a huge fireplace, surrounded by stonework that matched the outside of the house. Mrs. Rose showed everyone to their rooms. 'Take your time to freshen up. We'll have dinner when everyone's ready.'

The following morning over breakfast the group discussed their plans for the day. At Gordon's request Gunther had built in some free time to allow them to recover from jet lag, so they weren't planning to rehearse until four that afternoon. Jennifer's cellphone had already been ringing off the hook, and she made her apologies.

'Sorry guys, you won't see much of me outside our rehearsals. I have to meet with the Board this morning to finalize plans for tomorrow's fundraiser, and then I have to call a bunch of people to make sure they're coming, and schmooze them over lunch and coffee.'

Gordon toyed with a waffle, wrinkling his nose at the melted butter and maple syrup that Mrs. Rose had poured over it, and reached for the bowl of fruit salad. He took a sip of coffee and pulled a face at the bitterness.

'You'd think after not sleeping on the plane yesterday, I'd have been tired. But I woke up at one a.m. and I haven't been able to get back to sleep. I'm going to take some Benadryl and go back to bed.'

Jacek and Krzyzstof pored excitedly over a wine country map, asking Mrs. Rose for recommendations for wineries to visit.

'You're probably best off taking the shuttle – then you won't have to drive. Here's the route. I'd suggest you ask the driver to stop at these ones.' She marked the map with little x's.

Gordon headed back to his room and Jacek and Krzysztof headed to theirs to get ready for their wine tour. Jennifer had left. Gunther helped Mrs. Rose clear the dishes and then made his excuses, saying he had some business to discuss with Ed.

'You'll find him in his office, at the back. He starts work early; he has calls with Europe, you know. I'll be heading out shortly myself to the store.'

Gunther climbed the stairs to his room. He heard a car engine start up and looked out of the window. A Mercedes sports convertible headed down the drive with Mrs. Rose at the wheel. That was quite a car to take shopping. Once the house was empty, he took the envelope containing the original autograph from the secret compartment in his violin case, leaving its twin behind, and went down to knock on the door of Ed's study.

'Come in!'

Gunther pushed open the door. Unlike the rest of the house, which was decorated in modern, minimalist style, Ed's study had the air of a traditional, cozy library. He sat behind a large old-fashioned desk with a green leather top and a banker's lamp with brass base and cylindrical green shade. A bottle-green leather armchair, generously upholstered, its buttons gleaming with military polish, faced the desk. The dark wooden floor was softened by a Moroccan rug. All around the walls ran built-in cabinets with shallow drawers, and book shelves filled with what looked like first edition books, their spines beautifully tooled in leather.

Ed jumped up and came around the desk to greet him. 'Good morning Gunther. How did you sleep?'

'Very well, thanks. Your office – wow.' Gunther swept his hand around to point at all the books. Ed looked flattered.

'Yes, it's impressive, isn't it? My wife calls it my man cave.'

'Is this where you keep your collection?'

'Yes, it is. Would you like to see it?'

'I'd love to.'

Ed went back to his desk and took a pair of white gloves and a key from the drawer, which he then used to unlock the cabinet and pull out the drawers one by one to show Gunther the first editions and other Beethoven memorabilia that he'd amassed over the years.

'Here's the Opus 74 string quartet I mentioned. I'm going to put it in a glass display cabinet in the winery function room for the fundraiser tomorrow. That was a great suggestion of yours. I just can't decide which pages to open it at for the display. What do you think?' He pulled on the gloves and picked up the score, turning the pages carefully with a finger.

'Given the nickname 'The Harp', I'd suggest you turn to that passage. It's in the first movement. Keep going. There. Do you see where it's marked *pizzicato* and the cello and viola take turns? Just like plucking the strings of a harp?'

'Great – thanks Gunther!' He placed a slip of paper in the place and set the quartet score on his desk. 'I'll deal with that later. Come and sit down. Let's get down to business.'

Gunther glanced behind him to make sure the door was closed, and then sat in the large leather armchair and laid the envelope in front of Ed.

'Ah! I've been so looking forward to seeing this' said Ed, leaning forward and rubbing his still gloved hands together in anticipation. 'May I?'

'Please, go ahead.'

Ed opened the flap of the envelope and gently slid out the contents. Gunther had placed the autograph inside a plastic sleeve with card backing to keep it clean and flat.

'Oh my word – there it is! Quartetto …LV Beethoven. Let's compare the signature with the one in my book!' He strode across to a bookshelf and pulled out a volume, ruffling through the pages. 'Here's an example. Let's see. Oh yes, that big curly B, and the scoring underneath. It's Beethoven's signature all right.' He looked at Gunther. 'Don't take it the wrong way, I'm sure it's what you say it is but before I commit to buy I still need to verify its authenticity, as we discussed. I've an expert lined up in Sonoma who specializes in historical documents. Is it OK if I run over there this afternoon so that he can verify the age and chemical composition of the paper and ink and so on? Don't worry, he uses spectroscopic tests, just using reflected light, it's completely non-destructive. You can come and watch if you like.'

Gunther sat back in the chair, his arms resting on the padded rests.

'No problem. It's the real deal, I'm confident your expert can verify that. I won't come; remember no-one can know where you got this from. I'd rather not risk it; even if you don't tell him my name he might recognize me. The quartet's photo is on all the publicity materials for the concerts these next two weeks. Anyway, we are rehearsing at four today. I wouldn't want you to have to rush your testing to get me back here on time.'

'Great. Let's find some time to talk privately again after dinner this evening. Meanwhile let me put this somewhere safe.' Ed slid the manuscript back into its envelope and walked over to a painting of bison hanging behind one of the built-in shelves, which he swung forward, revealing a small safe. His back blocked Gunther's view of the dial, but Gunther couldn't help but hear the number of turns – eight in all before the door creaked open. Ed placed the envelope in the safe and closed the door, replacing the painting over the top.

'So, what's your plan for the rest of the day, Gunther?'

'I'd really like to take a look at the set-up for tomorrow's concert, and check the seating and lighting and so on.'

'Jason can show you around. He works behind the bar in the Winery tasting room. I'll take you over there. Oh, ask him for a tour too, if you're interested. He'll be happy to show you around.'

They found Jason in the tasting room, behind the bar serving customers. Today he wore his work uniform, a black shirt embroidered with a red rose, the winery's logo. Something about Jason's demeanor stuck a chord in Gunther. His thin, pale face and downcast eyes, the droop of his shoulders. It was uncannily like looking in the mirror at his younger self, before his fortunes had turned. It couldn't be easy, being the failed older sibling of a successful and confident young woman, who was clearly the apple of her father's eye. Gunther's scars from being Gordon's underdog until so recently were still fresh enough for him to feel empathy for Jennifer's brother.

Ed made his apologies and went back to work, while Jason took Gunther to the function room where the following evening's concert and reception would be held. The space was perfect for a concert with a floor of polished stone flags and a high arched ceiling supported by cedar beams. Contemporary tapestries hung on the walls. Gunther conjectured that the acoustic would be church-like.

'We can open up these doors to the patio, if you like, so the guests have an unobstructed view of the vineyard. But we thought it would be better to have the event indoors, it still gets chilly here at night, and we weren't sure about the acoustics if you played outside.'

'It would be ideal to open the doors at either side but to have us play in front of the window in the center. That way our sound will reflect back to the audience but the fresh air and night sounds will make it feel as if we are outdoors. Perhaps we could do a sound and lighting check in here later this evening?'

'Yup. We can do that. Anything else we need to go over?'

'No, I don't think so, not right now. Thank you.'

'Cool. You wanna taste some of the wines, while you're here?'

Gunther said he would love to. The tasting room was almost empty, with just one couple finishing up a flight of wines at the other end of the bar.

'We usually have a lull this time on a Friday. The lunchtime rush is over and it's too early yet for the weekenders to drive up from San Francisco.'

He set three glasses in front of Gunther and poured the wines, one white and two red.

'This is our chardonnay, the lighter red's our zinfandel and this dark one is the cabernet sauvignon.'

The chardonnay was a pale straw color and smelled of ripe peaches. Gunther took a sip and was surprised by the strongly oaked taste. He tried the zinfandel, which had a peppery bite to it. He was no judge of fine wine but he liked both of these. The young, fresh taste reminded him of Jennifer – he even thought he could detect a hint of the nutmeg scent that she wore. And the unexpected woodiness and pepper were like her strong and independent character.

'What d'you think? You're from Germany, aren't you, Gunther? How do they compare with German wines?'

'I'm no connoisseur, but they taste very – American – to me. German wines are sweeter – these are very different.'

Jason laughed. 'And is that a good thing, or a bad thing?'

'Oh, very good' said Gunther hastily. 'They remind me of all good things American.'

'Which are…?'

'Your optimism, your energy, for example.'

Jason narrowed his eyes. 'And my sister?'

'Well yes, we appreciate the youthful energy and optimism she brings to the quartet. It's easy to get jaded and stale after a while.'

Jason leaned his elbows on the bar and slouched down with his chin on his hands. 'Tell me about it.'

Gunther looked up from his glass and scrutinized Jason's face.

'How long have you been working at the winery?'

'Coupla years, I had to reach legal drinking age first.' He laughed sardonically. 'Dad thinks if I'm right here under his nose he can keep an eye on me.'

'But it's not what you really wanted, no?'

Jason shrugged. 'I dunno. I'm not cut out for business like my Dad. He's trying to train me to run the winery some day. I haven't figured out what I want to do yet, I never had any obvious big talent like Jen. I'm just a big disappointment to all of them.'

Gunther tried to think of something encouraging to say, but nothing came to mind. Jason reminded him too much of his own brother Otto, who was still figuring out what he wanted to do at the age of thirty. He picked up the third glass and took a sip, so that he wouldn't have to talk. The cabernet smelled and tasted of cherries. He complimented Jason on the wines and then thanked him for his help and made his excuses and went back to the house. Jason's obvious depression made him uncomfortable. It was a little too familiar.

He took a nap and then, being woken by the muffled sound of Gordon practicing at the far end of the house, was guilted into getting out his own fiddle and warming up for the four o'clock rehearsal. Mrs. Rose had suggested they use the living room, and he went down shortly before four o'clock to borrow four dining chairs for the quartet to use. He heard a car door slam outside, and Jennifer came in with Jacek and Krzysztof, whom she had picked up at the shuttle stop on her way home. Jacek's cheeks were flushed and his arm was flung around the younger man's shoulders. He whispered something in Krzysztof's ear and he giggled. Gunther rolled his eyes. Jacek, always the life and soul of any party, seemed to be on hyperdrive this trip. He'd not stopped smiling since he'd met Krzysztof at Heathrow airport the day before. He just hoped the pair hadn't had too much fun wine tasting and that Jacek, who had a surprisingly large capacity for alcohol, could play unimpaired.

The rehearsal went well. Once they had run both pieces, Gunther suggested they walk over to the tasting room to check the layout and the sound. The tasting room had already closed and the illumination from the setting sun that flooded through the westward facing window cast its dim recesses deeper into shadow. Jason opened the side doors as Gunther had suggested and they became aware of the evening songs of crickets and roosting birds. They pulled some chairs over to the window and Jason experimented with lighting, so the quartet could see and be seen by the audience rather than just silhouetted against the scene outside.

The Roses had organized a barbecue for dinner, back at the house in the garden. Ed managed to catch Gunther's eye and the two slipped inside while the others were noisily discussing their day's activities over more wine. Jason, who tended the grill, was the only person to see them leave.

Ed took Gunther into the study and closed the door.

'I took the document over to Sonoma, this afternoon.' He paused and looked at Gunther.

'Well?'

'He says it's the real deal. The spectroscopy checked out. He said the paper and ink chemical composition are consistent with other examples of similar documents from central Europe at the time, and the handwriting analysis confirmed it. I'd love to get this deal done. Twenty-five thousand dollars?'

'Very good. Yes.' Gunther and Ed shook hands. Ed walked over to the safe. Gunther expected him to pull out the document but instead when he turned around he had a small bankers' envelope in his hand, stuffed with bills.

"Here you are, twenty-five thousand all in cash. Hundred dollar bills. You can check it if you like.'

Gunther was caught unprepared. He hadn't anticipated that Rose would offer him cash on the spot. He'd planned to switch the original and forged manuscript after Rose had taken the original to be examined. The forgery was up in his room in his violin case, he needed to stall for more time. He slowly counted the bills while he thought frantically what ruse he could use to make the switch.

'Thank you, the amount is correct. But I don't have anywhere secure to keep such a large amount of cash – could I leave it in the safe, with the document, until we leave on Sunday? I'd feel much better knowing it was in there.'

'Why, of course, no problem. I'm sure I can slip it to you on Sunday morning. I can pass it off as paperwork related to the concert.'

Gunther nodded. He felt a little better, but he still needed to find a way to make the switch. He decided to sleep on it. He still had time.

Chapter 21 – The Switch

The following day, the quartet members were each taken up with their own plans. Jennifer spent the morning rushing about, organizing the room set-up for the Strike Up fundraiser, and overseeing the floral arrangements, the printed programmes and the caterers. Gordon mooned around the house trying to get his anxiety under control and practicing his introductory speech on behalf of the quartet. Gunther, not wanting to be caught unprepared a second time, had zipped into his jacket the forged frontispiece in an identical plastic sleeve and envelope to the original, its telltale Post-it note now removed. He lurked in the living room, pretending to be relaxing and reading a book as he sat stiffly on the large couch with his jacket on, trying not to crush the hidden envelope, while watching and waiting for Ed to leave the house so he could sneak into the study unnoticed and make the switch. Jacek and Krzysztof announced with secretive smiles that they would be going out for lunch and would be back later but the other barely noticed as they were so preoccupied with their own concerns. At last, Jennifer came into the house.

'Dad, we're ready to set up the display case with the first edition. Please can you come and help?'

Ed ducked into his study and emerged with the Opus 74 score held in his gloved hands. He followed Jennifer over to the winery, leaving the study door ajar. As soon as they were out of sight, Gunther seized his chance and slunk into the study, He closed the door behind him, and made straight towards the bison painting, pressing the left edge as he'd seen Ed do to release the catch. The painting swung outward revealing the door of the safe. Gunther paused. He was going to make a wild guess at the combination, the eight digits that Ed Rose was most likely to remember. If he was wrong, he was screwed, failing a miracle. He took his handkerchief from his pocket and covered the dial with it to avoid leaving fingerprints before delicately holding it between two fingers and turning it forward and back, listening to the clicks as he did so. 10071995. Jennifer's birthday, July 10th, 1995. He held his breath and tugged. Nothing. The door remained locked. He buried his head in his hands. He'd been so sure that would be the code that Ed had used. What else could it be? He looked wildly around the room for a clue, ran to the desk and pulled open the top drawer to see if he could see anything like a passcode. Could it be the phone number? No, American numbers were ten digits, not eight. His eye fell on Ed's desk calendar. Something odd about it niggled at his mind. What was it? Ah yes, the Americans put the month first, not the day. His mouth fell open. Of course. He rushed back to the safe and dialed 07101995. The latch clicked and he pulled on the dial with trembling fingers. The door opened. The small fat envelope from the bank sat on top of the larger one whose twin was zipped over his heart. He pulled out the large envelope and peeked inside. Thankfully the frontispiece was still there.

He unzipped his jacket and laid the forgery in the safe, which he closed and put the painting back in place, and then, stuffing the original inside his coat, he tiptoed to the door. He looked back over the room to make sure that everything was undisturbed and then listened at the door for voices. Hearing none, he cautiously turned the knob, opened it a chink and peeked through. No-one was there. He slipped out and left the door ajar, to the same degree as he'd found it, and then walked quickly and silently back to take up his position on the couch with the book. His heart was pounding and he forced himself to take slow, deep breaths until his heart rate returned to normal. Then he walked nonchalantly upstairs, passing Gordon on the landing, and went to his room. He removed his jacket and secreted the original document in his violin case and then went into the en-suite bathroom and flushed the toilet and ran the faucet for a minute as if washing his hands. He'd done it! Although he wouldn't rest easy until he had left Napa, in fact, until he had left the United States, and was safely home with the dollars deposited in the bank.

Gunther wandered downstairs and decided to go and take a look at the tasting room. Jennifer was still there, laying Strike Up brochures on the seats. Gunther picked up a pile and went to help her. The room had been transformed – tall tables had been set up at the back with white linens artfully draped and tied with broad yellow satin ribbons, with a mason jar of yellow tulips atop each one, and boughs of flowering forsythia were fastened along the front of the bar. The stage area at the front was demarcated with four tall column vases each filled with an arrangement of willow branches complete with their fuzzy catkins, some kind of sword-shaped variegated leaves and tall yellow and white gladioli. The effect was like bringing springtime indoors.

'What do you think?' asked Jennifer, tucking a stray strand of hair behind her ears. Her hand left a dusty smear where she'd wiped her forehead.

'You've done a great job. It's beautiful.'

She beamed back at him. 'Come and see Dad's first edition. Over here.'

The Opus 74 score took pride of place on the table where Strike Up would be taking donations. It sat inside a light oak case with a glass lid, open at the page Gunther had suggested with the pizzicato arpeggio passage in the first movement. Jennifer flicked a switch and hidden LEDs illuminated the page. More forsythia branches decorated the front of the table.

'Dad's taken a real liking to you, Gunther. He kept talking about you and saying how much he liked your entrepreneurial spirit. He says you'll go far. That's high praise from him.'

Gunther smiled warmly and grew an inch taller in his shoes. It wasn't just that he felt like a new person; the confidence that radiated from him ever since he'd taken the Beethoven manuscript was visible to other people as well. He was glad he'd made a good impression. He couldn't help thinking back to Jason's comment from the evening before, though. Ed was disappointed that his son hadn't inherited his entrepreneurism.

'Thanks for telling me. No-one's ever said that to me before.'

'You're a man of hidden depths, Gunther Erdogan' she twinkled back at him. 'And you're a good listener. I like that.'

Her compliment caught him unawares and he was momentarily tongue-tied. He didn't know how to respond so he redirected the conversation onto safer ground.

'How many people do you expect this evening?' he asked.

'I'm hoping for around two hundred. I've been working my ass off distributing flyers, and if the number of phone calls I've been making the past few weeks is anything to go by…' her voice tailed off, ruefully.

'Well, let's go put our feet up and get some rest before we play.'

Ed had sponsored a pre-concert reception to welcome the quartet. By the time the quartet arrived, Gordon, Gunther and Jacek wearing their tuxedos and Jennifer in a stunning strapless yellow satin gown that matched the color theme she'd selected, the party was in full swing. Jacek took Krzysztof by the arm and swung him off to the bar, while Gordon glanced appreciatively around the room at the women, who to his eyes looked incredibly healthy and fit, with their sleeveless dresses showing off tanned and toned arms, doubtless the result of hours spent on the tennis court, and their perfect white teeth a testament to the excellence of American dentistry. Ed proudly took Jennifer's arm and whisked her off to meet some of his wealthy contacts. Gunther spotted Jason standing off to the side. He was talking to a younger man with a ponytail and full beard wearing a grey leather jacket over tight black designer jeans. Gunther watched as the man furtively passed Jason an envelope and then sidled off into the crowd.

Jason slipped the envelope into his jacket pocket and then wandered over to one of the tables, where he pretended to read a Strike Up brochure. Gunther's heart sank. Surely Jason wasn't dealing at Jennifer's fundraiser, of all places? He decided to give him the benefit of the doubt. The man with the ponytail was younger than most of the guests. Perhaps he was the son of wealthy philanthropists who had dragged him there as company for Jason. Or perhaps he was one of the staff hired for the occasion, helping with something technical behind the scenes. Jason cut a forlorn figure, standing on his own, toying with the brochure. Gunther's heart went out to the young misfit, knowing exactly how he felt, a fish out of water. He walked over to Jason and tried to think of something encouraging that he could say. All that came out was a lame 'Great turnout, isn't it?'

'I s'pose so. I don't know most of them – they're all friends of Jen's or Dad's.'

'Didn't you have any friends you could invite?' Gunther decided to fish a little.

Jason shrugged. 'This isn't my friends' kind of scene, if you know what I mean. They're more at the receiving end than the giving end. I'm just the example that well-meaning people trot out to show what happens when you give someone another chance.'

So maybe Gunther's hunch had been right. The other young man must be someone's son, not a friend of Jason's after all.

'It must be difficult for you, having a sister like Jennifer. I have a younger brother, Otto, who's a little like you. He and I were very different and he always resented having other people tell him that he should try to be more like me.'

Jason looked interested. 'So, what does Otto do now?'

'I have to be honest, we're not in touch very often. He spent some time in jail for dealing, while I was studying at the Royal Academy. I don't think he's ever forgiven me for not coming home to bail him out. He still lives in Essen, our home town, as far as I know.'

'Sometimes I feel like I'm doing time here, but in a luxury jail. My freedom's only illusory.'

Gunther squeezed his arm. There wasn't much more he could say.

Suddenly the sound system squealed and Gunther heard a familiar plummy tone announcing,

'Ladies and Gentlemen', followed by throat clearing. Oh no, it couldn't be…

Gordon had taken it upon himself to take to the stage and make the speech he'd spent the afternoon practising. Gunther wished the floor would swallow him up. Did Gordon not realize the evening was not all about him? He glanced at Jennifer. Her face said it all. She'd planned to give a welcome speech on behalf of the Board and to speak about the work of Strike Up with first-time offenders. Gordon had totally stolen her thunder.

Gordon finished his remarks. 'Ladies and Gentlemen, let's have a round of applause for London quartet cellist and Strike Up Board member Jennifer Rose!' As the crown clapped and whooped, Jennifer walked briskly up to the microphone, her mouth fixed in a rigid grin that was more like a rictus while her eyes darted pure hatred at Gordon. She snatched the microphone from Gordon's hand and gave her speech, finishing with 'Now, please make your way to your seats for our concert program, which will start in a few minutes.'

The quartet stepped outside to the makeshift green room to pick up their instruments. Jennifer cold-shouldered Gordon, sweeping imperiously past him with her cello, her satin skirts rustling as she ignored him completely.

'What's gotten into her?' asked Gordon plaintively of the others. Jacek shook his head and whistled.

'Gordon, Gordon, you've cooked your goose now. D'you have no idea what you did back there? This is Jennifer's baby, not yours. What possessed you to give a big speech?'

Gordon looked deflated. 'But I'm always the spokesperson for the quartet. I don't get what the big deal is.'

Jacek replied. 'Never mind, we have a concert to play. Let's go out there and do our best.'

They filed after Jennifer on to the stage. Jason adjusted the lighting to dim the audience and highlight the quartet. They started with the Shostakovich. Jennifer's mouth was set firm and she narrowed her eyes as she put all her hatred of Gordon into her playing. The music sizzled and crackled with fury and the audience rose to their feet at the end with cries of 'Bravo, Bravo'.

The Beethoven Harp quartet was to be the grand finale. Gunther glanced over at Ed Rose. He sat back in his seat, eyes closed, a blissful smile on his lips as he listened to Beethoven's masterpiece. Being able to share his love of the composer and show the First Edition to the guests who had stopped by the display case during the reception made hearing his daughter play with her first professional quartet even more rewarding.

Gunther spotted Krzysztof in the front row seat that Jacek had no doubt reserved for him. Krzysztof's gaze was locked on Jacek and a radiant smile played on his lips as he twisted a ring around his finger. Gunther peeked at Jacek's left hand on the neck of the viola. He too wore a ring on the third finger of his left hand, one that looked suspiciously new and shiny. That was a weird coincidence. He focused back on the music.

The quartet came to its quiet conclusion and the audience scrambled to their feet, cheering and clapping. The four players stood, hands held high, and bowed. As they raised their heads, Gunther felt Jennifer's hand twitch in his as she gasped. He darted a look at her to see what was the matter. She was staring at the man with the ponytail whom Gunther had seen with Jason earlier.

'Oh my god – it's Kent' she whispered. Her hand went limp in his and then she squeezed it hard with sudden determination and hissed at Gunther 'Kiss me.'

Gunther thought he must have misheard, amid all the noise the audience was making. They bowed again and while their heads were down she hissed again frantically. 'Kiss me as soon we stand up, right here. I'll explain later.'

Gunther saw the glint of panic in her eyes. It was impossible to resist her when she was like this. As they straightened up, he slipped his hand down around her waist, drew her to him and kissed her on the lips. The roar of his own blood beating in his ears drowned out the whistles of the audience. He'd dreamed of this moment, not quite imagining it would be so public. Her lips were softer than a whisper and she trembled in his arms. He didn't know what was going on, but he offered a split-second silent prayer of thanks to the spirit of Beethoven for making the impossible happen.

He released her and looked into her eyes. She smiled at him, softly and weakly and mouthed a thank you, and as they made to leave the stage, she whispered 'Stay close by. Don't leave me alone.'

Ed was waiting by the tall vases of flowers. He hugged Jennifer and looked between her and Gunther.

'Well, that was a pleasant surprise. When were you going to tell me?'

'Oh Daddy, Kent's here! I spotted him in the crowd when I stood up to take my bow. How did he get here and who let him in? Please, can you get rid of him? I don't want to see him. He terrifies me.'

Ed's face became serious. 'Where did you see him?'

'Near the back, close to the display case. I'd recognize that beard and ponytail anywhere.'

'Gunther, can you walk Jen back to the house? She shouldn't be alone. That Kent's a psycho. I'll go find him and kick him out before he can frighten her any more.'

Gunther hesitated, wondering if he should speak up. Jennifer seemed freaked out. He decided he owed it to her. 'Ed, you should ask Jason where he is. I saw them talking before the concert, and he slipped Jason an envelope.'

Ed's mouth hardened. 'Unbelievable. OK, thanks, I'll go find Jason and get to the bottom of this.' He strode off.

Jennifer was shivering, so Gunther took off his jacket and put it over her shoulders. They went back to the green room to put their instruments away. Gordon and Jacek had already headed back to the house for the after-party.

'I'm so sorry, Gunther' she burst out, as soon as the green room door closed. She had her back to him as she put her cello into its case, securing the straps and snapping the clasps on the lid. 'I didn't mean to be so unprofessional. But that creepy guy with the ponytail is my ex-boyfriend from New York. We had an awful break-up after I got the job with the quartet and left for London, and he's been cyberstalking me. I had no idea he would come to the concert – he would have to fly all the way across the country to get here. I guess I did too good a job on publicity.' She turned around to face him and smiled forlornly at her little joke. 'But I can't believe he paid off my ratbag of a brother to let him in to the concert. All I could think to do on the spur of the moment was to pretend I'm in a relationship with you, just to show him it was really over. But now I'm afraid he might do something – he's the jealous type.'

'So, you were just using me' said Gunther flatly.

'Well, yes…and no.'

'What do you mean by that?'

'Well, actually I like you – I like you a lot, Gunther. You're my best friend in London – did you know that? And I feel so safe with you.' She looked down coyly at him. 'And it turns out you're a fabulous kisser.'

'What do you want from me, Jennifer? One minute you are apologizing for being unprofessional and the next minute you are complimenting me. I don't understand.'

She looked at him and her mouth crumpled like a little girl. 'Right now, I want you to hold me.'

Gunther stepped forward and caught her as she fell on his neck and started crying. He held her in his arms and stroked her back awkwardly. Her long hair fell forward over her face and he couldn't see her eyes, but her mouth found his and she kissed him again.

He kept stroking her hair as it tumbled down her back, and murmured to her. 'It's OK, whatever you want. I love you and I respect you as a musician. I'll keep you safe, don't worry.'

She sniffed and wiped her eyes, and tried to smooth her hair.

'I must look a mess. Thanks Gunther. I just don't know what I want, but I'll figure it out in time if you'll be patient with me. We should get back to the house. The others will be wondering where we've got to.'

'You look fine. Come on.'

He held her hand as they walked back up the driveway to the house. The front door was wide open and the lights blazed out from the hall. The hubbub of conversations and the clinking of glasses greeted them. Ed stood by the front door, looking for them.

'There you are. It's OK, I told Jason to personally escort his "friend" off the winery. He's gone. I'll deal with Jason in the morning. And you two can fill me in on all the details tomorrow. For now, your fans are waiting, Jen, honey. Give me your cello, and Gunther, I'll take your violin too and put it somewhere safe, and you two get in there.'

The hall heaved with partygoers, and Gunther and Jennifer had to squeeze their way through to the side table to get a glass of champagne. Jennifer seized a fork and climbed half way up the stairs to tinkle it on her glass to get everyone's attention.

'Hi everyone. Thanks so much for coming. We so enjoyed playing for you and I hope you enjoyed the music. I'd like to thank my Mom and Dad for hosting, and all our Board members and volunteers for the great turn-out and making the event such a success. On behalf of Strike Up and the London Quartet – thank you!' She raised her glass to make a toast.

Jacek leapt to his feet, dragging Krzysztof with him. 'I too would like to make a toast – to my husband, Krzysztof!' He raised his glass in his left hand, deliberately flaunting the new wedding ring that Gunther had noticed during the concert, and showing off its twin as he held Krzysztof's left hand aloft.

Jennifer shrieked from her vantage point on the staircase 'Oh my God! You two got married! Congratulations!'

Gordon wheeled round in amazement and slapped Jacek on the back. 'You dark horse! When did all this happen?'

The quartet clustered around the newlyweds as Jacek related the story.

'I got the idea to propose when we were on the wine tour yesterday. We were sipping wine under a rose arbor on the patio of one of the wineries and chatting to the waiter, who told us it was a popular spot for weddings. We looked at each other and thought, why not take advantage of being in California where we can legally get married? I rushed into the shop and bought a set of those little rings that you use to slip around the stem of a wineglass at a party, so that you know whose glass is whose. I got down on one knee and proposed to Krzysztof on the spot and slipped a ring on his finger, to claim him as mine, and he said yes. The waiter arranged all the rest for us - license, officiant, wedding rings. We went back this afternoon and tied the knot there under the arbor.'

Gordon shook Jacek's hand. 'I'm truly happy for you both'. Jennifer kissed them both on the cheek.

Jacek twinkled 'Well, if you'll excuse us, we have a wedding night to celebrate…' He led Krzysztof upstairs while the partygoers jeered and clapped. Well-wishers swamped Jennifer, and Gordon held his own with a bevy of ladies who, tipsy with champagne, exclaimed over his British accent and swooned over his artistry. Gunther in the mood for solitude. He retrieved his violin from the dining room and stole upstairs to his room to ponder all that had transpired that evening. He relived the memory of Jennifer's tender kisses. He'd told her that he loved her – the rest was up to her. Things were moving fast. He wasn't sure whether it something in the wine or the Californian sunshine that inspired romance. He was certainly happy for Jacek and Krzysztof and their love for each other. But in his own case, he was immune to the charms of California, and he was increasingly convinced that the Beethoven autograph he carried around in his violin case was a good luck talisman, an amulet that would protect him and bring nothing but good fortune his way. He suppressed a sudden urge to take it out, gaze on it, touch it. It seemed a risky thing to do in this house. If he was discovered, his whole plan could be blown. He struggled with himself and then gave in to temptation. Just touching the page gave him a power surge of confidence. He inhaled deeply, stroked the paper and then put it away, back in his violin case.

The next morning as the quartet was packing the van to depart on the drive up to Sacramento for the next leg of their tour, Ed pulled Gunther aside.

'Gunther, I haven't forgotten our deal. But I wanted to thank you for taking care of Jen last night. She means the world to me. I can't believe her own brother accepted a bribe to let her ex into the concert. I've already had words with him this morning. He's sulking in the winery. And to think, she organized this fundraiser to help little shits just like him.' He looked Gunther in the eye. 'I'm relying on you to keep Jen safe. I don't want that creep Kent showing up at your other concerts. I can see she's sweet on you – you make sure you treat her with the care and respect she deserves. Whatever you do, don't break my baby's heart, OK?' Gunther nodded, mute. 'Very good. Well, don't forget this.' Ed slipped him the envelope of cash. 'Thanks again for everything.'

Jennifer was calling to Gunther from the van. 'Come on Gunther, are you ready? We're waiting for you.'

He ran over and jumped in the back seat. Krzysztof, sitting in the middle, slid over closer to Gordon to make room for him. Jacek drove, with Jennifer riding shotgun. She wound down the window and waved to her parents. 'Bye, love you, see you soon!'

Jacek was in high spirits. He turned up the radio and fiddled with the dial until he found a country music station and then belted out the songs at top volume as he drove. Jennifer was in charge of navigation and lost no opportunity to point out of the windows and call the quartet's attention to various landmarks and tourist attractions as they passed. Gordon complained peevishly that he had a headache, and Jennifer passed him some aspirin and a bottle of water. He leaned his head against the window and closed his eyes, trying to rest.

After an hour, they arrived and checked into the hotel that Jennifer had picked, close to the California State University campus where they were booked to perform for the local Chamber Music Society that evening. Gunther was unpacking his suitcase and hanging his tuxedo up in the closet when he heard a soft tap on the door. He went to investigate. It was Jennifer.

'Hi Jennifer. What is it?'

'May I come in?'

He stepped aside and waved her in. She closed the door softly behind her, and then without warning, leaned in and kissed him full on the lips.

'I've been wanting to do that all morning' she murmured. Gunther was pleasantly surprised that the feeling was mutual. He'd been daydreaming, gazing at the back of Jennifer's head for the whole duration of the drive, longing to touch her hair and liberate a waft of her nutmeg scent. 'Guess what – we've got adjacent rooms and there's a connecting door.' She went over and turned the handle. 'I've unlocked my side. If you unlock yours, we can go from room to room without being seen.'

'Do you mean…?'

She nodded. 'After the concert, later tonight.'

'Are you sure?'

She looked confused. 'I know, I'm breaking my own rule about keeping relationships strictly professional. But ever since Poland there's just been something about you that I can't resist. You're kind and considerate, and fun to spend time with, and you're a great listener. And my Dad thinks very highly of you. I trust his judgment. That means a lot to me.'

Gunther put both arms around her waist and kissed her back, feeling her relax as he held her. She kissed the top of his head and pulled away.

'OK - after the concert. Leave the connecting door unlocked and wait for me. I'll come to you.' She slipped through the door and pulled it closed behind her.

Gunther sat back heavily on the bed. He couldn't believe his luck – this was like a dream come true. Anticipation gave an edge to the rest of his day – colors seemed brighter, the scent of the lilies in the hotel lobby more intense, and during their afternoon rehearsal the music seemed to linger in the air, each note clear and limpid.

He lost all sense of time during the performance, when catching Jennifer's glance, he felt suspended in a single musical moment. The pieces seemed timeless, in that each movement lasted forever. He bowed mechanically to the applause and then sat through dinner with the quartet at a local Mexican restaurant that Jacek had picked out, willing away the minutes until he could be alone with Jennifer, together at last. He sat in a daze chewing his fish taco (although he couldn't recall the next day what he'd eaten there) while the others conducted a vigorous post-mortem of their performance, nodding or saying 'Mmm' politely at intervals, although he wasn't really listening to what they were saying.

At long last, they drove back to the hotel. By this time Gunther was beginning to feel nervous. Should he shower and get ready for bed? Or just sit and wait for Jennifer as he was, in his tuxedo? He sniffed under his arms – he'd been sweating at the concert and his jacket smelled of corn tortillas and oil. Better take a shower and put on something more comfortable. He hung up his jacket and showered as quickly as he could, and then put on a clean pair of slacks and a fresh white shirt. He resisted the temptation to touch the Beethoven autograph for luck, and instead put his violin case away in the bottom of the closet, out of sight. He sat on the bed and turned on the TV, changing channels until he found an audio channel with classical music playing. He could see the connecting door from where he sat. He watched and waited.

At last the door handle turned, and Jennifer slipped into his room. She'd changed too, from her long concert dress into a flowing sundress printed with palm trees and tropical flowers.

'Hi Gunther' she said, and stood still, looking at him.

Gunther gazed back. She looked like a vision standing there and for a crazy moment he thought he might be hallucinating, but then he realized she was waiting for an invitation to come in. He smiled shyly, slid off the bed and, taking her hand, led her gently back there to join him. It felt strange to hold his colleague in his arms, and at the same time, the most natural thing in the world.

Afterwards, she knelt over him and tenderly kissed the tip of his nose, stroked his hair and then moved back towards the adjoining door. Gunther propped himself up on one elbow.

'Are you leaving already?'

She turned her head back, her hair a tousled mane on top of her graceful neck.

'You don't mind, do you? I'll be here next door if you need me.'

Gunther watched her vanish through the door. He shook his head in amazement. That was one independent young woman. He collapsed back on his pillows and pulled the sheets and comforter back up to his chin, basking in the warm afterglow. Within minutes he was asleep.

Chapter 22 - Retribution

London, May

Back from their US tour, the London quartet had two brief months to complete the busy season before summer. Gordon began experiencing shooting pains in his left hand, and to his dismay, on consulting a specialist, learned that he had developed tendonitis, for which the only cure was rest. 'Complete rest – you'll need to wear a support brace 24/7 and no violin playing for five weeks.' He summoned the quartet to his Edgware home for an emergency meeting. Gunther arrived first, and was shocked to see the brace on Gordon's wrist when he opened the front door. Gordon's hair was uncharacteristically disheveled and one of his shirt buttons was missing.

'My god, what happened to you?'

Gordon grimaced. 'I'll tell you when everyone gets here.'

When Gunther and Jennifer were seated on the couch, and Jacek in the armchair, Gordon paced up and down in front of his fireplace, not looking at them, his words tumbling out breathily.

'We're going to have to find a sub for me for the next month or two. Doctor's orders. I can't play. Tendonitis. Anyone have any suggestions?'

The other three looked at each other, mentally running down lists of people they knew.

'Is there anyone in the New London Sinfonietta who might be able to cover for you?' asked Jacek. 'Your co-principal maybe?'

'He's more of a hard-core orchestral player. He doesn't know the string quartet repertoire.'

Gunther piped up 'I know someone who does know the chamber music literature – David, the second violin from my gigging quartet, the Nightingales. But he prefers to play second.'

Jennifer dug Gunther in the ribs 'Gunther, couldn't you play the first part? You know the programme, you know our interpretation. I'd much rather have you lead us rather than have to adjust to a new first violin at such short notice. Then your friend could come in on second.' She looked around at her colleagues. 'What do you think?'

Gordon scowled. Not content with stealing Jennifer's affections right under his nose, it seemed Gunther was on the verge of stealing his job as well. But due to his competitive nature, he hadn't ever seen the point of befriending other quartets' first violinists, and he couldn't think of an alternative.

Gunther considered Jennifer's suggestion. Why not, indeed? He certainly knew Gordon's part by ear, he could work it up in a couple of practice sessions. He sat up straight with a big smile.

'I think I can do it. Let me call David right away and check his availability for our concert dates.' He went into Gordon's kitchen to use the phone, and came back beaming.

'We're in luck. David can do all but one of the dates, but he thinks he can get a sub for the one that conflicts, which would free him up to play with us. Oh, and he can come to our rehearsal tomorrow afternoon so we can get started working with him as soon as possible.'

Jennifer and Jacek high-fived each other. Gordon looked glum.

'Did you talk money with him?'

'He's asking five hundred pounds a concert. Can we do that?'

'Yes, we can cover that. Fortunately, I have an injury insurance policy that should tide me over until I'm back to playing again.'

'I'm glad you had the foresight to put that in place. Don't worry Gordon, it sounds like we've got the concerts covered. You rest up and we'll take care of the quartet until you're better.'

Gordon managed a shaky smile. 'At least I can work on my conducting skills with the New London Sinfonietta. You only need a right hand for the baton.'

Gordon showed them out, and Gunther kissed Jennifer on his doorstep.

'That was a stroke of genius – how did you know? I've been itching to play first for so long but I never dared suggest to Gordon that we try switching. I hate to say it, but his injury's a godsend.'

'I believe in you Gunther – I know you can do it. I think you'll be great.'

Gunther once again thanked the gods of fate and Beethoven. Six months ago, he couldn't have predicted this turn of events. Everything was going his way.

He and Jennifer were dating now. She'd rented a flat in St. John's Wood, just a couple of tube stops away from Kilburn. They went to concerts together and out for dinner and then would go back to Gunther's flat to make love. But Jennifer always insisted on going home afterwards. This evening, Gunther was glad of the solitude as he wanted to practice the first violin parts to the Beethoven and Shostakovich. He turned to the first movement of the Beethoven quartet with the violin bariolage passage and worked at it until it was in his fingers. He was surprised that the notes sat so well under his hand. Gordon was such a showman, he made it look very virtuosic but in fact the notes were easier to play than they sounded.

David arrived early at their rehearsal the following day, keen to make a good impression. Used to playing second fiddle to Gunther's first in the Nightingale Quartet, he slotted in easily to the London Quartet. Jacek marveled at the ease with which Gunther took Gordon's place. There were none of the histrionics or the ego that Gordon displayed. Just a clear and solid lead. For the first time in the fifteen years of the London Quartet's existence, Jacek could relax and just play.

Gunther's cellphone rang, and he glanced at it as he played. The number that flashed up had a +49 country code and he recognized the phone number of Nike Wagner, director of the Beethovenfest in Bonn that he would be playing at in the fall. He broke off and apologized to the others

'So sorry, I should get this, it's about my festival job.' He laid down his violin and stepped outside the studio to answer the call.

While Gunther was gone, David looked at his bow and wrinkled his nose, and asked if anyone had any rosin he could borrow.

'Mine's cello rosin, you probably don't want that' said Jennifer. 'I'm sure Gunther will have some violin rosin in his case. Let me look.' She walked over to Gunther's open case and started going through the pockets looking for his cake of rosin.

Gunther walked back in the room to witness Jennifer bending over his case, systematically searching through its compartments. He froze. Jennifer valued honesty above all else. If she were to accidentally open the bow compartment and find the manuscript, she would recognize it at once and she'd know where he'd got it. Even worse, if she mentioned it to her father in their nightly phone calls, that would open a whole other can of worms.

'What do you think you're doing?' he barked from the doorway.

Jennifer straightened up 'I'm only looking for some rosin for David.'

'Don't go looking through my case. No-one but me goes in there. Understand?'

She looked at Gunther with big, hurt eyes, not understanding why his voice was so harsh. She held his rosin in her hand.

'OK, OK, I won't do it again.'

Gunther muttered 'Thanks', realizing he'd gone too far. He looked at David, who was clearly trying to pretend he wasn't there. It hadn't been the most auspicious start for their newest member. 'I'm sorry. It's OK David, you can borrow my rosin. But next time ask me first.' He felt ashamed for snapping like that and wondered fleetingly if being first violin of a quartet automatically made you behave like a shit. A doubt gnawed at him – was the Beethoven autograph and the success it had brought him changing his personality too? During the rehearsal, he tried his hardest to be kind and considerate to the others, listening to their opinions and suggestions and not domineering the group the way Gordon did.

Chapter 23

Bonn, September

At the close of a golden summer, Gunther arrived in Bonn to start rehearsals, a week before the festival opened. Jennifer had traveled with him, having managed to persuade Hyperion to fund a video shoot at the Beethoven Haus in Bonn to accompany her DVD, which would be coming out in January. For the first few days of their trip while Gunther was tied up in rehearsals, she was intensely occupied with filming, meeting early in the morning with the make-up artists to get ready and have her hair done, and then shooting scenes with her cello at the Beethoven Haus in concert dress, the yellow satin she'd worn in Napa, as well as in business attire talking about Beethoven's life and about the cello sonatas.

After the filming was completed and the video crew returned to London, Jennifer stayed on with Gunther in Bonn. He'd negotiated a festival season ticket for her so that she could attend all the events and concerts, and she was looking forward to taking a few weeks' vacation before the new season started in earnest.

The opening night concert programme featured three of Beethoven's early period works – the Creatures of Prometheus Overture, the Triple Concerto for violin, cello and piano, and his Choral Fantasy. Gunther sat at the back of the second violin section. Back in January his request to Heimlich for a seat in the orchestra had seemed a bold leap for someone whose only professional accomplishment to date was being asked to join the London Quartet by a college buddy. He marveled at how far he'd come since then – now a *bona fide* member of the London Symphony Orchestra, with a successful American concert tour under his belt, and a beautiful and talented girlfriend to boot. The old Gunther would have felt intimidated by the orchestral pros with whom he shared the stage in Bonn, which included members of the renowned Berlin and Vienna Philharmonic Orchestras. But now he was their equal, that he had every right to be there. Luck played just as much a role as talent in a successful career, and he'd chosen to make his own luck. Who would have guessed that he'd been able to turn around his initial frightening encounter with Heimlich to his own advantage? He accepted that he'd got into the Festival Orchestra through a connection, so he didn't mind his lowly seat at the back.

When they'd walked onstage for the dress rehearsal he'd looked across the empty hall and up to the balcony, trying to remember in which seat he'd sat as a teenager all those years ago when this very same orchestra had captured his rapt attention. As the orchestra tuned under Maestra Wagner's baton, he'd had a lump in his throat, wishing that his adolescent self had known then, that he would be performing on that same stage some twenty-five years later. He'd brought the Beethoven manuscript with him – it lived in his violin case and he took it everywhere. Gunther had developed a kind of superstition for the autograph, believing it would bring him continued luck. When his case was close by, he was confident and assured, but when he left his home without his violin he felt naked and vulnerable without his talisman at his side.

The doors to the concert hall opened at seven and the audience flooded into the auditorium. Gunther took his seat on stage early, wanting to have plenty of time to tune his instrument and get comfortable. The piano tuner was still working on the concert grand, a Bechstein, rapping on the keys and making fine adjustments under the lid. Gunther scanned the audience to see if he could spot Jennifer. She was sitting in the stalls looking very grand – she'd put up her hair and wore a short black velvet dress with a crystal choker around her neck that glittered under the lights. She'd joked with Gunther that she hardly ever got to wear short dresses since she had to straddle the cello to play, so she'd enjoyed having an excuse to wear this one to his first concert with the Festival Orchestra.

By seven twenty-five the house was packed, with every seat taken, filled with the buzz of excited conversation. The concertmaster walked on stage to polite applause and the audience quietened down as he tuned the orchestra. Right on time at seven thirty the Maestra took the podium and began the Overture. Gunther was immersed in the music, intently focused on the conductor's baton and making sure he matched exactly the bow strokes of the player sitting in front of him. Next came the Triple Concerto and the first violins shuffled their chairs back to make room for the violin and cello soloists to sit in front of the piano. As they played, Gunther fantasized about playing the piece with Jennifer. The violin and cello were written in octaves in many places and in others enjoyed a dialogue with each other and the piano, answering each other phrase by phrase.

Before the grand finale began, the choir filed on to the tiered steps at the back of the stage. Gunther watched the audience as he waited. Most of the concert goers chatted quietly with their neighbors. One young man, Turkish-looking, near the front, stood out, since he was neither deep in conversation nor buried in his program, but looking up at the stage, staring fixedly at the podium. His stiff upright position suggested he was in some degree of discomfort – he wore a bulky coat despite the heat inside the theater. Gunther looked further back to where Jennifer was sitting, and caught her eye. She waved gaily to him and blew him a kiss.

The Choral Fantasy opens with the solo piano stating the theme reminiscent of Beethoven's ninth 'Choral' Symphony – in fact this early piece was an experimental sketch which Beethoven later developed into his better-known masterpiece and final symphonic work. The orchestra joins, expanding on the theme, and finally the choir enters, singing not about Brotherhood and Joy as in the ninth Symphony, but about Love and Strength. The final coda section was approaching when from the corner of his eye, behind the conductor, Gunther caught sight of the young Turkish man he'd spotted earlier, rising to his feet, and shouting as he waved one hand in the air. In a horrible instant Gunther realized what was about to happen, and he curled himself into a ball, to protect his violin and rolled backward into the curtain behind him as the blast went off.

The theater filled with smoke and screaming as shrapnel from the bomb flew into the front of the stage and the first few rows of the audience. Gunther lay where he was, curled in fetal position, swaddled in the thick velvet curtains, stunned and hardly able to breathe. All he could hear was a high-pitched squealing in his ears, above a muffled roar.

The sweet sickly smell of blood filled his nostrils and the sulfurous stench of cordite filled his lungs. He became aware of bodies stumbling past him, jostling him, as the orchestra members who were able, ran to get off the stage. He scrambled to his feet and blindly followed the crowd. And then he remembered Beethoven's autograph. He had to get to his case! He couldn't bear the thought of leaving his lucky talisman backstage to burn. He stood against the back wall of the stage, and began to make his way deliberately back to the green room where the orchestra had unpacked their instruments and left their coats and cases, shoving his way through the panicked throng of musicians streaming towards the emergency exits.

When he reached the green room, it was quite empty. He ran over to his case and pulled out the manuscript, sinking down to the floor and holding it in his hands. The luck of Beethoven continued to protect him. Apart from his ears which were still ringing, as far as he could tell he was unharmed, with not a single mark on his body. The velvet curtain of the stage had protected him from the flying shrapnel. Perhaps Beethoven's spirit had even guided him to look up at the right moment, to give him a premonition that something was not right about the young Turk, to duck a split second before the bomb went off. But as he gazed at the familiar autograph, instead of drawing comfort from it, he saw nothing but reproach in the angry scrawl. He dropped the paper and pressed his hands to his head. The tinnitus was unbearable. Was this how Beethoven had suffered for so many years as deafness encroached upon him? He heard Beethoven's voice in his head rebuking him. 'How could you do these terrible things, Gunther? This is my quartet, not yours. I wrote it. How could you cut my name from the score? And then steal it, not once but twice over, first from your own fatherland and then from the father of the woman you say you love. How could you deceive the people who have trusted you and who love you? Shame on you! Curses on your head for exploiting my work for your own selfish ambitions.'

Gunther howled 'No! Stop! No!' He scooped up the paper and dropped it back in his case, slamming down the cover of the secret compartment and then piling his violin and bow on top. He snapped the catches closed and took the case in his arms, cradling all that was dear to him. He'd better get out of the theater, to save himself.

Jennifer stood outside on the sidewalk opposite the theater, sobbing and looking frantically up and down the street for Gunther. She'd been swept up in the crowd rushing for the exits, someone had trodden hard on her foot in the melee and she'd only realized when she touched something wet on her forehead that she'd been cut on the head by a piece of flying debris from the explosion.

She shivered violently in her short black dress, her teeth chattering involuntarily in the cold September night air. Her heart jumped whenever she saw a figure in a tuxedo carrying a violin, but then her spirits were dashed when the figure came closer and it wasn't Gunther. Ambulances began arriving, their sirens wailing, and she hovered anxiously watching as the paramedics emerged from the theater carrying stretchers. She ran between them, looking and looking but Gunther wasn't there.

Some instinct made her head back up the street towards the stage door. A squat and stocky lone figure came running out, carrying a large custom-made violin case in one hand, rubbing its eyes with the other. Gunther! She darted towards him but he kept running, straight out into the street, directly into the path of an ambulance racing to the scene. Jennifer closed her eyes in anguish as she heard the dull thud of the impact and the screech of skidding tires as the ambulance driver braked hard. She opened her eyes and saw a small black heap in the road in front of her. Her legs crumpled under her and she collapsed to her hands and knees in the street with a silent scream. Gunther!

The next couple of hours passed in a blur. Jennifer couldn't remember how long she spent curled on the pavement in the cold before someone found her and gently shook her to her senses. She didn't know how she found the right ambulance so that she could accompany Gunther to the hospital and formally identify his body. They asked if she was his next of kin and she shook her head, mute. Somewhere in the fog she remembered him mentioning his family, a younger brother Otto in Essen. Otto Erdogan? The nurse smiled and said that with such an unusual name they should be able to find a telephone number. They would send for his brother. The hospital staff were very kind. They cleaned and dressed the wound on her head, and brought her a blanket. More time passed, she wasn't sure how long; she dosed on and off under the blanket in the waiting room.

Then someone touched her arm and she looked up and almost cried out as he looked just like Gunther. Otto had come. They were going to release Gunther's body and personal effects to the family. Otto returned, crying and catching his breath, with a mangled custom violin case in his arms. 'What should I do with his violin? I know nothing about musical instruments.' Jennifer opened the clasps and pulled back the lid, bursting into fresh tears when she saw the bows, their sticks snapped like pencils, the horse hair dangling loose, and the front of Gunther's beloved Vuillaume violin completely crushed in like a broken eggshell, its neck severed in two pieces, the metal strings twisted like a garrote.

'It's beyond repair' she said softly. 'Such a beautiful violin, his pride and joy. He always kept it close by. You should check his insurance policy, it was worth a lot.' She looked up at Otto with tearstained eyes. 'If it were up to me, I would bury him with his violin. If you believe in an afterlife at least he would always have it with him.'

And Otto took her advice. He placed the Vuillaume in its case, and unknowingly, the frontispiece to the Harp Quartet bearing Beethoven's signature still hidden inside, in his brother's arms before he sealed the coffin. He looked on as the casket rolled into the crematorium furnace. Gunther's ashes became inextricably intermingled with those of Beethoven's autograph and dissipated back into the air with the smoke that rose from the crematorium chimney.

And so, Gunther's secret inspiration died with him. While Jennifer went on to build a successful career, and fell in love again, she could never again bring herself to play Beethoven's Harp Quartet.

BIBLIOGRAPHY

'Manuscripts Found in the Jagiellonian' by Włodzimierz Kalicki, Gazeta Wyborcza, March 30. 2010

'The Music Collection of the Former Prussian State Library at the Jagiellonian Library in Kraków, Poland: Past, Present and Future Developments' by Marek Sroka, Library Trends Vol. 55, No. 3, Winter 2007 ("Libraries in Times of War, Revolution and Social Change," edited by W.Boyd Rayward and Christine Jenkins), pp 651-664

'The Beethoven Quartets' by Joseph Kerman, W.W. Norton & Company, 1966

'Beethoven's Hair – An Extraordinary Historical Odyssey and a Scientific Mystery Solved' by Russell Martin, Broadway Books, 2000

'The Rape of Europa – The Fate of Europe's Treasures in the Third Reich and the Second World War' by Lynn H. Nichols, First Vintage Books Edition, May 1995

'Blitzed – Drugs in Nazi Germany' by Norman Ohler, Allen Lane, 2016

'A Travel History of Poland' by John Radzilowski, Interlink Books, 2013

ABOUT THE AUTHOR

Janet White was born and educated in the United Kingdom. She began playing the cello at the age of ten years old and remains an enthusiastic amateur musician, playing chamber music, including string quartets, in her spare time. She has studied Beethoven's 'Harp' Quartet with the Manhattan String Quartet and enjoys playing all of Beethoven's string quartets as well as those by other composers. She is Chair of the Board of Associated Chamber Music Players, an international network of musicians who like to play purely for pleasure.

Janet White lives in San Diego, California, with her husband and three dogs. Beethoven's String Quartet Opus 74 'The Harp' is her fifth novel.

BOOKS BY JANET WHITE

DAUGHTERS' DILEMMA
AN AFRICAN ABC
FROM SAIGON TO SAN DIEGO
CROWS' FEAT
SEEKING APHRODITE